TBR: DEAD BUT WELL READ

Sedona Ashe

Cover and Interior artwork by Inessa Sage

https://www.cauldronpress.ca/

A huge thank you to-

Allison Woerner for Alpha Reading.

Maxine Meyer for Copy Editing.

Emily LeVault for proofreading.

Meg Kelly my assistant for encouraging me and keeping my chaos wrangled as much as is humanely possible.

TBR

DEAD BUT WELL READ

SEDONA ASHE

CONTENTS

Sensitivity Note
(Spoilers Below!)

If you're the type to clutch your pearls while reading spicy romance books… then I suggest you run and grab those pearls, because you'll be needing them quite a bit 😌. This book does talk about death and dying (yes, I'm aware the title kind of gives that away). While there are definitely sad moments that pull at the heart, this book takes a humorous approach to the topic—unless we're talking about Death with a capital D (and a "D" in his pants that only gets hard for his soulmate). He's no laughing matter, and things get violent when Axelle is insulted.
There are steamy scenes where she's being told what to do because her men are bossy, and they know what turns their girl on. All intimacy in this book is consensual.
There are some fight scenes in this book, and Axelle is beaten badly in one of those battles.

CHAPTER 1

AXELLE

S trolling through the library, I smiled at the patrons who slouched on the couches, completely engrossed in their books. The whisper of pages being turned, and the faint clicking coming from the computers lining the far wall, were the only sounds to be heard.

It was a relief since my ears were still ringing from the weekly children's story time that had finished less than an hour before. With a smile, I bent and pushed in several books that had been pulled out by Kyle, one of the more energetic children.

Story hour was a weekly event, and chaos was guaranteed when the library doors flew open and the group of kids rushed inside, dragging their frazzled parents behind them. You'd think we'd be used to it by now, but every week we would stand in openmouthed shock as an army of squealing kids tore through the library like tiny Tasmanian devils who'd devoured twenty pounds of raw sugar before their arrival.

I loved when the kids visited and broke up the monotony of my week, but I couldn't deny I also experienced a sense of relief when they left and the library's peaceful silence was restored.

Glancing up at the large clock, I grinned. There was only an hour until closing. That was when all the patrons would be shooed from the building, and I could stretch out on my favorite olive-green leather sofa in the middle of the library with my latest read. Until then, I'd go hideout in the archive room and read a few chapters while I waited for the library to be all mine.

I headed toward the librarians busy re-shelving books.

"Did you notice Dr. Gerland's wedding band was missing today?" Bertha whispered loudly enough that two patrons glanced up from their books.

Tilly nodded her head. "I certainly did. You know, none of the ladies at Monday night's book club meeting have seen his wife in town in the past month. Agatha heard that Mrs. Gerland went to help her sick sister in Wisconsin. Maybe she decided to divorce him?"

"I wouldn't blame her. The single women in this town have increasingly questionable morals, and he works with them every day of the week." Bertha clicked her tongue against her teeth. "Just yesterday, one of the nurses checked out a monster romance. Can you imagine?"

Tilly gasped as Bertha continued. "How is an attractive man like Dr. Gerland supposed to resist if one of those

young nurses set their sights on him and use the wicked-
ness from those books to tempt him? Mrs. Gerland is probably saving herself the inevitable embarrassment of her
husband having an affair."

I rolled my eyes. Or he had simply gained a few pounds
and had to have his ring resized, and he'd used his bonus to
pay for his wife to go to a spa retreat with her best friend
because he appreciated how she'd tirelessly supported him
over the years. It was amazing what you could pick up
from one-sided phone calls.

Turning sideways, I squeezed between the two gossips.
Neither woman gave me so much as a nod of acknowledg-
ment, but I didn't mind. I'd always been on the introverted
side, but over the last three years, I'd become downright
antisocial. No longer being subjected to tedious small talk
was quite possibly the best thing that had ever happened
to me.

I was living every bookworm's dream. No longer having
to worry about keeping a job to get a paycheck, no stressing
over where I was going to live, and no wasted time trying
to decide what I was going to eat.

Nope. For the last three years, I'd been free to spend my
days and nights reading to my heart's content.

Even so, my to-be-read list was still about fifteen miles
long. I really felt for the incredible women who were trying
to keep up with an actual life, advance their careers, grow a
family, and still managed to whittle away at their TBRs.
They were doing the impossible.

Heck! I was beginning to have serious doubts about

whether I'd ever make it through my list, and I was lucky enough to be able to focus all of my attention on reading. It had become a full-time job.

I might be dead, but I'd never give up on my to-be-reads.

"Dead, but well read" had become my afterlife's motto.

I made my way down the dark hallway, walking by several storage rooms, before finally reaching the archive room. Without stopping, I strode through the closed door into the dark room.

Unbothered by the dust and ancient cobwebs, I walked through a large spiderweb that had been abandoned by its owner. I could walk through spider webs, roll in dust, and never get dirty or end up sneezing. It was my second favorite ability—second only to not needing to worry about adulting.

Yep. Being a ghost came with some amazing perks.

The only time I could touch things on the earthly plane was when I gathered a surge of energy. That had proven challenging at first, and to my endless frustration, I'd been stuck reading over people's shoulders. I was a speed reader, so waiting for someone to turn the page was a special kind of torture.

But with stubborn determination, I'd learned how to move small items like books. And eventually, after countless hours of practice, I'd gained enough finesse to turn pages.

Better yet, with each passing year, it had grown easier to touch things, and I found myself less exhausted afterward.

In the past six months, I'd even learned how to work the computers so I could borrow books from other libraries in our system. Unfortunately, that had caused my TBR list to nearly triple in length.

The archive room was dark, but that wasn't an issue for me since I could see as well in the dark as I could in the light.

I glanced around at the six-foot-tall shelves mounted against three of the archive room's walls. Each shelf was stuffed with large leather-bound books that looked like they belonged at Pigworts Academy, rather than the back room of a small-town library.

When I'd first claimed the room as my bedroom, I'd tried to open a few of the volumes to see what was inside, but they'd been too heavy, and my energy had been exhausted by the strain.

Hmmm. Maybe I should try again…

I would. But not tonight.

Walking to the back of the room, I floated from the ground, rising toward the ceiling. On top of the wide shelf, far above the librarians' line of sight, folded stacks of thick brocade curtains that had once adorned the library's windows were folded neatly and stored on top. It wasn't the plush pillow-top mattress I'd owned while alive, but it gave me the illusion of sleeping on a decently comfortable bed.

Reaching the top of the shelf, I stopped short at the two dark eyes staring into mine.

Squeak!

"*Wasabi!*" I yelped, clutching at my chest. "We've already talked about this. I'm the ghost and the only one who should be doing the scaring around here."

The dove-gray rat twitched his nose, looking decidedly unapologetic and almost amused.

Jerk.

Shooing him from the middle of my bed, I drifted down on the fabric. With a happy little hop, he moved to my side and curled into an adorable ball beside me.

I summoned a small burst of energy and scratched behind his tiny ear. His fur was soft against my ghostly finger, and I couldn't help but smile when he tilted his head to give me better access.

"You know you shouldn't be out in the library during the day," I scolded. "If Mrs. Sourpants sees you again, she's going to call the exterminator."

Wasabi cracked open one eye as if to say, *you think I'm worried?* before closing it again.

I really wished he could talk to me, but apparently communicating with animals wasn't a ghostly perk. With my only friend—and the only being who knew I still existed—cuddled beside me, I sighed and reached for the book I'd started that morning.

A half-hour later, heavy footsteps echoed down the hall. I stiffened, craning my head to hear better.

Odd.

No one came to this side of the library unless they were planning to dig out the Christmas decorations that were stored in the room across from the archive room. And since it was March, that couldn't be the reason.

The door handle turned, the hinges shrieking in protest as the door opened. At the shock of the ear-splitting noise, I jumped and nearly threw my book.

What the heck, Ax? Your ghost game is seriously slipping if you're getting spooked twice in the same hour.

My nose wrinkled in thought. Did ghosts even have game? And why did I have to spend my life after death with my kind-of-mean inner monologue? I could say with certainty that there would be no resting in peace—or peace at all—as long as my inner critic was still alive and well in my head.

Besides, was jumping out and saying, "boo!" part of a ghost's job description? I had no clue. When I died, no one had been waiting to welcome me to my ghosthood with a handshake and a job manual.

The overhead light flickered and emitted a high-pitched hum. Grinding my teeth, I narrowed my eyes at the newcomer, then my jaw dropped.

Sweet and salty chicken balls! This guy was all man... in all the best ways!

His raven hair was shaved short on the sides, but had been left longer on the top, and it fell to one side of his angular face as he ducked through the doorway. Dark stubble ran along his jawline, giving him the rough, yet alluring, look of a man who was too busy dealing with dangerous crap to worry about his appearance.

The guy strode to the stack of books and swiped away

the cobweb that stretched across the rows. His finger trailed down the dusty spines as he searched for the book he wanted, giving me a wonderful view of his profile.

He was the type of man who was featured as the main love interest in the paranormal romances that made up most of my TBR. Raising myself on my elbow, I studied every line of the man's face and body. The next time I needed to imagine the face of a sexy, brooding alpha male, I wanted to be able to call this man to mind.

"Are you going to say something? Or just stare at me like you've never seen a man before?" the guy said, his eyes never leaving the shelf.

Thinking I'd been so caught up in his looks that I hadn't noticed someone else enter, I quickly scanned the room, searching for whoever he was speaking to. There was no one, other than Mr. Tall-Dark-and-Dreamy, Wasabi the rat, and me.

But no one could see me, so who was he talking to?

The man pulled a book from the shelf, then lifted his gaze and stared directly at me. "You look like you've seen a ghost." He raised an eyebrow and his lips twitched.

"You can see me?" I whispered, even though I knew he couldn't see or hear me. "That's not possible."

Only Wasabi and the occasional gifted child had been able to see me.

"Of course I can." The man leaned back against the shelf and flipped open the book, sending a cloud of dust billowing out around him.

I glanced down at the book in my hand, weighing my

burning desire to finish the current chapter against my curiosity to speak to someone for the first time in three years.

Deciding an opportunity like this might not come around again in my afterlife, I reluctantly closed my book and pushed myself up into a sitting position.

"But how?" I asked, drifting down to the floor. "I'm a ghost and humans can't see me."

"Simple." The man shrugged, not bothering to look up from the heavy volume. "I'm not fully human."

"Then what are you?" I stepped closer to the man, something I never would have done when I was living and timid as a mouse.

I'm dead, so I have nothing to fear. He can't lay a finger on me. Which is unfortunate, since I want him to lay more than just a finger on me...

Huh. It seemed that in death, my inner voice had grown a spine. I'd certainly never been bold enough to approach a guy while alive, and definitely not one who looked like he could take on a grizzly without breaking a sweat.

Yep, my preferred type of men had always been book boyfriends... the type of guys who were confined to the pages of a romance.

"I'm a collector." His piercing gray eyes locked on my face, studying me as I stepped into the light.

"Collector? Like, antiques?" Far be it from me to judge a book by its cover, but he didn't fit the mold of an antique dealer. "Or do you collect money from terrified people for a mafia boss, and if they can't pay, you turn them into ghosts like me?"

"Neither." The deep timbre of his voice added to the edge of danger that rolled off him. He changed the topic. "How long have you been a ghost?"

The man was tall enough I had to tilt my head up to look at him. Letting my curiosity win, I floated up until we were at eye level.

Sugar honey iced tea! He was even more perfect up close.

Well, it was decided; I'd definitely have naughty thoughts about him later. Being dead had killed my sex life, but it didn't stop me from imagining it in my dreams.

Realizing I hadn't answered his question, I shrugged. "Three years, give or take a few weeks. Time begins to run together after a while."

For the first time, the man looked taken aback, and his eyes widened. "Are you sure?"

I snorted and lowered myself back to the floor. "Uh, yes. I'm pretty sure I remember how long it's been since I kicked the proverbial bucket. Death is considered a fairly important milestone in most people's lives."

Slowly, as though afraid of spooking a wild animal, the man lifted his hand toward my face. If I'd still been a card-carrying member of the living, I would've darted out of the room like a bat out of Hades. But being dead had done wonders for both my dry skin and my confidence.

Holding the breath I didn't actually need, I waited to see what he would do. After all, he couldn't physically touch me, let alone hurt me.

Boy oh boy, was I wrong.

His fingers brushed my cheek, and I shivered at the heat of his warm skin against my ghostly face.

This was impossible.

He shouldn't be able to touch me. Even with my dazzling ghostly party tricks, I hadn't been able to touch a living human's skin.

The overhead light flickered and hummed, but I barely noticed as electricity sizzled through his fingers. It surged through me, heating me from the inside out before finally returning to him.

"You can touch me?" My voice cracked. "I... I don't understand."

Unable to stop myself, I reached up and pressed my palm to his cheek. There was another pop of static and heat poured into my body from where our skin met.

"I live my life crossing between the planes of this world and the other. I can interact with you the same way I can interact with humans," he answered almost absently, his fingers slowly tracing my jaw. "You are just as alive to me as the people sitting in the library."

My eyes went to his lips, and I blamed the years spent reading romance for the direction my thoughts took. But since he could touch my face, I couldn't help but wonder what other things he could do.

"How'd you die?" The guy took a step closer until our faces were only inches apart.

Ha! Like I was going to tell him the truth. Not a chance in this life—er, death. "I got run over by Santa's sleigh."

"What?" His brow creased, and he blinked as he tried to process my words. Then he barked out a strangled laugh. "Santa isn't real."

I gave him a cheeky grin. "And neither are ghosts."

The gorgeous giant laughed, the sound husky and rough, as though he didn't use it much.

As though it had a mind of its own, my hand shifted, and my thumb slid across his bottom lip. I was being drawn to this guy like a hungry moth to an ugly Christmas sweater.

"You're beautiful," the man whispered, the mirth in his eyes being replaced by something dark and alluring.

I blew out a breathy laugh, trying to drag my wits back to me. "Yeah, if sweatpants-for-life girls are your type."

When I first started living the easy-breezy-ghost-girl life, I'd spent countless hours learning to visualize and finally swap my outfits. But after a while, I realized no one could see me, so why bother?

And for the past two years, I'd opted to stay in my favorite sweatpants, fuzzy socks, and an oversized white T-shirt. They didn't get dirty, and I didn't sweat, so they stayed clean. It was another ghostly perk.

I finished my look with a messy bun to keep my long hair out of my face—and to avoid looking like a certain unkempt and soaking wet ghost chick that scared the crap out of, well, everyone. The last thing I needed was for a kid to see me looking like that and convince the adults to perform an exorcism. I had no idea if it would work, but it was bound to cut into my reading time.

He shook his head at my words and caught my chin between his fingers. "I've never seen anyone so beautiful." His lips moved toward mine.

Holy hollyhocks!

Was he about to kiss me?

Was I about to let him?

After only a moment of hesitation, I tilted my head back, giving him better access to my mouth.

Just as our lips were about to touch, the library's intercoms crackled and I jerked back, clutching at my no-longer-beating heart as though I might have a heart attack.

It was another reminder that I was far too jumpy for a ghost.

A metallic voice announced, "The library is closing shortly. Please bring your books to the front to be checked out. Thank you."

"You should probably go." I backed away from him, not liking the feeling of loss that welled up in my chest as I said the words.

What was wrong with me? I shouldn't have felt anything over this stranger at all.

He took a step toward me, and suddenly afraid of the pull I felt toward him, I released my ghostly body and allowed myself to become one with the shadows.

Maybe he wouldn't be able to see me in this form.

Maybe he would leave before he messed up the perfect death I had going for myself.

"I'll come back." His eyes scanned the darkness, searching for me.

When I didn't answer, he returned the book to the shelf. Striding to the door, he flicked off the light and was gone.

Wasabi's twitching nose appeared at the edge of the shelf, sniffing in my direction. Calling my energy back, I put my ghost form back together.

"I have no freaking idea what just happened," I whispered, reaching up to scratch his ear.

"Impossible. You must've heard her wrong." Lochlan leaned against the counter and crossed his arms over his chest.

I tossed the paper bag with the fries and hamburgers onto the counter. "Ev! Dinner is here."

Grabbing one of the foil-wrapped burgers, I took a bite and turned to face Lochlan. "I know what I heard. Plus, I double checked. She was annoyed at me for questioning her."

"I guess there's a first time for everything," Lochlan mumbled, unwrapping his burger.

Evander came down the stairs, a book tucked under his arm. "A first time for what? Has Lochlan finally agreed to read a book?"

Lochlan scowled and took another bite of his burger. Unbothered, Ev snatched several fries from Loch's pile.

"No, we were talking about a ghost I met at the library this afternoon." Grabbing a bottle of ketchup from the fridge, I squeezed some out onto my wrapper. "She's been dead for three years."

Ev froze with a fry halfway to his mouth. "Three years? Even if that were possible, she'd be nothing more than flickering energy at this point."

I shook my head and picked at my food. "But she isn't. In fact, she's so vibrant I could've sworn she was a living, breathing woman when I entered the archive room."

My heart jerked in my chest at the memory of her gorgeous smile, inquisitive eyes, perfect curves, and her plump, kissable lips. I'd gone years without experiencing the stir of carnal desire, but today I'd been slapped in the face with it. Hard.

"Hello? Anyone in there?" Loch snapped his fingers in front of my face.

Blinking away the image of the seductive spirit, I brought the room back into focus. "Uh, yeah? I mean, did you ask something?"

"I asked if you knew how she died. But based on your expression, I'm thinking maybe I should ask how hot she was." A smirk lifted the corner of Lochlan's mouth. "I didn't think it was possible for the renowned, cold-as-ice Rhodes to be smitten."

Rather than denying my attraction, which would only have served to make him more suspicious, I answered his first question. "She claimed she got run over by Santa."

Ev choked on a fry and Lochlan slapped his back. When at last he could speak again, Ev wheezed out, "She said that?"

I chuckled. "Yep. With a straight face."

"Interesting. I like this chick already." Lochlan laughed, then turned thoughtful. "I think I'll visit the library tomorrow."

Ev choked a second time and spluttered, "You? At a library? Someone check the weather report; I bet hell has frozen over!"

"Whatever. Books might not be my thing, but I'm pretty good when it comes to ghosts." Lochlan leaned against the counter and raised a brow. "And I'm even better with women."

There was no denying the truth of the statement. We made a good team, each of us pulling our weight during our missions. While I tended to be more of the muscle, and Ev did the lion's share of research, Lochlan handled most of the communication with the living and the ghosts.

I knew most people considered me emotionless and cold, but since I preferred being left alone, I did nothing to change their perception of me.

With his perfectly messy golden hair, crystal-blue eyes, and boyish good looks, Evander could've had a different woman in his bed every night. But he preferred spending his evenings with a book. In fact, the man spent every waking minute with his nose buried inside the pages of a book. Heck, if it weren't for Lochlan and me, Ev would probably have died of starvation at this point.

So suffice it to say that Ev and I didn't have the best people skills. Lochlan was different though. He was good with both the living and the dead. And it wasn't just his cover-model good looks that had women falling all over him. No, he exuded a sincerity that had strangers willing to spill their deepest secrets within five minutes of meeting him.

Which meant he'd be able to get the library ghost's backstory far faster than I could. It made logical sense for him to go, so why did the thought of Loch meeting her make my stomach feel like I'd swallowed several lead weights?

Why did the thought of her big brown eyes with their beautiful green rings going all soft over Lochlan's boyish good looks make me want to punch something? Something like Loch's face.

"I still believe you must've misheard her." Ev's forehead creased as he tossed his wrapper into the trash can. "There are very few ghosts that haven't faded a year after their death. After eighteen months, even the strongest ghosts have disintegrated. In all my studies, I haven't run across a single record of a ghost who has survived two years past their death."

"You think I don't know that? I've been a collector since I was fifteen. I'm well aware of the ticking clock that starts the moment a person dies and what will happen if they aren't sent off the Earthly plane before the time runs out," I snapped, then regretted it when Ev dropped his eyes to the table.

Before we'd formed our posse, Evander had been placed with collectors who had little use for emotions and zero appreciation for his intellect. They'd eagerly worked to tear down his confidence, continuing the work Ev's parents had done on him for years.

We'd been a posse for five years, but Lochlan and I were still working to undo the damage that had been done before we met him. Having Ev be comfortable enough to question me out loud was a big deal. Now, my surly tone might have set us back.

Swallowing my pride, I sagged into the chair opposite him. "Sorry, Ev. There is something different about her and it has me unsettled, confused. Being near her was as though I'd stepped from the dark into the light."

Ev's eyes lifted to study my face, and he pushed his glasses up his nose. I waited, but he didn't question me further, his continued silence confirming that he'd retreated from me.

He'd become my brother, and I hated for there to be a wall between us. I didn't want him to feel as though he couldn't question me without fearing the repercussions. If I wanted to pull him back out of the shell he'd retreated into, I'd have to be vulnerable—something that would've been much easier to do if Lochlan wasn't leaning on the counter listening to every word.

Lochlan was also like a brother to me—the bratty little brother.

Deciding to pretend Loch wasn't there, and hoping he wouldn't use the conversation as blackmail later, I took a deep breath and admitted, "Ev, I wanted to kiss her. Hades! I didn't just want to, I almost did."

"What?!" My admission practically yanked Ev from his

shell. "You don't even like anyone well enough to let them in your personal space, let alone allow someone to touch you." His blue eyes glittered with interest.

"You're not wrong." I ran my thumb over the faint scratches on the table's wooden surface. "I'm fulfilled by the work we do. Chatting with you two is more than enough socialization for me. And that's what surprised me most at the library. I had to physically restrain myself from touching her."

Lochlan's laughter filled the kitchen. "Or maybe you've gone so long without getting your rocks off that you could barely keep it together when you met the pretty ghost girl?"

My jaw clenched at his vulgar comment, but I forced myself to relax. Loch wasn't entirely wrong.

"It wasn't just sexual. I wanted to touch her hair, hold her hand, stroke her cheek. It was an intense longing to be closer to her." This time, both Loch and Ev's eyebrows shot up nearly to their hairlines.

"She made you sentimental?" Lochlan's jaw hung slack. "So you're saying you didn't want to wrap her legs around your waist, pin her against the bookshelves, and take her on the spot?"

Dropping my eyes to the table, I avoided their gazes, trying to keep them from reading the truth written across my face. I was glad the table covered my lap so they couldn't see how a certain part of my anatomy had reacted to the mental image Loch painted.

I wanted her. Badly.

"She must be some ghost." Ev whistled and ran his

fingers through his hair. "But bro, you know we don't have sex with ghosts. We find them, help them get to the other plane before they disintegrate, and then we feed from the energy they leave behind. Doing the deed with a ghost just isn't part of what collectors do."

"I know that, Ev. Believe me, I know." Leaning back in the chair, I rubbed a hand down my face.

"Yeah. I haven't even done a ghost," Lochlan added, unhelpfully.

"She's different." I opened and closed my mouth, unable to find the words to describe the beautiful woman who'd stolen my breath. "She's... special."

"Then I can't wait to meet her in the morning." Lochlan gave me a crooked smile. "I need to see what kind of ghost can melt the heart of the ice king."

"Don't try me, Lochlan," I warned, sending a blade spinning across the room to embed itself in the wooden cabinet between his legs.

Unbothered by my threat or the blade that was a mere inch from his family jewels, Lochlan laughed. "Oh, don't look so worried, Rhodes. I won't steal her away." Pushing away from the counter, he headed toward the stairs, but paused and winked. "Besides, I'm fine with sharing."

I sent a second blade singing through the air, but Loch caught it mid-air, and with a flick of his wrist, sent it flying back at me.

It was an impressive feat, and pride swelled in my chest that he was part of my circle. We were three of the most powerful collectors on earth. Even the reapers, who enjoyed messing with my species, avoided ticking my circle off.

But just because I could appreciate his abilities and trusted him to have my back in battle, it didn't mean I wanted to share a woman with him. We'd bandaged each other's wounds and been in countless situations where privacy wasn't an option, which meant I could say with certainty that the male body did nothing for me. As far as I was concerned, I couldn't see any reason I'd want to share a woman with him.

"Some collectors share a wife. It isn't unheard of," Evander mused out loud.

"What?" Pulling my gaze from the dark stairway Loch had disappeared up, I squinted at Ev. "You'd seriously consider sharing a wife with Lochlan? With me?"

Ev shrugged. "I was raised by three dads and my mom, so the concept isn't strange to me. But honestly, it isn't something I've given much thought to. Probably because I figured Lochlan would never settle down with one woman, and I didn't think you'd ever get a girlfriend, let alone a wife."

Ev rarely offered personal details, and I couldn't resist the temptation to press for more.

"Did it work for your parents?" I asked.

Ev huffed out a soft laugh. "Mostly. My three fathers had separate rooms, and my mother would alternate which room she slept in. The problem was she made no secret of the fact that she had a favorite partner and a least favorite, so two of my dads never felt as though they were equally loved by her. But they made it work."

I'd grown up with a single mother who didn't know who my father was, so I couldn't imagine growing up like Ev. And knowing the extreme pressure they'd placed on him, I suspected that growing up with no dad was easier than growing up with three overbearing fathers.

"Rhodes, I've seen how girls look at you and Loch, and I know I can't compete with that. But if you or Loch took a wife, and she was happier being the only woman in the house, and you two agreed that sharing was the best for our circle, I would accept it." Ev fiddled with the edge of his book.

"Well, I don't think you need to worry about that. Despite what Loch says, I don't think either of us are the sharing type. You know we're too possessive and needy. We'd drive a woman crazy." Standing, I made my way to the fridge and pulled out two beers. "Enough about that. I want to know if you've made progress figuring out why the ghosts are flocking to this city." Grinning, Ev flipped open his notebook and began to go over the intel he'd gathered that afternoon. I sipped my beer and did my best to pay attention, but my thoughts kept drifting back to the sassy little ghost from the library.

CHAPTER 3

AXELLE

B iting down on my tongue, I squinted and concentrated hard on the rat trap in front of me. Apparently, Bertha the librarian was up to her tricks and trying to off Wasabi.

"If we don't get pest control to come in and take care of the problem, we're going to have rats chewing up all our books." Bertha tapped her fingernails on the countertop as she addressed the regional library director.

"Bertha, pest control was here three months ago, and they didn't find any signs of rats or mice. Are you positive you saw a rat in the break room? Maybe it was just a dust bunny that got stirred up by a draft?" To her credit, the director was trying her best to be patient.

The director had arrived that morning to do her bi-weekly check-in at our branch, and like every other visit for the past six months, Bertha was determined to convince her we had a rat infestation. Except we didn't.

We had a single rat, and he was an absolute gentleman who didn't tear up books or leave droppings around the library.

Bertha huffed in annoyance. "I know what I saw! It was a massive rat!"

"Are you ready for this?" I whispered near Wasabi's ear, even though I could have spoken in a normal tone since he was the only one who could hear me.

Taking Wasabi's blink as confirmation, I summoned every ounce of energy I'd gathered and slowly lifted him in my palms. For living humans, picking up an item the size of a rat was a piece of cake. But things were totally different when you were a ghost.

I caught the tip of my tongue between my teeth as I concentrated hard, not wanting to drop my little friend. Inch by inch, I raised him in the air until he was eye level with me. I was standing a few feet behind the director's back, so I knew she wouldn't see what was happening.

The moment Bertha turned to face the director, I carefully began moving back and forth, swooping Wasabi up and down as though he were flying or riding an invisible, slow-motion roller coaster.

"Eek!" Bertha's eyes bulged as she caught sight of Wasabi dipping this way and that. "The rat! It's right there!"

The moment her eyes darted to the director's face, I threw myself and Wasabi behind the counter. Lowering him to the ground, I smiled as he touched his nose to my hand, then scampered through the hidden hole behind the printer.

With Wasabi safe, I stood and leaned on the counter, eager to take in the unfolding drama.

"Where?" the director yelped, the fabric of her clothes whirling around her as she turned in circles. "I don't see anything!"

"It was right there! Flying around behind your head!" Bertha shrieked, waving at the air behind the manager. "The rat couldn't have gotten far!"

Bertha whipped her head this way and that, searching for the flying rodent. Her wide-eyed expression of determination, combined with the chaotic twisting of her neck, gave Bertha an unhinged sort of vibe. And judging by the deep creases in the director's forehead, I wasn't the only one who thought so.

"Bertha, are you feeling okay?" Tight lines appeared around her eyes and mouth as she watched Bertha's erratic searching.

Spinning around to face her boss, Bertha shoved at the hair that had escaped from her bun that was twisted tighter than a pair of hipster jeans. "Yes, of course! Why would you ask?"

But even as she spoke, Bertha's eyes continued to dart toward the ceiling, still searching for Wasabi.

"Because you just told me you saw a flying rat..."

"It *was* flying!" Bertha exclaimed, little bits of spit flying from her mouth. "I know! We'll go check the security cameras. Then you'll see!"

Breathing hard, she stomped toward the cramped office

the librarians shared. The director followed slowly behind Bertha, rubbing at her forehead as though already feeling the beginnings of a migraine.

I didn't bother to join them since I already knew what they would find. Nada. Only an amateur would forget to turn off the security camera before pulling a ghostly prank. Duh.

The last thing I needed was for the rumor to spread that the library was haunted. If that happened, the library would become a hot spot for ghost hunters who would spend all hours of the day and night asking me yes or no questions. Just thinking about it had a shiver skating down my spine.

My thoughts drifted to the hunk from the evening before. See? He was a perfect example of why it was best no one knew I was hanging around.

I'd lost a good chunk of reading time last night because I hadn't been able to get him out of my thoughts, and I wanted to kick myself for acknowledging him at all. Let's be real, a man would lead to a whole host of distractions that I didn't want to deal with.

Sure, I was dead and completely alone, but death had given me the freedom to read for hours. I had zero responsibilities or worries. What more could a girl need or want?

Heck! It was a good thing Wasabi was able to care for himself, because he would've joined me in death if I was in charge of keeping him alive. And I certainly didn't need a man if I couldn't even handle the responsibility of a pet.

I sighed, trying to ignore the tiny voice in my head that

dared to disagree. That was the part of me that devoured every romance book I could get my ghostly hands on, and desperately wished I'd thrown myself in his arms and kissed his lips as though it was the last kiss I'd ever receive.

And it probably had been my last chance at a kiss since he was the only person I'd met in my afterlife who could physically touch me.

In life, my dating experiences had been nothing like the steaminess I'd discovered inside the pages of romance books. Making out on dates had been rather lackluster, and my sex life had been dead long before I died.

So why had I let my last chance at riding the midnight train to pound town walk out the door? I rubbed my face and groaned. For all I knew, he might've been unwilling to do a ghost.

Although, he certainly hadn't seemed turned off by the fact I was among the *living challenged*.

"Pull it together, Axe," I murmured, propping my chin up against my palm. "You have a good thing going here, and you don't want to do something that will screw it up. Dudes are drama."

It would've been a whole lot easier to follow my advice if he hadn't been so dang yummy.

Shaking my head, I resolutely pushed the naughty images running through my brain into a box and locked them away. I didn't throw the key away, though. Who knew when a girl might have needed some inspiration for her spank bank?

"I'm telling you, I feel perfectly fine!" Bertha's loud huff brought my attention back to the melodrama playing out in front of me.

"Bertha, I appreciate how hard you work for us here at the library. I'd rather you take a few days off, than risking you having a breakdown. We all need a little R&R from time to time. There's no shame in it." The manager's voice was gentle but firm, and I couldn't help but grin.

Once the director made up her mind, there was no undoing it. Bertha would be taking a vacation whether she wanted to or not.

That meant Wasabi was safe from exterminators until she returned. And even then, I doubted Bertha would be so quick to bring up the topic of rats to the manager for fear it would only help to usher her into early retirement.

Wonderful! With that distraction out of the way, I could get back to tackling my TBR list.

The whoosh of the library's main door opening caught my attention, and I turned to find Tim, the delivery driver, carrying several boxes.

The library had received a large donation, and the funds had been earmarked for purchasing new books. Using my computer skills, I'd managed to add a few novels to the list before the director had placed the order.

Waiting for them to arrive had been more painful than my death. I rushed to Tim's side, practically dancing around him in unbridled glee.

"Hi, Tim!" Tilly called out, appearing from between two shelves and hurrying toward the counter.

"Well, hello there, Miss Tilly." Tim huffed, dropping the

stack of boxes on the counter. He shivered. "It's cold in here today."

Tilly clicked her tongue against her teeth and shook her head. "Yes, we've been dealing with a draft in here for the past few years, but no one has been able to figure out where it's coming from."

Grabbing a small handheld device from his belt, he began scanning the packages. "Probably just an old building thing."

I rolled my eyes and took a step away from Tim. The cold had nothing to do with the library being old and everything to do with it being haunted... *by yours truly.*

Right after my death, I'd haunted the one bookstore in town, but it hadn't worked out. The constant chimes from the cash register and the beeps of the credit card machine had nearly driven me to become a screaming banshee. Although, by far, the worst part had been the aromatic scent of coffee that wafted through the bookstore from the tiny cafe setup in the corner of the shop.

Coffee was one of the only things I missed about being alive, and I decided for everyone's wellbeing, I needed to find somewhere quieter to spend the rest of eternity. Other-wise, I might've tried my hand at possessing someone's body just so I could taste the caffeinated nectar of the gods one more time.

I was much happier spending my days and nights inside the quiet library, even though it meant I sometimes had to wait many months for new releases to make their way into the collection.

As Tilly and Tim continued sharing small talk, I shifted impatiently from one foot to the other.

"Come on," I whined. "Just admit you have the hots for each other so we can get this show on the road. There's a book in that box that I'd like to read before I die of anticipation!"

They didn't respond, not that I'd expected them to since they couldn't hear me. Sadly, I was forced to endure their awkward attempts at flirting for another ten minutes before Tim tipped his hat and headed out the door.

"Finally!" I sagged onto the counter in relief.

Tilly added to my agony by taking a full five minutes to find her preferred box cutter, but at last, she sliced the tape on the first box. I watched with bated breath as she lifted one book after another from the box and set them on the counter. She had removed half the books from the box when I spotted the book I'd desperately been waiting on.

The latest release from none other than Raven Kennedy.

"Finally!" I squealed, fighting the urge to snatch the book from Tilly's hands.

The library already had one librarian on a mental health leave. If Tilly started screaming about ghosts and floating books, we'd be down another one.

I clenched my fists at my side and stared longingly as she laid the book on the counter. But the moment she turned to put the empty cardboard box on the floor, my self-control snapped and I snatched the book. Laughing maniacally, I clutched my treasure to my chest and darted toward the archive room.

There were only two guests in the library at that early hour, but I wasn't worried about them spotting me. I was moving at a pace the human eye couldn't track.

My speed was a ghost perk that was thoroughly wasted on me. I could count on one hand the number of times I'd run since my death… which was exactly never.

Even when I'd still been among the living, I hadn't been fond of running. And the last time I'd attempted to run, I'd ended up dead, so look where it had gotten me. But a new book by my favorite author was worth the risk.

Reaching the archive room, I settled on top of the bookshelf I called my bed. I spent the next two hours lost inside my newest BILF—Book I'd Like to Finish.

Completely captivated by the story, it took me far too long to realize something was stroking against my cheek.

"Not now, Wasabi," I murmured, my eyes still fixed on the page. "Things are just getting steamy."

I'd expected a disgruntled squeak of protest from Wasabi, but instead, deep laughter filled the room and sent a thrill racing straight to my toes.

Jerking my head to the right, I came face to face with an unfamiliar man. He must have stepped onto the lower shelf because his arms were folded on the top of the bookshelf and he was resting his chin on top of them.

"*Ahhh!*" My shriek was loud enough to wake the dead, but the man only raised an eyebrow in response.

"Boo!" he teased, still chuckling under his breath. "Someone is awfully jumpy."

"You would be too if strangers were sneaking up on you! And that's my line!" I snapped.

My irritation at being pulled away from my book was only slightly dampened by the pair of glittering green eyes that were partially hidden by the blond hair that fell over the left side of the stranger's face.

He was pretty. Almost too pretty. With my mind still filled with romance and a fantasy realm, I couldn't stop myself from taking a quick peek at his ears to check if they were pointed. They weren't, which was an absolute shame because the man would've made one heck of a beautiful fae.

The infuriatingly alluring man was studying me, and his finger stroked along my cheek again. In life, I would've growled at any man who dared touch me without permission, sexy or not. So it had to be the lack of physical interactions I'd had over the past three years that had me leaning ever-so-slightly into his touch.

Realizing how close I was dancing to a whole world of trouble, I sat up and scooted away from him. "Nope!"

The man tilted his head, likely confused by my sudden change of mood. "Something wrong?"

"Yes. I'm living a bookworm's dream, and I refuse to lose my valuable reading time by getting sucked into a beautiful stranger's drama." I narrowed my eyes.

"Aw. You find me attractive, boo?"

"It's not like you didn't already know that. I'm sure you've been told how good looking you are since you were a kid." I blushed but lifted my chin, refusing to let him see how much he was muddling my brain and making my stomach quiver. "And don't call me boo."

"I've never been complimented by a woman as lovely as you though." The man purred. "If I can't call you boo, can I call you mine?"

Oh yes.

This man was definitely going to be trouble.

CHAPTER 4

AXELLE

"Axe. Well, actually, my name is Axelle, but I just go by Axe. Axelle sounds like a guy's name, although Axe isn't really any more feminine. I guess that's what happens when your mom gives birth and dips out, leaving you behind for your dad to raise." Realizing I was rambling, I snapped my mouth closed and looked up at the ceiling.

It was those stupid green eyes of his. They were a siren's trap, calling me to reveal my deepest thoughts.

Ha! Joke was on him. Deep thoughts were something I'd given up in favor of using my full energy for reading. So he was going to end up regretting any inner musing he pulled from my mind. Like why didn't we call a yeti's dick a *penisicle*? And if vampires didn't have blood flow, how could they get an erection?

"Axe. I like it." The man held out his hand. "I'm Lochlan, but you can call me Loch."

"It was a pleasure to meet you Loch." I shook his hand,

then picked my book back up. "Enjoy your visit here at the library. If you can't find something, ask for Tilly. She's the nice one."

Lying back down, I opened my book and pretended to focus on the crisp cream-colored pages. In truth, I was finding it hard to think of anything other than the scent of fir trees and leather that drifted around me. His scent.

"You're dismissing me?" Lochlan asked, a hint of surprise in his voice.

"I'm sorry. You caught me at a busy time." He probably wasn't used to having girls ignore him. Hiding my smile, I flipped another page.

Loch remained quiet for several minutes, watching me read. Then he hopped off the shelf, and from the corner of my eye, I watched as he pulled a book from another large metal shelf. Lowering himself to the floor, he opened the dusty cover and began slowly thumbing through the pages.

Interesting. He didn't seem like the reading type, but who was I to complain? I'd gotten what I wanted—peace and quiet to read my book.

Five hours later, I closed the book with a happy sigh. It had been even better than I'd hoped, but now I would have to wait months for the next book in the series.

Slinging my legs over the side of the shelf, I stretched.

"How was it?" The sound of Loch's deep voice had me clutching my chest.

"You're still here?" I yelped.

He shrugged and flipped another page in the giant tome he was reading.

Curiosity piqued, I drifted to the floor and soundlessly moved to sit beside him. Leaning forward, I skimmed the page he was reading.

"Ancient travel routes and temple locations?" I read aloud, then turned to squint at Loch.

He closed the book and set it on the floor beside him. "There's a lot of ghost activity in town and we are trying to figure out the cause."

"The guy from yesterday is with you?" I asked. They were the first two people who were able to see me since my death, so it made sense they would have arrived together.

"Yes. You left quite the impression on Rhodes yesterday." Loch reached up and tucked a stray piece of hair behind my ear. "And I can see why."

"Oh?" I breathed as my stomach twisted itself in knots.

My mind was still hazy with romance, and I was finding it difficult to remember my resolution to not get distracted or sucked into guy drama. Especially with this gorgeous man's scent tickling my nose and his attention focused on me as though I were the most fascinating woman on earth.

It was intoxicating.

I'd finished a book today, and my head needed time to bask in the story before I started my next. So maybe it wasn't the worst thing to let myself enjoy a bit of human interaction... How much trouble could that get me in?

"I'm sure you meet a lot of interesting people—er, ghosts."

"We meet a lot of ghosts, but there is something different about you." Lochlan rested his head against the wall.

His expression was open, allowing me to see the curiosity glinting in the mossy green pools of his eyes.

"Because I'm not hungover?" I asked.

"What?" Loch's forehead creased.

"You know what I mean! Every ghost I've bumped into since I kicked the bucket has seemed like they have the world's worst hangover. They shuffle around, squinting at the light, mumbling under their breath, shying away from loud noises, and stumbling through walls. Aren't all ghosts like that? Or just the ones I've met?"

Loch burst out laughing, and I watched, mesmerized by how every movement he made could be so perfect. Yep, he was definitely book boyfriend material.

"I never thought about it that way, but you're right. Ghosts do act like they just woke up after a two-day bender. Probably because the moment their bodies die, they begin to lose energy." Loch playfully squinted at me. "So what makes you different, Axe?"

I shrugged. "This is the first I've heard of ghosts losing energy. I was a lightweight when I was alive, so I have no idea why I'm not hungover in death too."

He rubbed at the five o'clock shadow on his jaw. "How long have you been dead?"

"Three years." I answered, a little distracted and a whole lot flattered by the way he was giving me his full attention.

How many insta-love stories had I read in the past three years? If I had to guess, probably close to two hundred. And every single time, I wanted to kick the leading female in the butt for not taking the hot man up on what he was offering. This was my chance to be adventurous and just go for it, but here I was doing the same thing as the women who frustrated me in books.

Loch rested his hand on my upper thigh, giving it a playful squeeze. I was pretty sure he meant for the gesture to be teasing, but it was hard convincing my body of that when I hadn't been with a guy in five years. It didn't help that I spent every single day reading love stories that stirred my heart and body with all sorts of desires.

I closed my eyes for a moment, soaking in the heat that was radiating from where his palm rested against my thigh. As a ghost, I was always cold. I wasn't freezing or in pain, but still, it was hard to ignore how comforting it was to feel warm... to feel almost alive again. It was a struggle not to wonder what it would be like to have more of his body touching mine. Or how amazing it would feel if there were nothing between us.

Whoa. Slow your roll, Axelle! I forced myself to put a stop to the dangerous direction my thoughts were moving in.

"Did you enjoy it?" Loch asked.

Confused, I blinked at him. "Um... what?"

Surely I hadn't spoken out loud.

"Your book. You were so focused while reading it that you barely moved for hours." Loch jerked his chin at the book I'd set on the floor beside me.

"Oh!" I gasped, retrieving the book and turning it over in my hands.

It was a relief to discover I hadn't humiliated myself by

blabbering my inner thoughts as I was prone to do since only Wasabi could hear me.

My relief was short-lived.

"Did you have a favorite part?" Loch asked.

His eyes, which had been so intently focused on mine, suddenly slid down to my mouth. Absolutely flustered, I dropped my gaze to the book in my lap.

"Yes, it's… um…" I tried to think of even a single scene from the book, but it was no use. My brain was too busy wondering what his lips tasted like. "It's big."

Seriously, Axe? Come on, you can do better! My inner pep talk only added to the chaos inside my head.

I turned the book over. "And hard."

"That's what she said," Loch crowed, his chest rumbling with laughter.

Embarrassment flooded my body. The overhead lights flickered, then with a pop, they went out. I was thankful for the cloak of complete darkness, since it gave me time to compose myself.

I like it big and hard? I mouthed the words, crossing my eyes and scrunching my nose as I mocked myself. *Open wide, Axe! Let's see how much further you can shove your foot down your throat.*

Dropping my head back against the wall, I looked toward Loch, taking advantage of the darkness to admire the man.

With his high cheekbones, gleaming skin, chiseled jawline, pale hair, and sultry lips, the man looked like he belonged in a Middle Earth kingdom. Honestly, if he'd sprouted a set of fluffy white wings, I wouldn't have been surprised.

He was one of those pretty people who were painfully attractive. Even if I was having the best hair day, and I perfectly nailed the winged eyeliner on both eyes, and I slid on a pair of jeans without having to do the wiggle dance to get them over my hips, I'd still feel like a frumpy bridge troll in their presence.

My eyes traced the lines of his face before focusing on his lips. With his thumb rubbing soft circles on my upper thigh, I was having trouble thinking about anything other than how long it had been since I'd been kissed.

I wished I had the confidence of the strong female characters in my books. They knew what they wanted and had the courage to go after it. I wanted to straddle his lap, sink my fingers into his hair, and capture his lips in a kiss. But I wasn't brave or spontaneous, so I remained motionless beside Loch.

My internal struggle came to a screeching halt as a male ghost in a pinstripe business suit walked through the wall and into the archive room. Without looking left or right, he strode across the floor and through the wall that led to one of the library's storage rooms.

Before either of us could comment, a young woman in denim shorts and a crop top walked through the wall directly behind us. She bumped into me, the movement pushing me away from Loch. For her part, the woman didn't seem to notice. Rubbing my arm, I stared at her back as the ghost disappeared through the same spot on the far wall.

I was jostled again when a third ghost, this time a man wearing swim shorts and a sun visor, strolled through the wall.

"That's weird," I murmured, staring at the wall the third ghost had disappeared through. "I don't think I've ever seen three ghosts in this room."

"Yeah. Unless there was a mass casualty disaster nearby, this isn't normal." Loch's denim jeans rustled as he stood. "I'm going to go check it out."

Reaching out, I caught his hand. "It's dark and you don't know the library. Maybe I should check it out, since I can see just fine in the dark?"

"I can see just fine in the dark. Perk of not being human." Loch winked, lifting my hand to his lips and placing a soft kiss on the back of it.

My mouth opened and closed, but no words came out. Did that mean he knew I'd been checking him out? A horrible thought slapped me in the face. He'd watched me make faces at myself. I went pale, which was saying something since I was dead.

Loch smirked, then turned and headed toward the door.

"Why not follow the ghosts?" I tried to clear the lump of embarrassment from my throat.

"Because I can't walk through walls." He opened the door, causing light from the hall to stream into the room.

Apparently, my electrical surge earlier had only blown the lights inside the archive room, which was good. The first time I'd lost control of my emotions and surged, I'd accidentally fried three computers and blew every light bulb in the building.

Loch blew me a kiss, stepped into the hall, and closed the door behind him. With him gone, I felt like I could finally take a deep breath—which was absolutely ridiculous since ghosts didn't need to breathe and I only continued the motions out of habit.

Not wanting to sit alone and dwell on my awkwardness, I jumped to my feet and headed toward the spot the ghosts had vanished through.

"THIS IS EXACTLY the kind of distraction I was trying to avoid," I muttered under my breath, glancing around the storage room.

"Is that why you've done your best to ignore me today?" An arm snaked around my waist, pulling me back against a hard chest. "Aw, boo. Are you struggling to resist me?"

"Loch!" My yelp of surprise came out more like a moan —a sound that encouraged him to double down on his flirting.

Wrapping both arms around my middle, Loch bent and nuzzled my neck. Heat rushed through me, raising my body from room temperature to almost alive. It was glorious, and a whimper tumbled from my lips.

I quickly clamped my mouth shut, but it was too late. Loch knew my willpower was wavering. Cradling my body against him, Loch brushed his lips against the bare skin of my neck.

"W-we are supposed to be looking for ghosts," I whispered, my voice quivering.

His chest rumbled with a soft growl. "You can keep looking, but I'm already holding the ghost I wanted to find."

Holy Headless Horseman!

Being in his arms was like being caught in quicksand. Except I didn't want to escape from him.

Come on, Axe. Where's your spine?

A man could be fun, but having one would make it even more impossible to get through my to-be-reads. Swallowing hard, I reluctantly wiggled from his arms. Not trusting my legs to carry me, I floated a few feet away from him.

"We can't get side-tracked. You're in town to figure out what's up with the ghosts. This is our chance to get more information." I was proud of how confident I sounded, despite my regret that I'd never know where things might have gone if I'd stayed in his arms.

Loch studied me for several long seconds before nodding. "Okay. We'll focus on work. For now."

Outwardly, I rolled my eyes, but an electrifying thrill zig-zagged through me.

We spent the next five minutes maneuvering our way

through dust-covered boxes that had been arranged into haphazard stacks. Twice, I caught a glimpse of a ghost from the corner of my eye, but they disappeared before I could follow them.

The overhead lights hissed then whirred as they flickered to life. Blinking hard in the sudden light, we spun toward the door to find Tilly standing there with her arms folded across her chest.

"Sir? What are you doing back here?" she demanded.

"Uh-oh. You're in trouble," I teased, knowing she couldn't see or hear me.

Loch shot me a sly look before smiling at Tilly. "I'm sorry, miss. I'm terrible with directions, and I got confused when I left the archive room. I guess I turned the wrong way."

He rubbed at the back of his neck, causing the hem of his shirt to rise and giving the librarian a peek at his toned abs. Catching his bottom lip between his teeth, he looked at her with his big green eyes.

I snorted. "Come on! There is no way she's going to fall for the innocent puppy eyes from a guy who looks like a sexy stripper!"

Tilly gave a girlish giggle and patted her hair. "Oh! It happens all the time!"

It was my turn to cross my arms over my chest. "No it doesn't."

Tilly couldn't hear me, but I caught the twitch at the corner of Lochlan's mouth.

"Well, the library is closing in a few minutes, so let's get you back to the lobby." She waved for him to follow her, then bustled down the hall.

Loch waited until she was far enough away so she wouldn't overhear him speaking to me. "I'll be back later tonight to look around."

"Sounds good. I have plans, but I wish you success." I grinned and headed toward the archive room.

Loch's eyebrows rose. "You have plans?"

"Yep." I grinned over my shoulder at him. "I have a date!"

Not giving him a chance to respond, I disappeared into the shadows.

CHAPTER 5

SAUL

I watched the collector move away from the ghost and follow after the bossy librarian. Remaining in the shadows, I stayed hidden. If the collector knew I was near, he'd have questions. Or worse, he'd try to create small talk.

As long as I stayed in the reaper plane, the collector wouldn't be able to see me. Although it was possible that a collector of his power would be able to sense the presence of a reaper in the area.

Earth was made up of several layers that were each superimposed or overlaid on the others. Humans were stuck on one layer or plane, and most could only see other humans. There were a few special humans who could sense the beings on the ghostly plane, but no human could travel to another plane.

When humans died, their ghosts could travel between the human and ghostly planes. Unfortunately, ghosts were made of energy, and they couldn't survive very long on either layer, and if they burned out before getting an escort to the beyond, they were lost forever.

That was where reapers came in. We came to collect souls as the human body breathed their last. But the world's population had grown to a point where there simply weren't enough reapers.

It had left my kind struggling to keep up with the demands placed on us—especially with the loss of our leader a few years before. So sometimes, during times of chaos or mass casualties, a soul or two would slip away before a reaper could gather them.

And that was where the collectors came in. They were able to hunt down the souls who'd slipped through a reaper's grasp.

Collectors had the ability to interact with those in the human and ghost planes. They collected the wandering ghosts and delivered them to one of Earth's vortexes where the different planes were the thinnest.

When ghosts were pulled into the vortex to the beyond, they left behind what remained of their energy and the collectors absorbed that energy. Reapers looked down on collectors as lesser beings due to their need to feed on ghostly energy.

It was pathetic, just like the vampires who required the blood of the living to survive. Just thinking about it caused a shiver to run down my spine. Regardless of my disgust, I couldn't deny that the collectors provided a necessary service to both the living and the dead.

I couldn't imagine how different the world would be if

the collectors had decided to murder humans in order to feed off their fresh ghostly energy. Instead, they'd chosen to use their abilities to help the lost souls.

Reapers were far superior in all ways but one. The collectors still possessed the ability to breed, thus ensuring their kind's continued survival.

The last female reaper had died almost five hundred years before, and she had produced only two children—my older brother and I. While reapers were immortal, and it was rare for one of our kind to be killed, we all knew it was only a matter of time before our species was extinct.

Before his death, my brother had fallen in love with a female collector. Yet despite their hopes and years of copulation, they'd been unable to produce offspring. When my brother had been murdered, the slim hope that our species could continue by breeding with the collectors had also died.

Pushing back the morose thoughts, I made my way into the lobby and up to the second story that overlooked the library. Until the collector left the premises, I wanted to keep an eye on him. Perched on the iron rail, I stared down at the collector male, watching as he finished chatting with the librarian and then headed out into the last rays of the setting sun.

Once he was gone, the librarian turned off the lights and did a final check for any stray guests. When she finished closing down the library and locked the door behind herself, I dropped soundlessly to the floor beneath me.

Something bothered me, and it wasn't just the fact that a collector could create complications for our plan.

Collectors were committed to their jobs. They had to be because their lives depended on seeking out lost ghosts and devouring the energy they left behind. So why would he allow the ghost to remain? His kind could teleport to the vortexes, so why had he been fraternizing with a ghost instead of teleporting her straight to the nearest vortex?

I needed to let Zacharias know collectors were in town, since their presence could create an issue for us. But first, I wanted to learn more about this ghost and what made her special to the collector.

Following the scent of her energy, I found her curled up like a feline on a plush sofa in the back corner of the library, her attention focused on the book in her hands. Tilting my head, I took in her opalescent skin, soft pouty lips, and the messy, dark hair that framed her heart-shaped face.

Her clothes were baggy, but they did little to hide her curves. As my eyes trailed over her body, something stirred in me... something dark and ravenous.

I'd reaped more than a million souls, and not once had I given a second glance to any of them. So why did she cause me to feel... unsettled?

My reaction couldn't be natural. Needing to get out of there and clear my head, I turned on my heel and strode away.

Right before I moved out of sight of the sofa, I gave in to the urge to take a last look at the female. But when I glanced over my shoulder, I was stunned to find her brown eyes staring right at me.

It was as though she were seeing straight into my soul.

Impossible.

I was walking in the reaper plane, which meant only another reaper could see me.

Her eyes slid back to her book, and I realized she must have been looking at something else that just happened to be in my direction. Of course she couldn't see me.

My fingers clenched into a fist. Why did that bother me?

Because I want her to see me.

Shaking my head to clear the foolishness from it, I strode through the wall and out into the dusk.

Zacharias and I were close to finishing our plan, and getting revenge for my brother's murder was the only thing on earth that mattered to me.

There was no way I'd allow my curiosity over a wayward ghost to jeopardize it.

CHAPTER 6

LOCHLAN

I sagged onto the couch, blowing out a long sigh.

"Well? Did you learn anything?" Evander asked, pushing his glasses up his nose and peering at me over the top of his laptop.

Leaning my head back against the couch cushion, I closed my eyes. "There's a reaper in town."

"Are you sure? Did you see one?" Rhodes' footsteps were heavy as he entered the room.

Cracking open one eyelid, I glanced toward him. "I didn't see anyone, but I sensed his presence nearby. He must've been walking in the reaper plane."

Ev closed his laptop and leaned forward to set it on the coffee table. "Maybe it's the reaper's presence in the area that's drawing the ghosts to Amberwood? Ghosts are drawn to reapers like moths are to flames."

I snorted. "Not just ghosts. Have you seen how humans act when they're around a reaper? They should fear death, yet they fawn all over reapers. Those dicks might as well be a type of sex god with the way panties hit the floor whenever they enter a room."

"You sound jealous," Evander chuckled. "Don't worry, bro. Reapers wouldn't even consider dating a human, so they aren't in competition with you."

I didn't care who the reaper was interested in dating, as long as it wasn't Axelle. He could have every female ghost, human, and collector out there if he wanted. But he wasn't getting Axelle.

That morning, when I'd stepped inside Amberwood's public library, I'd been greeted by the scent of floor polish, old lady rose perfume, and dusty book pages. It had brought back memories of being in elementary school.

Unlike Evander, who would be thrilled to live in a library, I would've been content to never step foot inside one again. Oh, the things a man would do for a beautiful woman!

My brow furrowed. I knew the guys thought I was only there to check out some ghost booty, but they were wrong. We each had a set of skills that made us a valuable part of the circle, and one of mine was the ability to read body language.

Sure, I might've gone a little too far when teasing Rhodes about his attraction to her, but it had served a purpose. While he'd thought I was simply being a dick, I was reading his non-verbal cues.

There was no doubt in my mind that he would jump the ghost's bones if given the chance. What surprised me most was that his interest went deeper than just getting his rocks off.

Rhodes had never shown sexual interest in a ghost, and he'd never shown serious interest in a human or collector. Probably because having a relationship would require him to talk to people other than Ev and me. I'd known the man long enough to know he wasn't a virgin, but he might as well have been.

There was something about the library ghost that had captured his attention in a way I hadn't witnessed from him before. We were there to study the unusual ghost activity going on in town, so it had only made sense for me to figure out what made her different. It might have helped us answer some questions.

Instead, I'd spent the day sitting on the floor and reading maps, just so I could study her face while she devoured her book.

In a single day, the beautiful bookworm had me doing two things I swore I'd never do.

First, I'd read a book. Well, part of a book.

Second, I'd fallen in love.

The idea of love at first sight was something I'd spent my life scoffing at, but I'd left the library a believer.

After seeing Axelle in person and tasting her sweet skin, Rhodes' visceral attraction to her the previous day had made perfect sense. It wasn't just her looks that captivated me. No, something deep inside me was pushing me toward her and causing my skin to burn with the need to touch her.

Glancing at Rhodes, I wondered for the thousandth time

today how this could work. We both wanted her, and we were each far too stubborn to give her up.

What if she wanted us both? Could we work things out, or would we end up killing each other?

I was a selfish man, and I'd only been joking about my willingness to share. Hades! Even if I found the strength to share Axe, I'd lose my mind if she spent the night in another man's room and I was left alone with my thoughts and insecurities.

If our circle was going to share, we'd need a single bedroom with a large bed. But that would pose a major problem for Rhodes.

He was the most private man I'd ever met. He liked Ev and me, but we weren't even allowed in his bedroom. Could he be happy sharing not only a mate but also his living space?

Ev tapped his fingers on the arm of his chair. "But to draw this number of ghosts to him, the reaper would have to be staying in town. I've never heard of a reaper staying in one location for more than a few hours," he mused out loud.

"True. So, either Lochlan is mistaken about a reaper being nearby, or this particular reaper is involved in the weirdness going on in Amberwood." Rhodes sighed. "That doesn't really help us, though. Because even if we find the reaper, he isn't going to tell us what's going on. I can't remember the last time we bumped into a reaper who acknowledged our existence or spoke a word to any of us."

Groaning, I sat up. "I'll reach out to a few contacts. Maybe someone has heard rumors about what's going on in the reaper realm. Let's stay careful and watch each other's backs until we untangle this mess."

"Agreed." Rhodes and Ev nodded.

I pushed to my feet and stretched. "I guess I'll go make those calls."

"Sit." Rhodes packed enough command in the one word to have my body obeying before I'd even processed his order.

Lifting a brow, I shot him a questioning look. I had a suspicion I knew what he was going to ask next, but I hoped this was one of the rare occasions when I was wrong.

"Did you meet her?" Rhodes asked.

It was hard being Mr. Right all the time.

I locked gazes with Rhodes. "Yes, I met Axelle."

She didn't belong to him, so I'd done nothing wrong. But I'd heard his admission last night, and I couldn't deny I felt a tiny twinge of guilt.

"And?" Rhodes prodded.

"And what?" I snarled, feeling defensive. What I did or didn't do with her wasn't his business.

Tense silence descended on the room. When Rhodes spoke again, his voice was soft. "And what was it like, kissing her?"

My eyes snapped to his face. "How could you know that?"

Rhodes rubbed his forehead. "You're glowing. Unless

you managed to collect a year's worth of lost souls and deliver them to a vortex in"—Rhodes paused to glance at his watch "—less than twelve hours, then you found a new way to feed. My guess is you kissed her."

"I didn't kiss her lips, but I did kiss her neck." At my admission, displeasure flashed across Rhodes' face, but he was quick to hide it.

"You can't be serious! You think just kissing her neck could do this?" Evander's voice rose, cracking slightly. "If that's true, imagine what having sex with Axelle could do to your energy!"

Rhodes and I groaned in unison. Ev hadn't met her, so he had no way of knowing the strange effect she was having on us. He didn't understand that just her name and the word *sex* in the same sentence was a special kind of torture.

Needing to go to my room and relieve some of the pressure that had built over the last few hours, I pushed to my feet again. "I think we should go back to the library and see if we can pick up the ghosts' trail."

My suggestion had nothing to do with the fact I was a jealous man and I wanted to find out what kind of date Axelle was going on. It was simply because our records on ghosts said they didn't date, and I wanted to know if that needed to be updated.

Yep. I only wanted to ensure that our books contained accurate data.

"Sounds like that's our best lead." Rhodes stood and stretched. "I got a glimpse of the security system yesterday.

It was pretty low-tech, so it shouldn't be difficult to disable it."

"I guess I'll go change and print off a copy of the library's blueprints." Evander tucked his laptop under his arm and headed toward the stairs.

Snickering, I followed him up the stairs. "The library isn't big. I'm pretty sure we won't get lost."

"It never hurts to be prepared. I'd rather not be caught off guard," Evander quipped.

I watched him disappear into his room and couldn't help but smirk. Like it or not, if we bumped into Axelle, he was definitely going to be caught off guard. She was different from every other ghost I'd met.

Axe was special.

"THIS WOULD BE SO MUCH EASIER if we could walk through walls like the reapers," I grumbled, watching Evander work. For an old building, it was proving a challenge to unlock the ancient steel door.

"Where did they get this thing? An estate auction at Alcatraz?" Rhodes snarled and glared at the unmoving steel as though he could intimidate it into allowing us entrance.

"Lochlan, I thought you said this door would be a piece of cake? I'll try for another minute, but we might need to resort to more drastic measures or try the other door." No sooner had Evander spoken the words, than the door swung inward.

"Good work, Ev." Rhodes clapped him on the shoulder as he moved past him and into the library's dark interior.

"I didn't do that," Ev whispered, standing and pocketing his lock-picking tools. "Maybe the ghost helped?"

Following Rhodes inside, I searched the darkness, trying to feel for Axelle. I couldn't see her, but her scent lingered in the air. Ready to get to work, we headed straight for the security cameras, only to find the two screens were dark.

"Huh. Maybe they were rearranging things in here and forgot to plug them back in?" Evander suggested.

Rhodes shook his head. "No. Axelle was in here recently."

"So she's helping us? Shouldn't we take her to a vortex before she fades out?" Ev's gaze bounced between Rhodes and me.

"Not unless she asks us to. So don't even think about it," I warned him.

"She's different. If she was going to fade, I think she would have already done it," Rhodes added. "Now, let's get to work."

"I think we should start in the storage room. That's where the ghosts seemed to be headed this afternoon. Follow me." Without waiting for them to respond, I turned and headed deeper into the library.

To my disappointment, I didn't see Axelle when we passed through the archive room. It was odd though; I almost thought I could feel her. But ghosts couldn't hide themselves from reapers or collectors, so if she was there, I should've been able to see her.

The memory of her blending with the shadows in the storeroom came to me. At first, I'd simply chalked it up to the dark room, but I could see just as well in the dark as I could in the light. It was a skill I'd never appreciated more than today when Axe had blown the lights in a fit of embarrassment.

The expressions she'd made as she mocked herself had been on the level of an animated movie character. It had taken every ounce of discipline I possessed to keep from laughing... or pulling the adorable woman onto my lap and kissing her pouty lips.

When she finally stopped poking fun at herself, I'd thought I was in the clear. But then Axelle had turned her attention to studying my face. I wasn't a mind reader, but the shift in her energy and the way her eyes had darkened as they focused on my lips told me she'd liked what she saw.

It had been physically painful to keep my muscles relaxed when I wanted nothing more than to taste her. I'd managed to mostly keep my hands to myself until we'd been in the storage room. It was the way her hips swayed that had pushed me over the edge. I'd needed to touch her —to feel her body against mine.

Recalling the way Axelle had melted against me caused my cock to harden. When I'd tucked my face against her neck, she'd tilted her head the slightest bit, unconsciously giving me better access, and my heart had melted.

I was a stranger, but Axelle trusted me. She'd wanted my touch. Sure, she'd pulled away before things could escalate further, but I didn't care. She was attracted to me, and that was all I needed to know.

She might have been the ghost, but I was going to haunt her sweet booty until I'd made her mine...

CHAPTER 7

AXELLE

"**A**rgh!" I flopped back on my makeshift bed on top of the bookshelf. "Stupid men!"

I was on a date with the latest release in my favorite series by Eva Chase. It should have been a perfect evening. The book was just as amazing as I'd come to expect from the author, but my mind kept wandering to Lochlan and Rhodes.

Less than twenty-four hours ago, my life—well, death—had been perfect. It was uncomplicated. Now I couldn't shove aside the thought that I should help the guys.

"Don't do it, Axe." Even as I warned myself, I was already accepting the fact I would ignore the advice. "This has nothing to do with you. If you get attached to them, it's going to get messy."

I reread the page in front of me three more times before I finally snapped the book closed and drifted to the floor. Wasabi appeared in the doorway, his whiskers twitching as he glared up at me.

"Yeah, I know I'm breaking my rules. But my conscience isn't going to let me sleep until I do something to help."

And my libido isn't going to let me rest until I give in to desire.

Bending to give Wasabi a quick scratch under his chin, I tried to reassure both of us I was still in control of the situation. "All I'm going to do is open the back door and turn off the security camera. Then it's right back to my book."

My rat bestie gave a reproachful squeak, not buying my excuses.

Turning off the cameras took less than sixty seconds. I was getting good at this whole ghost thing. I approached the back door, then stopped at the soft rumble of male voices that came from the other side.

Pressing my ear against the cool metal, I closed my eyes and tried to listen for a voice I recognized. Imagine how terrible it would be if I unlocked the door to a group of robbers? Or worse, a pack of raccoons looking for trouble? Robbers would take whatever electronics they could find and the meager contents of the cash drawer.

Raccoons would climb all over the shelves, wrecking my precious books. The chubby masked marauders were like vampires—once they were invited inside, it was almost impossible to get them out.

"Lochlan, I thought you—"

Hearing Loch's name was all the assurance I needed. Flipping the deadbolt on the door, I gathered my energy and twisted the door handle.

As soon as the door began to creak on its hinges, I hid

myself in the shadows and hurried to the upstairs reading nook where I'd stashed my book.

I'd helped, thus proving I was a good ghost. Heck, I might have changed my name to Caspera. Yep, I was going to leave the stray ghost wrangling to the professionals.

Blowing out a long sigh, I released the tension in my body and curled up on the worn velvet reading chaise.

I flipped open the book and began to read.

What if they got lost in the library?

Stop being stupid, Axe. These men have been doing this longer than you've been dead.

My eyes slid over the words on the page, barely taking in what I was reading.

Maybe I should have told them about the giant, scowling guy I'd seen in the library after Lochlan. Caught up in my book, I'd given him a quick once over, then assumed he was one of Rhodes or Lochlan's buddies.

But something about him had been tickling the back of my brain, leaving me slightly unsettled. I replayed the memory of him glancing over his shoulder at me before he'd left the library. Every hair on my body had stood on end and the temperature around me had dropped to near freezing levels.

Tonight, Lochlan and Rhodes had struggled to unlock the door. Which meant Collectors had to go through doors.

Since I'd watched the purple-eyed stranger walk through a wall, he couldn't have been a collector.

The man hadn't been like any ghost I'd encountered since my death. Closing my book, I popped my knuckles and tried to recall every detail I could about him. It didn't help, and I still had zero clue what he was.

The guy hadn't appeared until after Lochlan had left. Was he purposely avoiding the collectors? Did Rhodes and Lochlan even know that another paranormal being was loitering around the library? What if the stranger was the one causing the ghosts to congregate in town? The guys could be walking into very real danger while I relaxed with fictional drama.

My stomach churned, something it hadn't done since I'd eaten bad sushi a week before my premature demise. Wasabi appeared from beneath the chair, peering up at me with his shiny black eyes. Then the ungrateful rodent nipped the bottom of my foot.

"Hey! Stop that!" I scolded, quickly pulling my foot up onto the chair.

Wasabi was undeterred, scampering onto the chaise and nipping harder at my foot.

"What is wrong with you? Have you been sharing secondhand breadsticks with the raccoon in the alley again? We agreed he was sus, and probably rabid." I tapped Wasabi's nose and gave him what I hoped was a stern glare.

The famous talking mouse wasn't the only rodent that wore pants, because Wasabi seemed to be wearing the pants in our relationship. Unbothered by my disapproval, he bit me again.

"That's it. I'm going ghost!" I yelped, stifling the emotional energy that had caused my form to stabilize enough that I could interact with Wasabi.

I swear the chubby cheese boy rolled his eyes.

"Maybe I'll let them call the exterminator next time Bertha catches you stealing a midday snack." My threat lacked any heat, and Wasabi knew it.

He hopped off the chair and took off toward the storage room.

"Okay, Lassie. Let's go save them." I made the comment in jest, not seriously thinking it was possible the two perfect specimens of manhood could actually need my help.

If they were searching for books with tropes like enemies to lovers, second chance romance, morally gray heroes, fated mates, vampire royalty, fake relationships, jilted brides, love triangles, forced proximity, or reverse harem… I was the ghostess with the mostest.

If they wanted recommendations for books with the most unique male anatomy… I held the world's only PHD on the subject. And by PHD, I meant I was the Poltergeist of Hung Dudes. Or was it Phantom of Huge Dicks?

If they wanted a romance that would give them a good cry… I could suggest several books capable of causing heartache that would haunt them for years.

If they wanted a book to raise the heat level in their bedrooms… I had a list of titles capable of creating phantasmic orgasms.

But if they wanted trained backup while taking on an enemy force, they needed to look elsewhere. Heck, I was dead because I was easily spooked and struggled to think clearly during moments of panic.

Yet there I was, floating around the storage room, searching for the guys.

But they weren't there. Where else could they be?

An animated string of squeaks from the back wall caught my attention. "Wasabi? You okay, bud?"

I found him sitting next to a large opening in the floor. "That's odd."

The trapdoor had been designed with attention to detail, and unless you knew it was there, it would have been impossible to find. So how had the guys found it? I'd gotten the impression from Rhodes and Lochlan that they weren't familiar with the town.

Bending over, I looked down the dark tunnel, then backed away. "Nope. I don't care if the creepy crawlies down there can't touch me, I'm not doing it."

Hadn't the guys ever watched a horror movie? This tunnel was exactly the type of place you weren't supposed to explore if you valued being alive.

But I had one thing going for me. I was already dead.

Standing there, I stared down into the hole. It was the stuff of my old nightmares and it might as well have been Hades as far as I was concerned.

I backed away several feet, but instead of easing my anxiety, it had the opposite effect. With each centimeter of distance I placed between the hole and me, my trepidation grew.

My hair lifted around me, and static crackled in the cold air. Wasabi's breath looked like smoke billowing from a dragon's mouth.

They were in trouble. I didn't understand how I could possibly know that, but I was absolutely certain it was the truth.

Questioning my sanity and why I cared so much, I slowly descended into the tunnel.

As I reached the bottom, I sniffed the stale, moldy air. The tunnel had been built using bricks, several of which had worked themselves free and tumbled to the stone floor.

There wasn't a nightlight or torch in sight, and I thanked my unlucky stars for my ability to see just fine in the dark. Turning in a slow circle, I tried to figure out which way the men had gone.

I was standing in the middle of a cross point in the tunnel, and needed to pick which of the four paths to follow.

"Ahhh!" I screamed as a ghost stepped through the crumbling tunnel wall to my left. "You are supposed to announce yourself with some soft bangs or moans!"

The ghost either didn't hear me, or he was too dead to care about anything other than getting to wherever he was going.

Excitement bubbled in my chest. I knew how to find the guys. Darting down the tunnel after the specter, I crossed my fingers that he was leading me there.

M<small>Y GHOST GUIDE</small> led me deeper into the tunnel. At times, the path was so narrow I wondered if Rhodes' wide shoulders had even been able to squeeze through it. Some portions were wide enough that a vehicle could've driven through it.

Traveling deeper into the dark passageway, I looked for any clues that had been left behind that might hint at what the tunnels had been used for. But thus far, I'd found nothing of interest.

Currently, my working theory was that they were likely used for traveling unseen between locations or maybe to transport alcohol during prohibition. While history hadn't been my favorite in school, I think I would've remembered learning about a secret society with enough money to build extensive tunnels beneath the city. How many people in town were aware of the maze of passages running beneath their feet?

Amberwood had been a farming town from its founding, and those who lived there were known for watching out for each other. But clearly there was more below the surface of the town—pun intended.

At last, the vibrations of low male voices echoed down the tunnel. The male ghost picked up his pace and blurred down the tunnel. I followed, hot on his heels, torn between wanting to pass him and knowing I needed to follow him and help the collectors get the information they needed.

With each second that passed, it became harder to ignore the steady thrum of my anxiety as it turned to a thundering beat. Over and over, a single word chanted in my head.

Death. Death. Death.

The knowledge of what lay ahead of me should've had me tucking my tail and running for my life. But I wasn't afraid of death.

If given a choice, I would've chosen to live. Life was beautiful. It held endless possibilities, and every day provided a chance for a new beginning.

But I'd also been a pretty go-with-the-flow person, and rather than whining about dying, I chose to focus on the upsides. I hadn't wanted or welcomed death, but I'd learned to accept it and enjoy the benefits.

Death didn't scare me.

Is that so? Then why are you trembling like that time you decided to go hiking with work colleagues? Remember? You tried to score points with your hot new boss by saying you loved hiking. Then you were too stubborn to admit you'd never hiked to the top of anything higher than the pile of clean laundry you tossed on the floor at the foot of your bed?

I winced at the memory of the muscle pain I'd endured during that misadventure. Why did my inner voice have to be such a jerk? It knew how to hit me exactly where it hurt the most. I'd read some people didn't have an inner monologue. Frankly, that had been a harder pill to swallow than being dead.

Snarled curses and shouts bounced off the walls, making it seem as though they were coming from every direction.

"Lochlan! Get back!" Rhodes ordered.

The raw terror in his voice cleared my mind of every thought except one. My guys needed me. Now.

I streaked down the tunnel at a speed I'd never attempted before. My form twisted and warped as I moved. One minute, I was nothing but inky shadows and golden light, and the next, I appeared almost human.

Without slowing or even blinking, I surged through the wall in front of me and into a larger chamber. I took in the scene in front of me, and for the first time in my indecisive life, I knew instantly what I had to do.

They said no one could stop death, but I was going to give it my best shot.

CHAPTER 8

EVANDER

"**A**re you two ready? We'll move in on the count of three," Rhodes asked as he pulled twin blades from the hidden sheaths in his combat boots.

Lochlan and I nodded. This wasn't our first time facing the unknown.

We could have taken the path of the other collectors and traveled from one natural disaster or catastrophe to another. The reapers always lost track of enough souls during those events to keep most of my species fed. It would be so easy. A life of traveling the world and collecting ghosts without the threat of violence or even breaking a sweat.

Instead, our circle had embarked on a far more difficult path. We tracked anomalies in the ghost plane and areas with unusually high ghost activity or locations where ghosts were acting out of character. Then we headed out to investigate what was going on.

More times than I could count, we'd found the issue and

saved the lost ghosts, only to burn more energy rectifying the situation than the ghosts left behind after moving on from this plane.

I knew deep down in my core that this was going to be one of those situations. Which sucked, because it had been almost a month since I'd last eaten. Our last case had wrapped up two weeks before, and both Loch and Rhodes had been injured. They'd needed additional energy to heal the injuries that would have taken months to recover from without the benefit of our energy-fueled abilities.

I had claimed I'd already eaten and allowed them to divide the energy left behind by the ghosts. It wasn't the first time I'd told them that very same lie. They were large men, always running into danger head first, and it was rare to have a case where neither of them sustained some sort of injury.

Because of their protectiveness, I usually made it through our investigations without being sliced open, stabbed, shot, or blasted with magic. And through my training as a youth, I'd learned how to survive on lower feedings and minimal amounts of energy. It was a skill I was thankful to have and almost made the cruelty I'd faced under my parents' instructions worth it.

If we didn't wrap this case up soon, I'd need to come up with some type of excuse to leave for a few days so I could feed.

"One. Two. *Three!*"

The door flew open, slamming against the wall. Bricks worked themselves free and clattered onto the floor. Even through the dust billowing around us, the glowing scythe was visible as it sliced through the air.

Adrenaline shot through my body, and I pulled at my dwindling energy reserves, trying my best to force my body into action. But it was as though this moment in time had slowed and I could do nothing but watch in horror as the dark-cloaked reaper swung his weapon in what he intended to be a killing blow to the two men who'd become my brothers.

If a reaper's scythe drew blood, it also drew out the soul. Even a paper cut from the arched blade would be fatal.

Loch and Rhodes tried to dodge, but the attack was too fast and unexpected. Reapers had never attacked a collector before. And since my species weren't human, we didn't have our souls reaped at death. Never in a million years would I have imagined that one would be waiting on the other side of the door to murder us.

Torchlight caught the blade's edge, and it glinted as it sang the song of death itself. I wanted to close my eyes, but my body might as well have been frozen in ice.

A woman appeared out of thin air, standing in front of us, her body wrapped in golden light. Without hesitation, she reached out, pressing her hands to the reaper's scythe.

"No!" she screamed.

The goddess in front of us shoved hard at the blade. The reaper, having put all his muscle power into a swing meant to kill, was thrown off balance. He stumbled, giving us time to throw ourselves out of the range of his curved blade.

"What is wrong with you?" The reaper's voice shook with fury and... confusion?

Join the club, buddy.

He lifted his blade, ready to swing it again the moment he spotted an opening. Despite the way he towered over her, the tiny woman refused to back down. She crossed her arms and popped her hip out on one side. It was the pose of an angry parent at a school meeting, or that of a cocky cheerleader getting ready to throw down and knowing she was going to win.

What paranormal species did she belong to? Some type of warrior race was my guess, based on the steel spine she possessed, combined with her unsettling lack of fear.

The reaper swung again, and with an angry shout, she rushed straight at him. Reapers were at the top of the known food chain on Earth. They weren't used to being challenged or disobeyed, so he clearly wasn't expecting her attack.

She leaped forward and ducked beneath the blade, not even flinching as it sliced into her shoulder. Grabbing his extended arm, she turned and bit into his flesh. Hard. The reaper's scythe clattered against the stone floor as he roared in pain and tried to shake the woman off him.

Seizing the opportunity she'd given us, we scrambled off the floor. We rushed to help her, although I'm not sure she truly needed our help.

A reaper's blade was their most powerful weapon, but it wasn't their only weapon. Grabbing a knife from the folds of his cloak, he pulled back his fist, preparing to bring it down on top of her skull.

"Axelle!" Rhodes roared.

So this was the ghost who'd captured the interest of both my brothers?

I watched in awe as Rhodes and Lochlan moved in perfect harmony, protecting Axelle, while dodging the knife blade and delivering their own punches. It looked like a violent dance they'd practiced hundreds of times.

Despite our extensive skills, a reaper was as close to a final boss as you could encounter on Earth, and this one was powerful. We needed an escape plan so we could regroup.

"What's going on?" an unfamiliar voice boomed.

My blood turned to ice. I didn't need to see the speaker to know I was in the presence of Death with a capital D.

The first reaper took advantage of our distraction caused by the newcomer's arrival. With renewed energy, he lashed out with his knife. This time, the blade sliced into Rhodes' skin, opening his chest.

Rhodes stumbled back before dropping to his knees.

Axelle let go of the reaper and rushed to his side. "Rhodes!"

The reaper grabbed his scythe and rushed forward, lifting the blade over my fallen brother.

"Enough!" the new reaper shouted.

The first reaper was too caught up in his bloodlust to care. Lochlan and I lurched forward, raising our blades in a final fight. If he planned to take Rhodes, he'd have to take us all.

Before our blades could connect, the air was sucked from the room. Like water on the beach being pulled back into the ocean before a tsunami unleashed its fury on the land, it was all the warning we got for what was coming.

A heartbeat later, an unseen force slammed into Loch and me, flinging us through the tunnel walls like we were toys. My eardrums threatened to burst as his power flowed over and around my prone body. It burned as hot as a furnace, melting the blade I still clutched in my fist.

What kind of reaper was this?

Just as quickly as it had come, the power crushing me into the stone floor vanished.

I searched the room, worried the first reaper would launch another attack, but both cloaked figures were gone.

Axelle kneeled over Rhodes' prone body, her shoulders shaking and her cries echoing around us.

Rolling to my side, I tried to push myself off the floor, but my body was drained of energy. Across the chamber, I saw Lochlan was facing the same struggle.

The reaper hadn't killed us with his blade, but he might as well have. We wouldn't have the strength to get ourselves out of the tunnel until we fed.

There was a chance a ghost might wander by, but I didn't have the energy to teleport it to any of the vortexes. If a collector fed on a ghost, the ghost would fade and be lost forever. My kind had sworn to protect the ghosts in our care and could only feed on energy the ghost left behind after moving into the beyond.

No matter how desperate the situation, we'd starve to death in these forgotten tunnels rather than break our oath.

My trembling muscles gave way, and I collapsed on the stone floor. Twisting my head, I watched the tiny female ghost lay down beside Rhodes' motionless form.

I would've thought he was already gone if not for the nightmarish gurgling that accompanied his slow, labored breathing. He was dying, and I was powerless to save him. If I'd been well fed, I could have used that energy to heal Rhodes.

Lochlan's gaze met mine, and the same grief and hopelessness I was drowning in also shimmered in the depths of his eyes.

The dim chamber grew brighter, as though a dying fire was being stoked.

Sliding my cheek against the grime covered floor, I took in the heartbreaking scene in front of me.

Axelle had turned Rhodes' face toward her, and she was kissing him as though it was their first and last kiss.

Which was exactly what it was.

The kiss that had started gentle, quickly turned demanding. With a heroic effort, Rhodes lifted his hand to cradle the back of her head. I felt like a creep for watching such a private moment between them, but I couldn't summon the strength to look away... nor did I want to.

Rhodes was a force to be reckoned with during battle,

but privately, the man was a teddy bear who stopped the car to help turtles cross the road and had spent weeks bottle-feeding a litter of orphaned kittens around the clock. Which was why I was shocked to see the fingers of his right-hand hook into her hair, roughly hauling her toward him.

He hungrily devoured her mouth with an energy that seemed impossible for a dying man. As I continued trying to make sense of what I was seeing, his left arm grabbed her waist and hauled her on top of him.

It was when her glow flickered that the pieces clicked into place, and I understood what I was seeing.

He wasn't just devouring her mouth; he was devouring her energy.

"Rhodes! Your oath!" I sucked in a layer of dust from the floor and coughed.

"He's not breaking his oath." Lochlan's eyes glittered dangerously. "She's feeding him." The muscle in his jaw jerked as he clenched and unclenched his teeth.

"Oh," I wheezed.

He would drain her in a matter of minutes. Her energy would save him, and us, but she was sacrificing herself.

A flush traveled over Rhodes' gray skin as strength returned to his body, but the pair didn't break the kiss. Rhodes' hands traveled over her back, touching and exploring the body of the first woman he'd ever been enamored by.

It had been nearly ten minutes since they began kissing when Rhodes broke the kiss and slowly pushed himself into a sitting position. He brushed the dark hair from Axelle's face, then pulled her tight against his chest.

Her glow had dimmed, but she'd healed him without fading away.

"You saved me, love." He tucked her head under his chin and held her close. "My life belongs to you."

She pulled back and stared up at him. "I just did it for the kiss." A smile played at the corners of her mouth. "Totally worth it. I 10/10 recommend."

Axelle jumped as Lochlan's laughter bounced around the tunnels, reminding her they had an audience. An adorable blush spread across her pale cheeks, and she scrambled off Rhodes' lap.

"I can help you two." She caught her lip between her teeth as her gaze bounced between Loch and me.

Sensing her indecision, Lochlan made the decision for her. "Take care of him first. I can wait."

With a shaky jerk of her head, she moved toward me. Dropping to her knees, she gently rolled me onto my side.

I looked up into her face and caught my breath. She was the most beautiful woman I'd ever laid eyes on, and not just because of her outward appearance.

She was clad in a pair of white sweatpants, an oversized T-shirt with the words *'If you've got it, haunt it'* printed across the chest, and a pair of fuzzy leopard-print socks. Dark hair fell around her face.

She was a free spirit in all senses of the term and my heart twisted with a longing to be close to her. Rhodes and Lochlan's reactions to her made perfect sense.

"Hi. We haven't met. I'm Axelle, but you can call me Axe." She was struggling to make eye contact, but that didn't stop her from accomplishing what she'd set out to do.

Lying down beside me, she slowly scooted forward until her body brushed against me. Her chocolate eyes locked with mine, and another flush traveled across her cheeks.

"Is it okay if we kiss? Well, it doesn't have to be a kiss, I just need to stick my lips on yours. Or at least that's what worked to heal Rhodes, so hopefully it will work for you…" She was rambling, and I couldn't get enough of it.

Lochlan barked a dry laugh. "Axe, take a breath. I can assure you Evander wants nothing more than to feel your lips all over him."

"She can do whatever she needs to in order to feel comfortable, Loch. Shut up and wait your turn." I glanced at Rhodes just in time to see him glare at Lochlan.

"You're okay with it?" Axe whispered.

With her lips mere centimeters from my mouth, my mind short-circuited. Unable to speak, I simply nodded.

Her lips pressed against mine. The moment our skin touched, her energy arched up to meet me. It flowed through me, easing the pain caused by the yawning hunger that was my constant companion.

I discovered feeding from her energy differed greatly from all my previous feedings. Axelle's energy spread through me, stroking and caressing everything it touched. It was comforting, yet also insanely erotic.

I wanted her to know how she was affecting me, and I craved more. Not of her energy, but more of her touch.

Hoping I wouldn't make her uncomfortable, I gently placed my hand on her hip. I moved slowly, giving her plenty of time to bat my hand away or give me a sign that she didn't want my touch.

Instead, when I didn't make another move, she pressed tighter against my body. When her body made contact with the bulge in my pants, I couldn't swallow back my groan. Axelle stiffened.

It was my turn to flush. I couldn't control what that part of my anatomy did, but what if she thought I was a pervert for getting aroused while she was trying to help me?

Axelle wiggled her hips as though confirming what she'd felt pressed against her. My hand on her hip jerked, and her shirt must have ridden up because my thumb brushed against bare skin.

In response, she made a sweet whimpering sound that stirred another kind of hunger inside me. My lips moved against hers, teasing and tasting.

To my relief, Axelle eagerly kissed me back. We were strangers, but I felt as though I'd known her forever. Her hands moved to cup my face, deepening our kiss with a wild abandon that was such a turn on.

Grasping her thigh, I hooked it over my hip and impulsively ground my erection against her. We were separated by our clothing, but the movement still managed to steal the air from my lungs.

SEDONA ASHE

My muscles trembled as I fought the all-consuming desire to thrust against her again.

Tightening her leg around me, she hesitantly rocked her hips. The gentle friction sent pleasure zinging through me.

"Axelle." I breathed her name between kisses.

"Evander." Her voice was husky with need. "Please don't think badly of me—"

"Never," I assured her.

"I'm so turned on." She moaned as I moved to suck and kiss my way down her neck.

Her hips rocked against me again, her movements stiff and unsure. Did she think I was going to get mad if she used my body for her pleasure?

"Is this what you want?" Gripping her thigh, I ground against her.

I took my time and watched her face to see what movements pleased her most.

"Oh!" she gasped. "Please..."

Axelle had given me permission to do exactly what I'd longed to do. Without wasting a second, I rolled her onto her back. I tucked my left hand under her butt and supported my weight on my left hip and arm.

Gripping her thigh again, I wrapped it around my waist and lined our bodies up. The first time I thrust against her, I was slow and gentle. She trembled and her right hand slid beneath my shirt to press against my bare skin.

This woman had protected us, saved our lives, fed us, and now she was asking me to give her release. I rolled my hips hard and fast, a thrill shooting through my chest at the soft sounds of pleasure the move elicited from her.

If I'd been an experienced lover, I would have known how to draw this out and tease her. Enthusiasm and raw desire were all I had to offer, so hopefully it would work for her.

I ground against her, my movements hard and fast until we were both gasping from the delicious friction. My erection was engorged to the point of being painful, and I was fighting a losing battle against the pleasure that was building embarrassingly fast.

"Axelle, I'm so sorry. I won't last much longer," I panted.

My words seemed to send her over the edge. "Evander!" she moaned my name as she climaxed.

Her back arched off the floor, and her nails dug into my skin. She was beautiful in her pleasure, and I couldn't help but imagine how amazing it would be to feel her bare skin against mine.

I rocked against her once more and felt my body go stiff as the intensity of my orgasm turned my vision dark and roared in my ears.

For however long I lived, I knew this was the only woman I wanted to share my life with. If she was willing to accept us, I preferred the idea of her being loved, satisfied, and protected by our circle. But if Rhodes and Lochlan tried to keep her from me, I was prepared to fight.

I was certain this woman was ours to treasure.

CHAPTER 9

AXELLE

I clung to the man I'd just met… a man who'd just rocked my world without either of us needing to take off even a single piece of clothing.

"Can you carry her?" Rhodes' question cut through the post-orgasmic bliss clouding my senses.

"Easily." Evander scooped me into his arms and stood. "I've never felt this good."

"I bet," Rhodes growled under his breath. Leaning down, he looped his arm around Lochlan's waist. "If you've got Axelle, I'll help Loch."

"Wait!" The word came out garbled, forcing me to clear my throat. "I haven't healed him yet. It's his turn!"

"And you can heal him—after you've had a chance to recharge," Rhodes answered in a tone that was meant to end the conversation.

Well, too freaking bad. He wasn't the boss of me.

"I'm fine. Let me heal him," I protested, squirming in Evander's arms.

My mind must have still been high on pleasure, otherwise I would've remembered I was a ghost and could easily get away from him.

Or maybe you like being held because you're enjoying the physical contact and you aren't ready for it to end...

It was true. I loved my books, but the tiniest part of me was questioning my determination to remain alone. Death didn't scare me, but clearly attachments did.

Evander moved into the tunnels with the confidence of a man who'd traveled them countless times.

Tilting my head, I stared up at him. "Have you been down here before?"

He shook his head. "This was my first time."

"Then how do you know which way to go?"

Evander shrugged. "I brought a map that showed the sewer system below the library. Only it wasn't a sewer system that someone built. The blueprints were about these tunnels."

"And then the boy genius memorized those blueprints as we navigated this maze, so he doesn't need to check the map anymore." Lochlan's voice drifted through the tunnel from behind us.

Twisting in Evander's arms, I peeked over his shoulder. Lochlan was leaning heavily on Rhodes, but his steps were steady and his color was good.

"Stop worrying, Axe. I'm fine. I'd rather have my turn, as you put it, at the house." Loch's wink had butterflies taking flight in my stomach.

Then his words settled in. "House?"

"We're taking you home with us," Rhodes stated.

I scoffed. "I'm not a stray cat you can just decide to adopt and take home."

There were stacks of books that needed to be read. These men were messing up all my carefully laid plans for my future.

A lonely future…

"Boo, in case you hadn't realized it, you belong with—" Loch hesitated for a moment. "Us. You'll just have to accept it and tell us what we need to do to keep you happy."

"Us?" Surely he didn't mean what I thought he meant.

My gaze darted between the three men.

It was Evander who answered. "Our kind usually works in groups we call circles. It isn't uncommon for our species to choose to only have one female in the circle."

My brain began running a series of complicated math equations I didn't have a hope of understanding as I struggled to process what he was saying. Surely he didn't mean —

Loch snickered. "Yes. It works exactly how you're thinking. The woman is kept satisfied by her own personal harem."

My throat tightened. "And you three want to share… me?" My words came out as little more than a whispered squeak.

"We don't want to, but we're willing to go this route because none of us are willing to give you up." The muscle in Rhodes' jaw flexed.

Evander gave me a shy smile. "I like the idea of sharing.

We often get distracted by our work and we each have our own quirks. This way, we can make sure you get everything you need and deserve... even when one of us is being an idiot."

The tender sincerity in his voice chipped away at the walls I'd built to protect my heart.

"If you agree to give us a chance, we'll need you to be patient. We aren't used to sharing." For the first time since I'd met him, Lochlan's tone was serious.

I was being offered a harem of the three most beautiful guys I'd ever laid eyes on. Anyone in their right mind would jump at a chance like this. I read romance stories because I was obsessed with love. But when I got the chance to have my own happily ever after, I was too scared to take the risk.

Because I didn't want to get a taste of being loved, only to end up alone. As an introvert, I'd struggled to make friends and my life had been painfully lonely.

Bloody Mary! It was so bad that when I died, none of the people I shared blood with, and who loved to remind me they were my family when they needed a favor, had cared enough to claim my body.

The city had buried me in an overgrown field, which I suspected used to be a landfill before the city decided to use it as a graveyard for the unclaimed. And since most citizens of Amberwood were born and raised here, and very few strangers moved into town, people weren't exactly *dying* to get into the city's graveyard.

So my grave, with the tiny metal plaque engraved with

the identification number the coroner had assigned me, was the only grave on the entire ten-acre property. Even in death, I was all alone.

It would've been hilarious if it hadn't been so pathetic.

Now, three sexy men wanted to claim me as theirs and treat me like a queen, and I was too scared to say yes.

"You don't have to answer until you want to. I'm not going anywhere. Ever," Evander assured me.

His words sent a trickle of happiness through me. Acting impulsively, I caught his face and brought his lips to mine in a soft kiss.

Pulling away, I gave him a small smile before hiding my face against his chest.

How could these men be strangers yet feel so familiar at the same time?

WHEN WE ARRIVED at their house, Evander carried me to his room. He tucked me into his bed, then disappeared into the bathroom.

"You know ghosts don't sleep, right?" I protested when he returned five minutes later.

Evander was wearing only a pair of flannel pajama pants. When he ran his fingers through his wet hair, causing droplets of water to slide down his bare chest, I lifted my finger to the corner of my mouth to make sure I hadn't started drooling.

"I know a bit about ghosts." He moved to an oak shelf in the corner of the room. Turning back around to face me, he held a book in each hand. "That's why I figured we would read."

I nearly swooned on the spot. "Will you marry me?"

Evander's forehead creased. "What?"

I hadn't meant to say that out loud.

Thinking quickly, I stammered out, "Uh, I wanted to know if you would cuddle me?"

Smooth, Axelle. Not sus at all.

His eyes sparkled, and his lips twitched as if he were suppressing a smile. "There is nothing I want more than to marry you."

"What?!" I yelped.

"I said there's nothing I want more than to cuddle you while we read," he answered innocently, handing me one of the books he'd pulled from the shelf.

But as he stretched out on the bed beside me, I caught his sexy smirk and couldn't resist a smile of my own. The playful banter I shared with the men was doing a fantastic job of wrecking my resolve to distance myself from them.

I needed to decide if I was going to let them in, or push them away. And soon.

"Whatever you're worrying about can wait. You've had a hard day, and it's time to relax." Evander grabbed his glasses from the nightstand beside the bed. He slid them on and opened his book.

Great Gatsby's Glamorous Gambling Ghost!

I'd found Evander handsome before, but the whole sexy nerd vibe could have knocked my panties off. A wave of slick arousal rushed between my thighs, and my body ached with need. Evander turned a page, already lost in the book's story.

Lying down beside him, I opened my book and tried not to think about all the things I wanted to do to him. The book was a fantasy about dragons and elves, and while I missed the romance, I was quickly drawn into the story.

We'd been reading for about half an hour when the bedroom door opened and Rhodes appeared with Loch behind him. Both men had changed into pajama pants, and without a word, they moved toward the bed.

Loch laid down beside me, pulling me against him. I murmured in pleasure as heat seeped into my cold body.

Rhodes stretched out across the bottom of the bed. Lifting my feet onto his stomach, he began to massage them with a gentleness that surprised me for such a large man.

Snuggled between their bodies, I relaxed, letting the tension drain from my body. I was protected. Instead of distracting me, the guys' presence allowed me to let go of the world and fully devour chapter after chapter. Maybe there was a way I could have my cake and eat it too… or in my case, maybe I could have my romance and read it too.

The hours ticked by, and when I finally slipped the bookmark into the book and glanced out the window, I was surprised to see the sun was rising over the horizon.

Evander's eyes were closed, and his book was slipping

from his hand. I gently took it from him and placed it on the nightstand.

Rhodes' palm slid up my calf. Sitting up, I looked at the giant man cradling my calf in his sleep. Did they crave physical touch as much as I did?

Shifting my attention to where Loch lay on my right side, I was startled to find his moss-green eyes fixed on me.

"You're incredible." His whispered comment sent excitement rippling through me.

Carefully extracting my leg from Rhodes' grasp, I rolled over to face Loch and melded my body to his. "I bet you tell all the girls that."

"No, I don't." His arm curled around my back, and he buried his nose against my neck. "You were magnificent facing off with the reaper, but I've never felt fear like that in my life. I thought I was going to watch you die."

I huffed a soft laugh. "I already died, remember?"

His teeth nipped my neck, and he growled. "Yeah, but you can be ended in this form, too. Now, remind me, how did that happen?"

"I was target practicing with cupid and there was a freak accident." I blew out a sigh. "It happens. Wrong place, wrong time. You know how it goes."

Loch pulled back to stare at me. "You have a twisted sense of humor, boo."

Eager to change the subject, I slipped my arms around his neck. "You haven't fed. Now seems like a good time."

"Are you sure you're okay?" Hunger glowed in his eyes, but he was still worried. "You grabbed a reaper's blade yesterday, then took a bite out of him, and followed that up by feeding Rhodes enough energy to heal a fatal wound. Not to mention taking care of Ev. I can wait another day or two."

"I'm fine. Let me do this." I didn't tell him I was feeling tired, because I didn't want him to worry.

My energy was replenishing itself, and I still had enough to feed him. Dark circles marred the skin beneath his eyes, and I'd caught the slight tremor of his hand. I was new to collectors, but you didn't have to be an expert to see he was struggling.

Not giving him a chance to protest further, I pressed my lips to his. The energy that made up my entire being responded like a puppy eager to greet her master.

The moment the energy touched his tongue, Lochlan gave up fighting his hunger. He latched onto my mouth with a desperation that tore at my heart. Why hadn't he let me feed him in the tunnels?

In a single smooth move, Loch rolled us so that I was trapped beneath his body. His left hand slipped from where it cupped my cheek, to curl his powerful fingers around the delicate column of my neck.

I knew he could have snapped my neck without effort, but I wasn't worried. Not even when his kiss grew demanding, and he sucked the energy from me at a frantic pace. I didn't think he'd ever kill to eat, but right now, I was still his prey and his body was in survival mode.

Rather than struggle, I wrapped my legs around his waist and pulled him closer. The oversized white T-shirt I'd created to sleep in rode up over my hips, leaving only a lacy thong covering me.

Loch's thumb brushed along the bare skin of my neck. It was a tender gesture, and a sweet reminder that I was more than a meal to him and he wouldn't hurt me.

I did my best to ignore the ache between my thighs that was growing more demanding. Apparently, I couldn't share energy without getting turned on by the physical contact. Only, they didn't call it sharing, they called it feeding. My brain swirled with questions. Was this something they needed often? Did they feed from other ghosts? And did those ghosts get turned on too? An uncomfortable surge of jealousy caused my chest to tighten and ache. It didn't matter that I barely knew these guys, or that I'd been so determined about not wanting to make space in my life for them... I couldn't stand the idea of another woman experiencing this with my guys.

My guys.

Were they mine? They'd made it clear they wanted me, and my heart knew we fit together. But how could this work?

Lochlan's mouth pulled me from my thoughts as he moved from my lips, down to my neck. The hand that had gripped my throat moved to my thigh, then trailed over my butt.

"You need to focus on feeding," I protested, my voice husky with need.

Unhooking my legs from around his waist, I dropped onto the mattress. He shifted slightly down the bed and I bent my legs and pulled them toward me to give him more room for whatever he was doing.

When his strong fingers gripped my legs and began parting them, I tried to wiggle away. Lochlan was having none of it and held me in place.

His eyes bore into mine. "If you don't want this to go any further, say the word and I'll let you go."

I hesitated, still embarrassed over the raw neediness I'd shown with Evander while Lochlan and Rhodes watched.

As if reading my thoughts, Lochlan purred, "You were beautiful in your ecstasy. I was jealous, in awe, and painfully turned on watching the show you two put on. Getting to watch you being pleasured by him, put to rest any doubts about my ability to share you with another man. I still wanted to be the one touching you, but I enjoy watching you, too."

"How did you know what I was thinking?" I asked in a hoarse whisper.

"Boo, your face is far too expressive. Plus, your blush, combined with the flickering overhead light, made it easy to guess. But you don't need to feel embarrassed." Loch leaned forward and pressed a gentle kiss to each of my legs. "Let me see you. Please."

"What about your, um, you know... feeding?" My voice squeaked and my muscles trembled. "Shouldn't we focus on that, instead of..."

The overhead light flashed on and off like it was at a rave. Until I'd met these men, I had no idea that ghostly embarrassment would take such an embarrassingly obvious form.

"Sweet, innocent woman. Collectors don't need to kiss in order to feed." Lochlan's delighted rumble of laughter was laced with a positively wicked note. "Do you really think I'm going to kiss Rhodes or Ev? That isn't going to happen even if I were in dire need of healing and they had the energy to spare. We can absorb energy through our skin."

As if to illustrate his point, Lochlan rested his open palm against my stomach. The heat from his skin seeped into me as my energy lurched toward his touch. I sucked in a breath as the energy flowed from me and into Lochlan.

What the fright?!

They could've fed just by holding my hand or touching my arm? My gaze jumped to Evander to find he was awake, likely due to Loch and I moving around, but he was looking everywhere but in my direction. I glanced at Rhodes, who'd awakened as well, but instead of guilt, he grinned unashamedly at me.

Lochlan's laughter deepened. "Yeah, he didn't need to kiss you to feed. But cut him some slack. We thought you knew, and no man in his right mind is going to turn down the chance to kiss you."

"Axe, I'm sorry. I was going to say something, but when you snuggled against me, I couldn't even speak. At that moment, I forgot all about needing to feed. All I could think about was how desperately I wanted to taste your lips."

Evander's eyes swirled with guilt and hunger. His

honesty made it hard to be upset with him. Especially when I'd wanted it too.

Pushing aside my shyness, I reached out and brushed my knuckles along his stubbled jaw. "I liked it. A lot."

"Good." Evander caught my hand and placed a soft kiss on each of my fingers.

"Alright, enough," Loch grumbled, his laughter dying away. "You had your turn, Evander. I'm hungry and it's my turn to feed."

Slick arousal rushed between my thighs as the double meaning of his words sank in. In my old life, I was not what anyone would consider adventurous when it came to the bedroom tango. But this was my second chance to be whoever I wanted. Whoever said reading romance was a waste of time didn't have a clue what they were talking about, because I was about to put my long hours of *research* to good use!

I could let go and *boogie*.

Relaxing my locked muscles, I watched Lochlan's tongue slide across his bottom lip as he guided my legs apart.

CHAPTER 10

SAUL

"What were you thinking?" I paced the length of the dining hall, too angry at Zacharias to sit.

My muscles flexed and the need to do something, anything, to burn off the rage that was consuming me from the inside out.

"Calm down. You're acting like I was trying to kill off all the collectors, rather than deal with three troublesome collectors who were sticking their noses where they didn't belong." Zacharias lifted his wineglass and sipped the burgundy liquid.

His nonchalance fanned the flames of my wrath.

"Troublesome collectors? Have you lost your mind?" I strode to the table to stand in front of him. Leaning down, I flattened my palms on the table. "Do you know who they are?"

Zacharias swirled the wine in his glass. "No. Should I?"

"They are the Knights Baudelaire," I hissed.

A perverse part of me enjoyed watching the blood drain from Zacharias' face as he realized how far the repercussions for his actions might travel.

Grabbing the wine bottle off the table, I lifted it to my lips and took a long drink. It was rare that I drank, but if anyone deserved a drink, it was me.

"Do you know if he survived?" Zacharias asked, voice tight.

Good. He finally understood the depth of the dung he'd dove headfirst into.

I shrugged, dropping into a chair at the far end of the table. "How many do you know that survive having their chest sliced open like they were being autopsied?"

The man had lived, but I wasn't going to let Zacharias off the hook so easily. Reapers formed families just like collectors—close-knit teams that worked well together and watched each other's backs.

Zacharias, my brother, and I had been a team. Then Philetus was murdered, and the reapers had refused to aid us in the hunt for his killer.

They claimed reapers weren't meant to be the judges of right or wrong, and we definitely didn't go around enacting justice. Our job was simply to collect souls and escort them to the beyond.

Unwilling to give up, I'd petitioned the court to make an exception more times than I could count, but they had denied the request every single time.

After their last refusal, I'd forced myself to accept the

decision and do my job. My loyalty to my species drove me forward, helping me to survive the loss of my brother.

That loyalty vanished the instant I'd learned the truth. The reaper court knew who my brother's killer was, and they had sealed the record away to ensure no one avenged Philetus' death.

I'd been furious, yet no one had listened to me.

No one except Zacharias. And it was Zacharias who'd come up with a plan for us to get that file.

No one could visit the court or enter the coliseum without a summons. And even if you had a summons, you were only permitted entrance if you had an escort at your side.

But once a year, the court threw an extravagant feast and sent invitations to every reaper. For one hour, we sat and ate, strengthening the bonds between us. It was a unique experience since reapers were reclusive by nature.

This was only possible thanks to an ancient agreement with the collectors. For one night, they made sure most of their collectors were out scouring the earth for stray souls, picking up the slack while the reapers were MIA. With the collectors' help, and long overtime hours, we could enjoy our feast and maintain order.

Zacharias had located a warlock who'd given him the recipe to make an energy explosive similar to the fireworks humans loved to include in their celebrations. It wasn't powerful enough to harm, but it would provide the perfect distraction.

It was timed to go off during the feast, and we could sneak into the records room without an escort, because all the reapers would be at the feast or investigating the explosion.

Zacharias was risking punishment to help me obtain the files on my brother's murder. He hadn't given up on doing right by Philetus, and for that, he had my unquestioning loyalty.

At least I'd never had a reason to question it until today.

The Zacharias I'd watched in that chamber was one I didn't recognize. He'd almost seemed to enjoy the violence.

Reapers had been created to be powerful. We could focus all our attention on our job because we knew no other paranormal could compete with our abilities. The reapers who had died throughout history were almost always due to freak accidents.

Our abilities were only supposed to be used for defense on the rare occasion that the need arose. Zacharias claimed he was only defending himself, but I knew what I'd witnessed. He didn't have a ghost with him, so he could have stepped into the reaper realm and he would have been out of their reach.

Well, everyone but the female ghost who'd clung to him with the stubbornness of a crocodile who refused to release their meal. She'd haunted my thoughts since that day I'd first laid eyes on her in the library.

Decade after decade, I'd watched as humans chose a mate and then became possessive over that person. I understood the grief that came from losing a family member.

What I didn't understand was how humans could

become so enamored with another person that their happiness in life was contingent on whether they could possess the one they wanted.

They didn't call it possessing on the marriage forms. But if you took away the flowery language, it was simple. In exchange for the right to claim their chosen mate as belonging to them, humans were willing to sacrifice the freedom to make decisions on their own, giving partial ownership of the things they'd sacrificed hours of their lives working to acquire.

All for what? The chance to have sex? I'd been called to reap countless souls who'd died during their orgasms. Nothing about the process seemed appealing or worth the effort. I'd even wondered if humans were faking their dramatic reactions.

Loyalty and friendship, I understood, but love and desire were things that never made sense.

Until her.

From the moment I'd laid eyes on her, I felt as if my soul was being called to her. I'd been called to reap millions of souls, but this was different.

It took seeing her in danger for me to grasp what my body had been trying to tell me. I wanted to protect her and destroy everyone who dared hurt her... because my body already considered her ours.

When I'd yanked Zacharias away from her in the tunnel, it hadn't mattered that he was as close as a brother to me. My loyalty to her was already stronger, and I'd barely resisted the urge to rip his heart from his chest.

She was changing me, and we'd never even spoken to each other.

My jaw clenched at the memory of the energy Zacharias had blasted at the small group, causing my stomach to spasm and my heart to bang against my ribcage.

I'd teleported right into the path of the blast, standing between it and the beautiful ghost who was weeping over the dying Rhodes. Quickly tossing the other two Baudelaire men out of the blast's path, I'd braced for the impact.

The amount of power he'd put into the attack would've destroyed much of the tunnel system and killed anyone trapped inside. I'd wanted her to survive, so my only choice was to absorb the energy.

It was over in a matter of seconds and I'd grabbed Zacharias and teleported us away before he could do any more harm to them, or to my opinion of him.

My body shook with rage and the desire to make him pay for the pain he'd caused her. Not trusting that I could resist the urge, I'd left him on our estate halfway around the world from Amberwood.

Then I'd teleported back to the tunnels, staying in the reaper realm to prevent them from seeing me.

I'd watched with awe as she'd tried to heal the collector's wounds. Ghosts couldn't heal, but that didn't stop her from trying.

Pride swelled in my chest as she slowly and carefully manipulated the energy inside her and began sealing his wounds shut. She was a natural.

But one look at Rhodes told me he was beyond her abilities to heal. His soul was already pulling free of its dying vessel.

Remembering the way she had seemed to stare right at me in the library while I was in the reaper plane, I moved to stand directly behind her. When she buried her face in her hands and began to sob, I knew that was my chance to help without being seen.

Rhodes' soul opened his mouth and began the ancient call for death. While many people considered reapers to be harbingers of doom and gloom, we were closer to agents of mercy. Our presence eased the pain, confusion and fear the person was experiencing.

But not this time.

"Oh, no you don't," I'd snarled, covering his mouth with my hand to silence the call. "She wants you alive, so you're going to stay alive if you know what's good for you."

I'd none-too-gently crammed Rhodes' soul back into his body. Then, not trusting him to behave, I kept my hand pressed against his chest.

It was a lot like what would happen if you shoved a ticked off cat into a cardboard box, and then attempted to keep the lid closed with one hand, while trying to tear off a strip of tape to seal the box closed with the other.

Instead of tape, I was trying to use energy to repair the damaged artery that was causing him to bleed out. Just as I'd stopped the bleeding, she'd shifted positions to lie down beside him.

Their lips met, and she opened herself to him, and I

watched in a jealous rage as she let him devour her. He sucked up her energy at an alarming rate, leaving me confused about how a ghost could have stored away so much and how she could maintain a stable energy level. Ghosts faded a fraction with each passing hour after their death until they were simply gone. It was the natural order of things.

She was an anomaly that didn't make sense. But I knew with certainty that I didn't want her to exhaust herself. Not before I had a chance to figure her out.

The ghost's heart was tender, and she glowed with the purest of energies. There was no doubt she'd give her all if it would save a life, and it had my teeth grinding together in agitation. We needed to work on that.

I'd settled on the ground behind her, still wishing to remain unseen by the small group. One day, I would talk to her, but that wasn't the time. Lifting my hand, I lightly rested the tips of my fingers on her back and let my energy flow into her body.

It would've been more efficient if I'd sent the energy into Rhodes and healed him myself, but the grief on her face as she tried to save him told me she needed to do this herself.

For reasons I didn't understand, I disliked the idea that she would think back on this night and remember being helpless. No, I wanted her to look back and remember that she had saved him. Because that was the truth.

Sure, some of the energy she was using had come from me. But the only reason I was sitting on a cold stone floor, surrounded by collectors, was because of her. He would be dead if not for her desire to save him.

I was snapped from my memories and back to the present by Zacharias.

"Are you even listening to me?" He'd risen from his chair and was waving a hand in front of my face.

"No. And I'm done listening." Ignoring his pleas to let him explain, I turned on my heel and left the dining hall without another word.

CHAPTER 11

AXELLE

I could hardly breathe as Loch gently parted my legs. Unable to take my eyes from the man between my legs, I barely noticed when Rhodes rolled off the bed and moved to take Loch's previous place on my right side.

Sandwiched between Rhodes and Evander, I trembled as Loch trailed kisses along the sensitive skin of my inner thigh. I should have been expecting it, but when his mouth moved to press against the tiny piece of lace fabric, I nearly came apart.

And when Loch sucked the soaked fabric into the heat of his mouth, I cried out his name in surprise from the intensity of such an intimate act. My legs quivered, and I tried my best to scoot away from his mouth.

"No you don't." Rhodes caught my chin and tilted my head so he could capture my mouth in a slow, passionate kiss that had me seeing stars.

Not wanting to be left out, Evander's lips moved to my neck.

"You guys are going to be the second death of me," I panted between kisses. "I'm not sure I'm built to survive being with three guys at once."

"Imagine if you bring in a fourth," Evander teased, his hot breath teasing my overly sensitive skin with each word he spoke.

For a moment, I thought I felt my motionless heart jerk hard in my chest. "A fourth?!" My voice cracked on the last syllable.

"Yes. In our society, it's up to the female partner if she wants to bring in another male," Rhodes answered.

"I'm not sure I can handle the three of you. My brain might explode if I tried to bring in another." Even as I spoke the words, a fleeting image of the purple-eyed stranger in the library popped into my mind.

Stop being greedy, Axe, I scolded myself.

He was cute, but that didn't mean I wanted him. Because I totally didn't, right? I hadn't even talked to him for gourd's sake.

"Still, the decision is up to you. Things aren't as simple among paranormals as they are with humans. Just like there was an instant pull between us, you may feel that bond with another. We want you to know up front that as long as he understands he will be joining our family and not taking you away from us, we won't be upset with you. Fate has a weird way of meddling in matters of the heart. If you feel that bond, don't be afraid to trust yourself." Evander kissed the tip of my nose.

"Really Evander, I don't think—" I began, but Lochlan

had chosen that moment to slip his tongue beneath the fabric and trace along my slit. "LOCH!" Tiny spasms of pleasure ricocheted through my body as I screamed his name.

Needing to recover from the shock of that singular stroke of his tongue, I tried to close my legs.

"Behave, boo," Lochlan warned, gently biting the sensitive skin of my inner thigh. "I'm not finished feeding. You don't want me to starve, do you?"

Even in a moment like this, the man was teasing me. One thing was for sure, life with Lochlan would never be boring.

My panties were gone in the blink of an eye, causing a hot flush to run down my body and the lights in the room to flicker wildly. Lochlan remained motionless, his gaze burning my skin as he seemed to drink in the sight in front of him.

"You're so beautiful, Axelle," he whispered, sounding almost reverent.

Unsure how to respond, I remained quiet, simply waiting to see what his next move would be.

Lochlan's thumb brushed my slick, exposed sex. My back arched off the bed at the direct touch of his rough skin. Rhodes' lips reclaimed mine, swallowing my whimper of pleasure.

When Lochlan's tongue traced along my slit, I pulled away from Rhodes' mouth to stare down at him in a haze of disbelief.

Drinking in the sight of him, I wondered how a man

with otherworldly good looks like his, could ever desire me. I mean, I wasn't bad looking, but these men were on a different level. Yet there I was, with Lochlan's tongue thrusting into my tight heat as he pleased me in the most intimate way I could imagine.

It was overwhelming, and my climax built far too quickly. Closing my eyes, I fought against the storm swirling inside me. Instinctually, I knew I was teetering on a line that once crossed, I wouldn't be able to uncross.

Evander was placing tender kisses up my neck, and his large palm slid under the hem of my shirt to rest on my belly. Rhodes caught my jaw in his hand and his thumb stroked my cheek while his lips danced against mine.

Although I'd told myself otherwise, this was far more than a fling or a memory for the spank bank, rub hub, jill till, cover trove, or whatever it was called.

They were loving me.

Unable to think about anything other than how incredible it felt to have the heat of their bodies pouring into me, and Lochlan devouring me with the same feral hunger he'd shown when feeding from my energy, I gave in and allowed myself to enjoy this moment. An instant later, I climaxed so hard my back left the bed and I probably would have been levitating if my legs hadn't been clamped around Loch's head.

He didn't even give me a chance to recover. In a move so smooth it was deserving of an Emmy nomination, Lochlan grasped my thighs and flipped us over so that he lay on his back beneath me, and I was straddling his face.

"What are you doing?!" I protested, trying to scramble off him.

Loch's grip on my thighs tightened, refusing to let me go.

Rhodes caught my face between his palms, forcing me to look at him. "Stop fighting him and let him take care of your needs."

"What about *his* needs? You know, like breathing?" I yelped, worried they'd forgotten that only one of us in that room didn't require oxygen. Collectors still need that, right?

"Do you trust us?" Evander asked, peering into my soul with his piercing blue eyes.

"Yes." The word was little more than a whisper, but I meant it.

"Then relax and enjoy yourself," Evander reassured me.

The moment Lochlan's tongue began to stroke and thrust, I felt the energy in my body rushing to the apex of my thighs. But instead of devouring it, Lochlan was manipulating it and letting it build.

Maybe the fae were real, because that man knew how to work magic with his tongue. The flicking of his tongue, combined with the pulsing energy he'd called to my core, seemed to touch every hidden sensitive spot I possessed.

It was too much. The orgasm that followed was violent with a pleasure so powerful that it bordered on pain. I screamed Loch's name until I was hoarse. The lights in the room pulsed on and off in time with the aftershocks of my climax until, one by one, the bulbs exploded.

When the last ripple finally ebbed away, I collapsed into Rhodes' arms. My body was satisfied but weak.

Closing my eyes, I basked in the joy of being surrounded by three men who truly cared about me. It was intoxicating and unlocked the memories of dreams I'd hidden away after my death.

Memories of the life I'd hoped to have. A life like this one where I felt safe, loved, and I didn't have to be alone.

Even though I knew I would never again be alive in the most literal sense of the word, I had a second chance at living the life I'd only dreamed about.

On the heels of those resurrected emotions, a sense of overwhelming terror washed through me. A sharp wave of irrational anger followed it.

Just when I'd found a way to be content with the cards fate had dealt me, these men had come along and flipped my life upside down.

If I took a chance with them and it failed, I'd grieve over the pain of losing them and this chance for however long I haunted this earth.

If I chose the safe route, running from them and the love they offered, I'd spend the rest of my years wondering if I'd made the wrong decision.

It was a special kind of cruelty to dangle everything I'd ever dreamed of in front of my face, forcing me to risk the only thing I had left on this earth... my happiness.

Even though I no longer needed to breathe, I felt as though my lungs were screaming for oxygen and my head swirled with raw panic. I needed to get away.

I needed space from them so I could work through the emotions threatening to swallow me whole.

Not stopping to think, I bolted out of the bed and streaked toward the library. I didn't stop until I reached the tiny archive room I'd claimed as my own. Collapsing onto the floor, I let the tears come as I cried in frustration.

Far too quickly, heavy footsteps thundered down the hallway toward my hiding spot. How had they gotten here so quickly? Had they broken in again?

I wasn't ready to face the guys. Reaching for the shadows, I allowed myself to melt into them, begging them to hide me from the men.

Usually, when joining the shadows, I remained in the same location. But this time was different. Maybe because I longed to be somewhere they couldn't follow me, or maybe I'd been too emotional.

This time, as the shadows welcomed me, the room flexed and warped. Darkness swirled around me, but just before the last pinprick of light vanished, there was an audible snap and the world came into sharp clarity once again.

Except I wasn't in the library anymore.

Blinking in confusion, I tried to figure out where I was, but nothing in the opulent purple and gold room was familiar. The wall in front of me was covered with various gleaming weapons, each one adorned with intricate carvings on their blades and polished handles.

When my eyes landed on the large curved blade in the middle of the wall, chills raced down my skin.

Oh crap.

"Well, this is a surprise."

Spinning around, I came face-to-face with the purple-eyed man from the library.

But he wasn't a man.

He was a reaper.

CHAPTER 12

AXELLE

I opened my mouth, but thanks to the terror clogging my throat, not a single sound escaped. My last run-in with reapers hadn't been friendly, and I'd had backup that time. I seriously doubted I'd survive an encounter on my own.

From the bits of conversation I'd overheard between the guys, they seemed to think reapers were arrogant, but not evil. Personally, I found that hard to believe after the events of the day before.

However, according to Evander, the reaper who attacked us had been the exception, not the rule. Still, the odds seemed really high that this reaper was one of the two we'd met in the tunnel.

It made little sense, though. Because if he was one of the pair who fought us, surely I'd already be dead... well, dead*er*.

The reaper moved toward me with the silent elegance of

a jaguar stalking its prey. I stumbled to the side, desperate to put space between us, but he matched my every move. Finally, he reached out and caught both my hands in one of his and twirled me. If anyone had been in the room, they probably would've thought I was dancing with him, rather than trying to escape.

Our impromptu dance ended when my back came up against something solid. Taking another step forward, his hard body crushed me against the unforgiving wall.

He kept my hands in his, pinning them above my head. The position forced me to lift myself on tip-toe so I wouldn't feel like I was dangling, but our height difference meant my head was still only level with the center of his abs.

"Tell me, naughty girl, how did you get here?" Rather than the threat I'd expected, his words were like a reassuring purr.

Despite my fear, my insides quivered in delight. Maybe this was how they lured their prey. It was the only excuse I could find for why I didn't want to fight against his hold, and why my body was practically melting against him.

What if, just like a mermaid, they had a reaper's song? That didn't flow off the tongue the same way a siren's song did. Reaper's Rap? Reaper's Rock? Reaper's Rhapsody?

The reaper grasped my chin with his free hand, yanking me out of the anxiety-driven chaos of my mind. Ignoring the way heat spread through me from his touch, I narrowed my eyes and waited to see what he would do next.

He slowly turned my face from side to side—almost as though he were inspecting me. His grip on my jaw was rough, but not enough to hurt me. Tilting my head back, he forced me to look up at him.

The reaper wore his straight, black hair loose so that it fell around his face and brushed his shoulders. Each time he moved, the light would glint off the silky strands, revealing hints of violet. It was breathtaking and reminded me of a raven's iridescent black feathers.

My fingers twitched with the desire to run them through his hair, but it was a desire that quickly faded as he spoke again in that same silken purr.

"Answer me. You don't want to make me angry."

I don't want to see him angry?

"Listen here, Sir Douchington. You really don't want to see me upset," I growled, conjuring up every bit of emotional turmoil I'd been trying to lock away. "I've had a rollercoaster of a day and I've exceeded the limit on what I can handle in a single twenty-four-hour period."

The reaper arched an eyebrow, and the corner of his mouth twitched.

My irritation rose another notch. "I swear, if you laugh, I'll poltergeist your arse so hard they'll think you need an exorcist."

He carefully schooled his face to hide the signs of amusement. Still, he looked more intrigued than angry. "Is that so? Why don't you tell me about it? I'm a good listener."

SEDONA ASHE

I responded with an unladylike snort. "I doubt that."

But it seemed he was serious. Lowering my hands, he took several steps back, pulling me with him until he sat down on a velvet upholstered chair.

I dug in my heels, determined to defy him if for no other reason than I was terrified of how badly I longed to throw myself into his arms. My efforts were futile and, with embarrassing ease, he settled me onto one of his thick, muscled thighs.

It reminded me of seeing adult women sitting on the lap of the local mall Santa... only this Santa dressed in all black. And instead of a red shirt that stretched over a jolly round belly, his black shirt clung to a wide chest and flat abs. The traditional white beard had been swapped for several days' worth of dark stubble along his jaw that shifted his looks from an underwear model to a menacing warlord who killed anyone who dared to cross him.

Maybe I should tell the sexy gothic Santa that I'd been a good girl, and I deserve a reward. Or would I be a good *ghoul*?

The stupid pun, combined with the absurdity of the situation, broke me. I dissolved into the slightly hysterical laughter that could only come from overwhelm, stress, and anxiety. Without warning, my boring world had been turned upside down, and if I didn't laugh, I was going to break down.

The reaper leaned back, watching me with open curiosity. "Please share what you find so amusing about this situation."

TBR: DEAD BUT WELL READ

As he spoke, he inspected my hands, turning them over to check my palms and each finger, and holding his up to compare the size. It was as though he'd never seen female hands before. Weirdo.

I wanted to be disgusted by his skin touching mine, but I wasn't. It was as reassuring and familiar as the collectors' touch... It felt right.

After reading countless romances where I'd fallen for the bad boy, was it any surprise I'd be attracted to the first one I met? This was a passing infatuation.

My mind drifted back to what Evander had said about bonds and fate. Was it possible I shared some type of connection with this reaper? It would explain the strange pull in my chest when he'd been at the library, and the way my body submitted to his touch without question. I stifled a snort. Not just submitting; every fiber of my being craved him.

I needed serious help.

Fate must have loved screwing with my life. Or maybe I was being used as a test subject for future ghost upgrades? I could see it now—

"Reapr, the dating app for the undead and unwed. Scythe left for those you don't take a Shining to, and right for those who might get The Ring."

At least there was one upside to the crazy attraction I felt toward this man. He might've been in the tunnel, but he wasn't the reaper who sliced open Rhodes' chest. Because the only connection I'd felt with that one was when I'd been clinging to him with my teeth buried in his arm.

"Tell me what you found amusing."

Dang. He would not let it go.

Warm fingers teased across my collarbone as the reaper moved the neck of my oversized white shirt this way and that. What was he looking for? If he'd been a vampire, I'd have guessed he was looking for the best place to bite me.

With a sigh, I caved and blurted out the truth. "It's just that you kinda look like a younger, sexy, gothic Santa. And I look like I'm about to tell you I've been a good ghoul and deserve a reward."

The ghoul pun got me again, and like an idiot, I snickered over my own joke.

"I see." His gorgeous mouth curved into a wicked smile and his hand slid up my thighs and beneath the hem of the T-shirt that barely came to mid-thigh on me.

It was the first time I'd seen him smile, and I was stunned at how it transformed him from dangerous to heartthrob. Logic blared a warning that I was in danger and should run, but the lust stirred by his skin against mine held me in place.

An intoxicating cocktail of horror and excitement swirled inside me as I remembered I hadn't stopped to grab my thong before leaving the guys' house. If I focused, I could change my clothing into something less revealing, but that would use energy I wasn't sure I should waste while literally sitting on Death's lap.

Yeah, I need to save my energy to attempt an escape, I told myself, because there was no way I was getting turned on by this situation.

The reaper's palm trailed over my hip, thumb brushing across my belly. His hand froze as he realized I was naked beneath the shirt. He sucked in a harsh breath, sending a thrill racing down my spine.

Okay, fine. I might be deceased, but I wasn't delusional. There was definitely something wrong with me if I was getting aroused by the enemy. I didn't get time to dwell on it.

Moving faster than I could process, he lifted me from his leg and sat me so that I straddled his lap, facing him. He grinned down at me like the cat that had caught the canary.

"Since you've been such a good girl, how about you tell me what you want?" He templed his fingers together and pressed them to his lips, waiting for my answer.

With an effort that should have earned me an Olympic gold medal, I focused hard on all the reasons I could not allow myself to be attracted to him.

Closing my eyes, I whispered the one question that was burning a hole through my brain. "I want to know if you were in the tunnels last night."

"Yes."

I waited for him to elaborate, but he remained silent, his purple eyes studying me.

Anger boiled in my belly. About freaking time! Fury was exactly the distraction I needed.

"Why did you attack us? We did nothing to you!" The lightbulbs in the ornate wall sconces flickered, humming loudly as my temper burned hotter. "You almost killed us!"

His expression didn't change. "I saved you and those men."

How could he be so calm and self-assured?

"Are you serious right now?" Lifting myself up onto my knees so that we were almost eye level, I glared at him, wanting him to see my mounting fury. "How do you think you saved us? By throwing Lochlan and Evander through a freaking brick wall?"

The reaper's hands moved to my hips, holding me still as he leaned in. His rough jaw brushed against mine as he whispered in my ear. "It's all about perspective, pet."

"I'm-I'm not your pet," I responded, hoping he hadn't heard the quiver in my voice. "And I don't need perspective! I was there! I saw with my own eyes what happened."

"Since you aren't leaving here until I'm ready to let you go, I think 'pet' works." His knuckles brushed against my cheekbone. "You're such a stubborn little thing. There is always more than one perspective."

The reaper's lips brushed against my mouth, and I fought to swallow the whimper that rose unbidden up my throat. How could this stranger hold such power over me?

"Consider the situation we are in now. From my perspective, it appears you must have used some type of magic to track me. Then you teleported into my private chambers smelling of sex and dressed in a way meant to seduce me. The only logical reason for you to do this is because you plan to murder me the moment I let down my guard."

I reeled back as though he'd struck me. "You can't be

serious! I didn't want to come here… I don't even know where here is! And you need to get over yourself, because I certainly didn't come to seduce you. Besides, you aren't my type!"

"Don't lie to me, pet." The reaper's hand traveled down my ribs. "There is a wet spot on my slacks that tells another story."

He took his time, exploring every inch of my body that he touched. What game was he playing?

I snuck a furtive peek down, and an instant later, the lights in the room flickered as horror rushed through me. He hadn't lied. There was a slightly dark spot on his slacks where he'd sat me on his thigh. Despite my humiliation, I refused to admit he had any effect on me.

Lifting my chin, I shrugged carelessly. "You said I was a pet. I guess I haven't been housebroken yet. That still doesn't mean I want you."

His purple eyes glowed a brilliant violet. "What have I told you about lying to me?"

Refusing to back down, I met his gaze and lied through my teeth. "I'm not lying."

He was motionless for several long seconds before nodding and leaning back in his seat. "I do enjoy a good game. What do I get if I prove you're lying?"

"What do you want?" I asked, more than a little curious about what I might have that he would want as a prize.

I owned nothing of value except two special edition hardcovers of my favorite shifter romances that I'd rescued from my house, and not even a grim reaper himself could pry them from my cold dead hands.

"You'll spend the night with me. In my bed." His fingers brushed lazily up and down my bare thigh, making it difficult to focus.

I narrowed my eyes. "And you'll let me walk away, the same amount of dead as I am now, at sunrise?"

He nodded. "You have my word that no harm will come to you."

"And what do I get when I win?" I pushed.

Sitting up, he ran his fingers through my hair and pulled me so close that our mouths nearly touched. "Whatever you want."

Hmm. I could use that to get more information about what was happening and why they'd been in the tunnels. Or maybe I could ask for protection for the guys.

"Alright, deal," I breathed, fighting the urge to lean forward a fraction so that I could feel his lips brush mine.

Leaning back, I stuck out my hand. Instead of shaking it, he caught my hand and placed a soft kiss on the back. My insides quivered, and I could feel my odds of winning plummet with that one suave move. This was going to be far harder than I thought.

The devilish smile that stretched across his face should've been the wake-up call I needed to realize the smartest plan was to abort my mission, stop playing with fire, and run. But my one good trait was that I never gave up. It was also my worst trait because it meant I was stubborn and never backed down from a challenge.

If I was being honest, I'd expected him to make an attempt at seducing me. I thought I would win by not caving into the desire that was building inside me. I just needed to practice self-control and think about chicken butts, anal glands, and garbage dumps.

Come on, how hard could it be to not jump his bones?

It turns out it was harder than finding a heartbeat in a graveyard.

The reaper stood, plopping me down in the seat he'd just vacated. He walked toward the weapon-covered wall, unbuttoning his black dress shirt as he moved. Slipping it off, he revealed a sleek body that was toned to perfection.

He tossed the shirt on a side table and reached for the scythe hanging on the wall. I was ashamed to admit I might have drooled a little as I watched his back muscles flex and ripple as he lifted it from the wall.

The reaper spoke in a language I didn't recognize, and the lights dimmed. He gave another command and music flowed from hidden speakers in the room—the kind of music with a bass line perfect for doing things that went bump in the night.

Unable to look away, I watched in fascination as his body moved in perfect rhythm, grinding his way down the handle of his scythe as if it were a pole. When he reached the floor, he gripped the handle with one hand and put the other behind himself on the wooden floor to support himself as he continued to move his hips in time with the beat.

I squirmed on the velvet cushion as raw lust tied my

insides together and made it impossible to sit still. But the show had just begun.

The music shifted, and he smoothly laid the gleaming scythe on the ground, rolling easily into a position over it. When he began to undulate and rock his hips while executing perfect pushups, my mouth went dry as my body sent a wave of slick heat rushing between my thighs.

If he kept this up, the scythe was going to end up pregnant.

And why am I feeling jealous over an inanimate object?

As if sensing my thoughts—or worse, smelling my lust —the purple-eyed reaper turned his attention to me. Rising to his feet in the type of fluid movement typically associated with felines, he made his way toward me. I jumped at the sharp crack from his belt as he removed it with a single flick of his wrist.

He continued to take his time, his movements unhurried, as though he could do this for hours. Unfortunately, I couldn't if I wanted to win this bet. My resolve was crumbling faster than a granola bar—and not the chewy kind; the ones that would nearly shatter your teeth when you bit into them and somehow you always end up wearing more of them than you got in your mouth.

In the blink of an eye, he had my wrists wrapped in the soft leather of his belt and was sliding them up his bare chest as he slowly pulled me from the chair. Electrical pulses shot through me as my skin brushed against his, and the lights in the room hummed loudly.

The desire I'd felt for him from the moment we locked

eyes in the library had turned into a hungry thing that paced inside me. I needed to admit defeat and stop this madness before I did something stupid. He was a complication my life didn't need.

Even as the thought crossed my mind, my heart spasmed in pain. Why did it seem like I belonged with him? Belonged *to* him?

The reaper lifted me so that I stood on top of his bare feet. Wrapping an arm around my waist, he danced around the room, letting me feel the play of his muscles against me with every move he made. It was sexy and ridiculously romantic... and I loved every minute of it.

When at last he guided me to another chair, I was nearly panting and trying my best to hide it. If this ended now, I still had a chance at winning...

A new song filled the room, this one feeling somehow naughtier than the others. As though he'd known and had timed it, the reaper straddled my chair. Grabbing the back of the chair, his body flowed and undulated to the erotic music. He still wore his black slacks, but there was no hiding the size of the bulge when he was this close to me. Looking up at him, I saw the same hunger I felt reflected back at me in the depths of his eyes.

This was quite possibly the worst decision I'd made in my entire life. So why did it feel so beautifully right? Why did it feel wrong to deny the feelings that continued to grow inside me?

Of all the dirty tactics I thought he might use to win the bet, this hadn't been on my list.

He'd barely touched me… and he'd won.

I'd gotten a lap dance from Death and lost.

But after seeing the way his hips moved against his scythe, I wasn't even mad about it. Maybe I was willing to be screwed by death again… I had a suspicion it would be a lot more fun this time.

CHAPTER 13

AXELLE

My eyes crossed as I stared at the abs flexing with each move the reaper made.

Don't lick them, Axe. You have no idea where they've been.

The scent of evergreens, burning wood, and a masculine musk overwhelmed my senses and fanned the flames of desire I was desperately trying to keep from turning into a wildfire. I needed answers.

Yeah, like what does he taste like…?

Deciding I needed a distraction before my intrusive thoughts got any creepier, I cleared my throat. "So, um, what's your name?"

"Saul." With a smirk, he added, "Are you ready to admit defeat?"

I'd accepted my loss, but the arrogance on his face ruffled my feathers. "Of course not. I could do this all day." I faked a long yawn, as though exhausted by the whole affair.

"Is that so?" Using his unsettling reaper speed, Saul lifted me from my seat and spun us around until my back was once more pressed against a wall.

Saul's mouth brushed mine in a touch so soft I might have imagined it, then moved down my neck. "Tell me the truth."

This had to be the weirdest interrogational technique ever.

"I feel nothing." I wasn't sure if I was denying it out of sheer stubbornness or the thrill of seeing how far I could push him.

"You can try to hide it, but you desire me." Saul's chest rumbled with a sound that could have been annoyance or laughter.

His large hand grasped my thigh, sliding me up the wall until he could hook my leg over his hip. When he ground his hard length against me, I barely swallowed my moan.

"Still not my type," I wheezed past the lump of need that had lodged itself in my throat.

"Such a stubborn little pet," he growled, his teeth nipping my neck. "One last time. Tell me the truth."

My body grew wetter at the unspoken 'or else' in his command. What the hex was wrong with me?

Monster romance really should come with warning labels, since the journey from enjoying reading smut in the quiet of your bedroom to getting turned on by taunting a sexy reaper was a lot shorter trip than I'd imagined.

"Fine. I lied." It was time to do the logical thing and

admit my defeat with grace and dignity. "I haven't been a good ghoul."

Shut the creaking haunted house door!

Why did I say that? And why didn't I recognize the husky voice coming from my mouth? I was possessed. It was the only thing that made any sense.

"I tried to play nice." Saul's tongue swirled up my neck. "Now we'll do things the hard way."

Prepared to admit my defeat, my lips parted. "Do your worst."

Saul's eyes grew brighter, casting a soft purple glow around us. "As you wish."

His arm clamped around my waist like a steel band, and the room darkened for a moment, just as it had before I'd ended up here. When the world came back into focus, I found myself flying through the air.

"Oof!" I grunted as I landed on a large bed.

A bed that smelled of a certain sexy reaper.

Crypts! I was in Saul's bed.

Trembling, I lay still as his large frame moved over me. Once more, he caught my wrists in one of his hands and lifted them above my head. The white shirt slid several inches higher, exposing more of my bare skin.

Dropping lower, but still keeping his full weight off me, Saul kissed my forehead, my cheek, and the tip of my nose. Everywhere except where I wanted to feel his lips. The man was infuriating!

His free hand traveled up my thigh, teasing the sensitive skin of my inner thighs and inching ever closer to the part of me that ached for his touch, regardless of all the reasons I shouldn't. But just before his fingers reached the apex of my thighs, he stopped.

"Pet, I will ask this only once, so think carefully before you answer." His breathing was harsh. Or was I just imagining it?

I thought he was going to repeat the same question, but this time, he asked something completely different.

"If you do not want me to touch you, you need to leave now. I will forget our little wager and let you go. But you need to decide now."

My heart melted at how adorable this big, bad reaper was. Saul could have taken whatever he wanted and sent me off to the beyond with no repercussions. And even though he could see the effect he had on my body, he wanted to make sure my mind was just as on board.

I didn't know why he'd been in the tunnels or how he was connected to the murderous reaper, but I knew this man had told me the truth. He hadn't tried to kill us.

This game we were playing was too intriguing to admit that I wanted him, so instead, I gave him a shy smile and whispered, "You can touch me."

The unsure look on his face vanished, instantly replaced with the arrogant one I found equal parts annoying and arousing. "Innocent little pet. You should have run."

He didn't give me a chance to respond before his fingers stroked along my slit. Clenching my fists so tight my fingers left tiny half-moons in my palms, I fought to keep myself from reacting.

Lifting an eyebrow in challenge, I waited for his next move.

Spurred on by my defiance, he shifted slightly so he could trail kisses across my collarbone and shoulders. Inch by slow inch, his mouth moved lower until his lips found the hardened peak of my nipple.

There was no hiding my gasp as his mouth sucked and teased my breast through the thin shirt fabric, sending tiny zaps of pleasure shooting straight to my core. The wanton part of me longed to rip off my shirt so I could feel his lips on my skin, but with my hands still above my head, I couldn't do anything without asking him for permission. And I was far too stubborn to do that.

"Your body betrays you," he murmured. "Admit you have lost."

"You'll never take me alive," I hissed, belatedly adding, "well, dead. You know what I mean."

His laughter sent delicious vibrations through me. "You're something special."

I was saved from another idiotic response by his finger suddenly burying itself inside me. Stars sparkled in my vision and, despite my best efforts, my hips bucked.

As his finger continued to thrust inside me, quickly finding the perfect angle to pleasure me, he watched my face. It was a look I couldn't fully decipher. He wanted to hear me say the words, but it was more than that.

With my body still worked up from his dance, my climax built far too quickly. He somehow knew exactly how I longed to be stroked... like I was meant to be his.

I was seconds from falling apart when his hand stilled. Blinking, I tried to clear the lust from my mind.

"Tell me," he ordered, his rough voice sending a fresh wave of heat rushing to coat his finger.

I tried to rock my hips, but he pinned my legs with one of his, trapping me beneath him.

His finger disappeared, leaving an emptiness inside me that was far bigger than just a desire to get laid. I wanted him. I wanted to belong to him.

Lifting his hand to his mouth, I watched in shock as he licked his finger clean with the thoroughness of a cat cleaning its paw. When he finished, he looked down at me with a wicked smile that set my world on fire.

The lights in the room buzzed and the lightbulb in the lamp nearest the bed popped. This time, it wasn't from embarrassment.

"You're mine." The words tumbled from my lips before I'd had time to think them through. "I mean, you're my type. You win. Are you happy now?"

I was rambling, desperately trying to distract him from what I'd accidentally confessed. Humans never mentioned getting married on the first date, and here I was declaring I was going to haunt his butt for the rest of eternity.

It must have worked, because rather than running away in panic, his grin grew. Slipping first one finger and then a second into my tight heat, he stretched me as he found that perfect rhythm again.

"Come for me, pet."

I obeyed and let myself fall... trusting this stranger would catch me.

EVENTUALLY, I came back to my senses. Feeling absolutely boneless on the mattress, I waited to see what Saul's next move would be. He'd won the bet, and that meant I would be spending the night in his bed.

Only it couldn't be anywhere close to night since the library hadn't even been open when I'd tried to hide from the men and had somehow landed in the reaper's lair. Glancing around the room, I found an open set of balcony doors that led out onto a marble porch. A tiny slice of deep navy sky was visible.

It *was* night. But how was that possible? It wasn't uncommon for me to lose track of time when I was reading a good book and miss several hours, but I'd never lost an entire day. How long had Saul's dance been?

Catching the confusion on my face as I stared at the open doors, Saul explained, "You are on the other side of the world. It's almost midnight here."

I cleared my throat and asked, "Where am I, and how did I get here?"

"You're in my home, and for now, I'm going to keep the exact location to myself. As for how you got here, I don't have an answer for you." Taking my hands, he gently pulled me into a sitting position as he spoke. "You shouldn't be able to walk into the reaper plane, and you shouldn't have been able to teleport to a location you had no way of knowing even existed."

"Hmm," I murmured, my brain working overtime as I tried to put together the pieces. "So when I've hidden myself in the past, do you think I've been going into the reaper realm, or plane, each time?"

"Yes, it appears so. Stand in front of me for a moment." Saul's voice was low and firm. It wasn't a request.

I stood, more confused over my willingness to obey him than the fact I'd been hop-scotching my way through the different planes. "Do you have some type of magic that makes people do what you say? Like an alpha werewolf command?"

Saul's rich laughter warmed my body from head to toe. "You have a lot of experience with werewolves?"

"No, I've just read a lot about them. In… In research books." I sounded defensive even to my own ears.

"I see." Saul's chest rumbled with another laugh as he turned me so that I faced away from him. "To answer your question, no, I do not have the power to control another being's mind or will."

His fingers gripped the hem of my shirt, gently lifting it over my head and leaving me completely bare in front of him.

"There is something about my species that attracts females. But it is not something that we control, at least not any more than a human male might use his looks to attract a mate." As he spoke, Saul's fingers trailed down my spine and each rib.

"Have you done that to me?" I whispered, the words so soft I didn't think he could hear them.

"Not until you refused to tell me the truth. When we made our wager, I will admit to trying to seduce you to prove my point." His fingers prodded a tender place along my shoulder blade, causing me to wince.

Saul froze, and hoping to distract him, I blurted out a question I never would have asked if I hadn't been flustered. "You only did it to prove a point?"

Why did that hurt my feelings? This was an erotic one-night stand, and he hadn't promised me anything more.

His hot breath brushed over my skin, stopping directly over the tender flesh. "No."

The skin beneath his mouth grew hot as energy poured into my skin, rushing through every cell in my body.

When he finished with my back, he spoke, his voice low. "Turn around, pet."

My legs wobbled as I slowly faced him, and I struggled with the urge to cover myself. I'd been a goody two shoes my whole life. This time, I wanted to do what I was never brave enough to do while I was living.

His hands held my hips and his thumbs absently brushed the sensitive skin of my stomach. His eyes traveled over every inch of my skin, caressing me in a way that was nearly more intimate than being touched.

Saul wanted me.

Very slowly, he began the same process as he'd done on

143

my back. Prodding and exploring, although avoiding my breasts. Each time he found a tender spot, Saul would lean in and kiss it, sending a fresh wave of his potent energy into me.

"You're healing me." My eyes closed as his mouth moved to heal a bruise just over my breast.

"Why did you give so much of your energy away? You should have healed yourself first." The harshness of his words was a stark contrast to the tenderness of his touch.

You should have healed yourself first.

"How did you know I healed someone else?" I asked, opening my eyes to study his face.

By the time I'd started healing Rhodes, the reapers had vanished. There was no way he could have known. Unless...

"I watched you," Saul admitted, kissing a slow path between my breasts that had nothing to do with healing injuries.

A chill ran through me. How long had he stayed? What exactly had he seen?

"Calm yourself, pet. When things became intimate with the second collector, I left." He brushed his lips across the swell of my breast, making it harder to focus.

I should be upset that he'd been lurking about like some creepy voyeur, shouldn't I? So why was I feeling all hot and bothered just imagining him there... imagining all four men in the same room?

"But I wanted to stay."

I barely heard the words, and for a moment, I thought I might have imagined them.

"You wanted to stay and... watch?" The last word came out as a groan thanks to his tongue flicking across my nipple.

I knew collectors were cool with sharing, at least to some extent, but I had zero idea of how reaper society functioned. Even if it was possible to have him in my life, would he be willing to share me with them?

He would have to be because I was drawn to the three collectors just as much as to him. We were an all-or-nothing sort of deal.

"Yes. If I couldn't be the one to touch you, then I wanted to watch your beautiful face as you found your release with him." His tongue swirled around my nipple, causing me to whimper.

Abruptly, Saul stood, sweeping me up into his arms. He moved to the head of the bed and, cradling me against his chest with one arm, he pulled down the comforter and sheet.

Yes! He was finally going to stop teasing me and get to the main event.

Saul lowered me onto the bed and then slid in behind me. His muscular arm wrapped around my waist, tucking me into the heat of his body. It felt incredible, but not as incredible as it would feel when he used his wiener-wand to clear the cobwebs from the crypt between my thighs—

"Are you sure you're a ghost?"

Despite the fact that we spoke the same language, it took

an embarrassingly long time to process what he had asked. It was something I blamed him for, since he was keeping me all hot and bothered.

"What? Of course I'm a ghost. I have a gravestone to prove it. Well, technically, it doesn't prove it since it doesn't have my actual name on it, but my flesh-and-blood body is buried under it." Annoyance flashed through me and the lights in the room flickered.

"Ghosts don't survive long on the human plane, and they definitely don't cross into the reapers' territory," Saul mused, not accusing me of anything, simply working through his thoughts out-loud. "We need to find a way to keep you from fading."

"Aw. You don't want me to disappear?" I cooed, shocking myself that I felt so relaxed in the company of the being that almost everyone in the world feared.

"You're mine, pet." Saul nuzzled my neck. "Tell me, how did you die and when did it happen?"

"I was in a charity boxing match with the Easter Bunny. He took me out with a mean roundhouse kick in the second round." I clicked my tongue against my teeth as though disappointed with myself.

"You have a strange sense of humor." Saul's teeth nipped the curve of my ear. "Now, how did you die?"

"Alright. It's just that I hate telling anyone because it's so stupid, it's humiliating. You see, Cupid had gotten in trouble for drunk flying and was caught with his pants—er, diaper—down. Literally. Thankfully, there wasn't much to see, but the court ordered him to take mandatory archery

146

lessons at the facility where I worked. Let's just say he showed up sloshed, and I caught a stray arrow in the back." I sighed theatrically. "I was struck down by a weapon of love."

Saul growled, and his hand slid down to pinch my butt. "Enough with the nonsense. If you won't tell me the truth of how you died, then tell me when you died."

I would give him that much. "About three years ago."

Saul rose onto his elbow, rolling me to my back so that I looked up at him. "Is that the truth, pet? You've been a ghost for three years?"

"Yes," I whispered. "It's the truth."

"You are a miracle." His purple eyes searched my face as though trying to figure out what made me different. "No ghost can survive that long without fading, yet your energy is stable."

I nodded.

Saul lowered his forehead until it pressed against mine, and again his energy surged forward. This time, instead of washing through me like a tsunami, it moved with purpose. Wispy tendrils of his power poked and prodded, searching for who knew what.

When at last he pulled away, his face was hard and his pupils had narrowed to thin, cat-like slits. "Your body is capable of storing an impressive amount of energy, but you have barely enough to function right now."

Unsure of what he wanted me to say, I bit my tongue and remained silent.

"You fed all three of the collectors, didn't you? Even

147

though you knew your reserves were low." All signs of teasing had gone from his tone. Saul was angry, and I couldn't grasp why.

"They were in worse shape than me. My energy will replenish itself. You can't tell me what I can and can't do with my body." Clamping my teeth together, I glared up at him in defiance.

Saul's eyes glowed, the thin slits of his pupils making him appear even more dangerous. The room grew dark as shadows leaked like ink from him to swirl around the bed, almost wrapping us in a cocoon. He moved over me, his large frame pinning me to the bed.

"You are mine, pet." The fingers of his right hand wrapped around my throat, caressing the skin as he tightened his grip just enough so that I felt his power. "And since I am Death, there isn't a thing in this world that is going to take you from me."

If I were a strong independent ghost, I would've told him he didn't own me. But frankly, Saul was freaking terrifying and a total hottie when he went all angry Grim Reaper. And why deny the truth?

Leaning down, so that our faces were inches apart, he hissed, "If you want to feed your collectors, then you will ask me for help. I don't care if I have to give you energy while the four of you bang to your hearts' content and I am forced to watch. But you will not allow them to feed back-to-back from you unless I am there. Do you understand me?"

I nodded.

His fingers stroked the column of my throat. "Use your words."

I wasn't his toy, and I would dang sure feed the men if they needed me. A spasm of irritation jolted through me, but a sharp spasm of desire followed hot on its heels.

It wouldn't hurt to agree with him... and it might even be fun to find out what happened if one day I had to disobey him. A thrill of excitement raced through me at the thought. Saul had no idea the amount of trouble he was signing up for if he was so determined to keep me as his pet.

Let the games begin.

Lifting my fingers to my forehead, I gave him a sassy salute. "Yes, sir."

"Good girl." Saul's hand moved to cradle my jaw. "Now take what you need."

I didn't get to ask what he meant because he captured my mouth in a demanding kiss. As though we'd kissed a thousand times, my body seemed to melt against his.

My lips parted, allowing him to deepen the kiss. Just as his tongue stroked against mine, I felt it. The rush of raw power pouring down my throat. Saul's power.

I never would have admitted it, but I had pushed myself too far in the tunnels. While the reaper's scythe hadn't killed me, holding it had burned through a large amount of my energy. Then healing the guys so soon after had depleted me to levels I hadn't experienced since I'd blown up half the computers in the library. I didn't regret my decisions, but it would have taken me weeks to build my energy back up to normal.

When I'd taken enough power to ease the tiredness and put me past the danger zone, I tried to break the kiss, but Saul wasn't having it. His hand moved back to my throat, and he held me still as his power continued to rush into me like a raging river.

This lasted for several more minutes before he finally broke the kiss and pulled back so he could look into my eyes. His pupils had returned to a circular shape, but his eyes still shone with an otherworldly glow.

Without saying a word, he shifted positions on the bed so that once more my back was tucked against his chest. His shadows were still wrapped around the bed, and pulsed in perfect rhythm with Saul's steady heartbeat.

Unable to help myself, I whispered into the darkness, "You healed me and you shared your energy with me." He'd also given me a mind-shattering orgasm, but I couldn't bring myself to mention that. "Why? What are you getting out of this?"

He remained quiet for so long that I thought he wasn't going to answer. Then he murmured, "I get you."

Tears sprung to my eyes as Saul buried his face in my hair and his large palm flattened against my stomach, holding me tighter to him. "Now go to sleep, pet."

I huffed. "Silly, reaper. Ghosts can't sleep."

"You underestimate my power." Saul's seductive purr was back. "As long as you are touching me, you can sleep. I can feel your exhaustion. Let me take care of you tonight."

The idea of sleeping sounded too good to be true. I didn't want the burden of needing sleep as much as a human, but the past day had been overwhelming, and my mind and body vibrated with the need to shut down and truly relax.

"Saul? I'm scared," I whispered, lacing my fingers through his against my stomach. "What if I don't wake up?"

"My love, I already told you nothing can take you from me. You are safe in my arms. Now go to sleep." Saul tucked my head beneath his chin and tossed a leg over me.

Safe in the shelter of his body, I closed my eyes.

When he'd won the bet and I'd known I'd be spending the night in his bed, my mind had swan-dived into the gutter. I'd envisioned all sorts of naughty things that might happen.

What can I say? I'm a smut loving girl and completely obsessed with tropes like forced proximity and only one bed.

I'd thought my night would have been one of seduction and sins.

Instead, my night was one of snuggles and sleep... and falling in love with a purple-eyed reaper.

I stared down at the woman in my bed, watching as her dark lashes fluttered. She was close to waking, and when she did, I knew our time together would be over.

Last night, she'd been distracted by the bond pulling us together, and the passion she'd kept bottled up for three years. When she awoke from her first sleep since death, supercharged on reaper energy, the submissive kitten would be gone. In her place would be the fiery independent woman who had taken on Zacharias without flinching, and who'd been ballsy enough to make a bet with death.

Two sides of the same exquisite creature.

The blanket had slipped from her shoulders, pooling around her waist and exposing her torso. Unable to help myself, I drank in the sight of her bare, milky skin.

My cock, which had been engorged since the minx had appeared in my chambers dressed in nothing but a flimsy white shirt and smelling of sex, throbbed painfully. Once more, I questioned if the pleasure of orgasming could be worth enduring hours of discomfort. Not wanting her to wake and find me staring at her like a complete pervert, I gently tucked the blanket around her neck.

At least the worry in my heart over her wellbeing had been satisfied. After the confrontation with Zacharias, I'd been unable to rest, needing to assure myself she was safe. And knowing the power Zacharias wielded and how much damage he'd done to the three collectors, I worried she'd been hiding injuries beneath her clothes.

Hoping to ease the chaos in my mind, I'd gone to find her. But when I'd teleported to the library, it had been quiet and empty.

It was easy to guess where she was, who she was with, and what they were doing. That knowledge had added to my sour mood.

When she'd healed Evander, their tender moment had turned erotic. I wanted to kill him for touching her, but I also wanted to watch her beautiful face as she gave in to her desire.

It had taken all of my willpower to leave, but I wasn't a demon. And being there for such an intimate moment without an invitation had seemed like a breach of the trust I wanted to build with her.

When she'd asked me how much I'd witnessed, it had been a relief that I could tell her truthfully that I had respected her privacy and left. She'd appeared relieved, but something else had flashed across her face—disappointment, and maybe even a hint of lust.

Which was perfect for my plans. If she was already imagining me as part of her circle, it would be far easier to convince her we belonged together. I would tolerate the collectors if it meant I got to keep my beautiful little pet.

As long as they didn't hurt her, they would live. If they made her shed a single sorrowful tear, there was nowhere they could hide from Death.

I just needed to wrap up some loose ends and then I could focus my full attention on her. My brother's murderer had to be dealt with before I could close that chapter of my life, and like it or not, Zacharias' plan was the best one so far. But with my newfound suspicions about Zacharias' true character, the one he'd kept hidden from me, I needed to do some investigating. Blindly following his lead would not work for me any longer.

Remembering how hard she'd tried to hide her injuries and her waning energy sent a fresh surge of fury through me. Why had those idiot collectors allowed her to follow them into a battle with a reaper? Why had Zacharias chosen to engage with them rather than simply hiding in the reaper plane? Nothing in that chamber had been worth killing over. No part of our plan would have been exposed.

The moment she'd appeared, I'd wanted to strip off her clothes and reassure myself she was uninjured. But that would have scared her away. So I'd taken my time, checking her face, hands, then neck.

When I'd told her to stand in front of me, I'd half expected her to argue. Her trusting and sweet submission as she obeyed me had caused my erection to strain against the seams. It had very nearly been my undoing. I'd wanted to take her hard, make her scream my name and tell me who she belonged to.

While she had arrived smelling of sex, it had been only her alluring fragrance that I'd breathed in. The collectors had pleasured her, but they hadn't mated with her. I'd witnessed the bond they shared and knew she would never give the collectors up.

That was fine.

But a jealous, primal part of me wanted to be the first to claim her body with mine. Instead, I'd focused on healing her injuries. Four of her ribs were bruised, and one was broken. She also had two torn muscles and a small internal laceration likely caused by the shattered rib.

It was a miracle she hadn't been hurt worse after grabbing a scythe, tasting a reaper's blood, and being tossed around the room like a doll. Ghosts faced very few dangers, as not much could hurt them or even touch them.

Reapers and collectors were the exception.

What had worried me most were the dark circles beneath her eyes. When I'd sent my power drifting through her, I'd barely hidden my shock at what I discovered. She was a ghost, but unlike any ghost I'd ever encountered.

When a human died, they had a finite amount of energy. Once they burned through it, it was gone and they faded—unless they were helped to the beyond by a reaper or collector first. But the mysterious little beauty was making her own energy. Her reserves had been dangerously low, but even then, they were at a far higher level than any other ghost I'd encountered. Given time to recover, she would have replaced the energy she'd used to feed her collectors.

Still, she was injured and exhausted… and they still fed from her. And yes, I knew they had been on the brink of death—Hades, I'd had to forcefully put one back together. And without a reaper's abilities, they had no way of knowing her true levels. But I didn't care about logic at that moment. And facts would not appease my rage.

She was going to feed them whether I wanted her to or not. It was something I had to accept. But I would make sure I was there to replenish everything they took from her, even if it meant holding her on my lap while they fed.

As if sensing my irritation, my sleeping beauty scooted closer to me, pressing her lips against my chest and hooking her leg over my hip. This new position caused her to press against the painfully rigid bulge in my boxers.

Stifling a hiss, I clamped my eyes closed and focused on steadying my breathing.

How long were erections supposed to last? Even the men who died after blue pill marathons didn't last for twelve hours.

Maybe the bet had been a bad idea. I'd been desperate to find a reason for her to stay with me willingly. I wanted to check her injuries. I didn't want her to be with the men. I wanted to know she was safe. I wanted to hold her.

And so I'd done the one thing I had sworn never to do.

I'd used what I'd learned in the stupid dance classes my brother had forced me to attend with him to seduce her.

At the beginning of the dance, her expression had been one of absolute confusion, but that had quickly shifted to shock, and then it had morphed into the one I was waiting for. Lust.

She had continued to deny her attraction to me, even though I'd felt the wet arousal she'd left on my pants. But as I danced, the way she kept licking her parted lips and the raw hunger in her dilated pupils told me I had won.

Her sweet fragrance hung heavy in the air, an animalistic call that her body was ready and begging for me to tend to her needs.

There was nothing I wanted more, and I knew I could easily seduce her into being pliant, and letting me have my way with her all night long.

Not all reapers were as indifferent about sex as I had been before meeting Axelle, and I'd heard plenty of talk about their so-called conquests. They found it amusing how little effort it took to get a woman in their bed and enjoyed comparing their times as though it were a race.

I wanted her to rest, but that wasn't the only reason I'd put her to sleep. The larger reason was my fear. I'd savored the opportunity to learn how to heighten her arousal with my body, touch, and even my commands.

But how much of her attraction was because of my species' allure, rather than me?

I didn't want her to have sex with me because I was a reaper.

I wanted her to feel the same way about me as I felt about her.

Until I knew those answers, I would happily give her energy and satisfy any itches she wanted scratched... but I wouldn't claim her body with mine. Once that happened, there would be no going back. She would be mine forever.

Assuming my cock didn't fall off before then.

BANG!

My sleepy ghost sat bolt upright as the bedroom door flew open. Not wanting Zacharias to see her naked body, I tossed the sheet over her head a fraction of a second before he walked in.

"Listen, Saul. I've never seen you so angry and I really think we need to talk—" Zacharias froze mid-step as his eyes landed on me lounging in bed wearing only my boxers and the sheet-clad figure beside me. "This... is... a surprise."

The hair on my body lifted as he sniffed the air. She was mine, and I didn't even want to share the scent of her desire. It was for me. Swallowing back a snarl, I forced my features into an expressionless mask.

"You brought a woman to your bedroom? I never thought I'd see the day." Zacharias chuckled and leaned against the doorway.

Arrogant, mannerless prick.

"Are you going to introduce me to the girl who got your V-card?"

An odd strangled sound came from beneath the sheet and her fingers curled around the hem as she prepared to lift it. Acting unbothered, I stretched out my legs, pinning the thin fabric to the bed and trapping her inside.

"I'd rather not. We're in the middle of something." I gave Zacharias a pointed look that told him to leave before I lost my patience. "We will talk later."

"Are you sure she's okay under there? Sounds like something might be wrong?" His words sounded caring, but a nasty smile curved his lips.

"Yes. We're roleplaying. Not that it is any of your business." I wanted to grab my scythe and demand answers for his actions in the tunnel, but I didn't want to show my cards. Not yet. For now, he needed to believe I trusted him.

"The Vanilla Reaper is roleplaying?" Zacharias snorted. "And what is she pretending to be? A ghost?"

"Yes. A ghost," I ground out between clenched teeth.

"This is some boo-sheet," the love of my immortality whispered, just low enough that I could hear.

I wanted to yank her out from the blanket and kiss her adorable self until she was breathless, but knowing I needed to keep her safe until I knew Zach's true plans, I remained motionless.

Zach raised an eyebrow. "You can't expect me to believe you seduced some girl into playing Ghost and Grim Reaper with you?"

We eyed each other for several long seconds, and I could see the growing suspicion flickering his pale purple eyes.

The sheet sighed. "Woooooo. Woooooooo. I'm a ghost here to haunt you all night longgg."

Zach's eyes widened as he stared at the sheet.

She wiggled, getting into her performance—or maybe just seeing how far she could take it. "I might be the ghost, but I wasn't the only one moaning last night. Woooo."

I bit the inside of my cheek to keep from laughing. Zacharias knew me far too well, and the only person who'd ever made me laugh was my brother. If I laughed now, he'd realize she was important to me. That would paint a target on her back and risk him trying to use her as a pawn to force me to do his bidding.

He needed to believe she was a random hookup I would use and throw away. Just thinking the words caused my stomach to roil.

"I'm light as a feather, and Saul's stiff as a board. How about you climb under this sheet with me and rattle my bones?" The sheet shook as she giggled and gave a last wavering, "WOOooOooo."

If I wasn't already in love with her, I would've lost my heart right there on the spot.

Zacharias pushed away from the doorway, his face scrunched in disgust. "You sure picked a weird one for your first. Maybe try a sober one next time."

The door closed behind him and I listened as his steps faded down the corridor. As soon as I knew he was gone, I sat up and lifted the sheet. Her mussed hair stuck out at wild angles around her face, and her eyes sparkled as she dissolved into laughter.

I'd never seen a sight more beautiful in my life.

Impulsively pulling her into my arms, I covered her face

and neck in kisses until her laughs turned to small breathy giggles.

"I'm sorry, pet." My lips brushed against hers. "I didn't want him to recognize you."

"He was the reaper I bit?" she asked, wrapping her arms around my neck.

"Yes. His name is Zacharias." Her skin pressed against mine, making it hard to think about anything other than the granite length in my boxers and how incredible it would feel to be inside her.

"Sounded like you two are pretty chummy. You're close friends?" She pulled away from me slightly.

Growling softly, I tightened my arms around her body. "I don't know what we are. There are a lot of things I don't know right now."

Ignoring my protests, she pushed away from me and scooted to the end of the bed to find her shirt. She was going to leave me.

"Where do you think you're going, pet?" I demanded, wincing at the sharp tone I hadn't meant to use.

"My name is Axelle. And until you figure out who matters in your life, I'm not your pet and I'm not your toy." She pulled the T-shirt over her head and turned to meet my gaze.

"I know your name. The collectors said it in the tunnels." Rising from the bed, I moved to stand in front of her, holding her delicate hands in mine. "I just prefer to call you mine."

Her eyes softened, her lips parted, and for a moment, I thought she might stay with me.

"The collectors are mine, and Zacharias tried to kill them. He is my enemy." She pulled her hands from mine and took a step away from me. "If you are friends with him, then you're my enemy as well."

With that, she vanished, taking my heart with her.

CHAPTER 15

AXELLE

T hanks to the time difference between wherever the hex Saul's residence was and Amberwood, it had been evening when I'd re-materialized in the library's archive room. Honestly, it had been a relief that I'd gotten myself back in one piece since I still didn't understand how this new continent-jumping ability worked.

The library had been silent other than soft squeaking snores coming from where Wasabi lay curled up on the top shelf. I'd been too angry to do anything except pace—float—the room.

It didn't matter what my heart or fate wanted. Any man who could act so enamored with me, and then turn around and crack jokes with the man who nearly killed me, couldn't be trusted. Saul wouldn't get another minute of my time, and Hades would be in the middle of an ice age before I gave him the chance to touch my body again.

I thought about going to see the collectors, but feared

they would start asking questions about my disappearance and why I was so angry. Those were questions I wasn't ready to talk about.

Shame washed through me and the lightbulb in the lamp closest to me buzzed. How could I have been so stupid? I'd known he was in the tunnels, yet I'd let him spin a tale about perspective. He was hot, and I'd wanted him, so I'd let my bean instead of my brain do the thinking.

I needed to tell the guys, but I wasn't ready. It was too raw, and knowing that made me even more upset with myself. I was acting like a lovesick fool over a stranger I'd spent one evening with. One unforgettable, enchanted evening.

"*UGHHHH!*" Throwing myself down into an armchair, I stared out at the empty street.

It was Friday night, but since this part of the town lacked any bars or clubs, it was quiet on the weekends. With the library closed, I would have the freedom to stretch out anywhere I wanted and read without any disruptions.

I'd been right. Men brought complicated issues and emotions. It was time to go back to the safety of my book boyfriends. Getting up, I hurried to the shelves to gather an armful of new books and a handful of comfort reads.

Let's get this party started!

"Not now, Wasabi," I mumbled fourteen hours later. Ignoring his gentle tug on my sweatpants, I turned another page in my current book.

I'd kept up with every book I'd read since my death, and in the middle of the night, I'd finished reading book number nine-hundred-and-ninety-nine from my TBR list. It had given me renewed purpose, and I was focused on hitting four figures before the end of the day.

Unfortunately, Wasabi had woken up that morning and chosen violence.

"Ouch!" I growled when he nipped my ankle. Tucking my feet under me, I glared down at the gray rodent. "What's gotten into you today?"

Wasabi stood up, balancing on his back feet as he glared right back.

Hang on.

He shouldn't have been able to bite me or pull my sweatpants. Usually, I had to gather my energy and focus to interact with him. Why was it so effortless this time?

There was the occasional brush of whiskers, but I had to focus my energy to touch him. Had I only imagined the bite?

Slouching down into the cushioned seat, I raised an eyebrow in warning before dropping my gaze back to my book.

Two sentences later, Wasabi scurried up my leg. His tiny paws grabbed hold of the book cover, and his glossy black eyes locked on my face.

Squeak. Squeakitty squeak squeakish squeak.

It was the most Wasabi had ever said, and I didn't have to speak rat to know he'd just told me off. "You better not have said what I think you said!"

Wasabi bobbed his head as though he wanted me to know he'd meant every word.

"I must be losing my grip on sanity, because sometimes—" I leaned toward him and hissed, "Sometimes I think you understand every word I say. Which is impossible."

Wasabi didn't bother to respond. With a plop that would have been cute if I wasn't annoyed at the interruption, he landed on the arm of the chair. I watched him make his way up the fabric arm before he clambered onto the windowsill. Standing up, he pressed his nose and tiny front paws to the glass.

"Wasabi, I don't have time to people watch today. I've turned the security cameras off, so why don't you go check the breakroom for snacks? Tilly had a plate of cookies there two days ago." Reaching out, I touched the tip of his pink tail, then turned my attention back to the sexy wolf pack and the girl they'd just kidnapped.

Tap. Tap. Tap.

I ignored the tiny claws clicking against the glass and turned another page.

Tap! Tap! TAP!

Refusing to give in to his tantrum, I reread the last paragraph for the tenth time.

TWACK!

I jumped, snapping my gaze to the windowsill to see what the troublemaker was up to now.

Wasabi's tail swished back and forth like an angry cat. Using it like a whip, he smacked the window pane a second time.

TWACK!

"Fine." I closed the book. "Let's see what has you so worked up!" Letting my curiosity win, I rose on my knees to look out the window.

It was mid-morning and only a few people were out on the quiet street. "I really don't see why you are so agitated..." My words trailed off as my eyes landed on the source of Wasabi's bad mood.

Lochlan was eating brunch at the quaint cafe across the street. Sitting across from him was a tall blonde who looked like she'd just walked off a Paris fashion runway.

"She could be his banker, or maybe she's a realtor," I offered.

Wasabi growled, and his tail whipped hard against the glass.

"We don't need to leap to assumptions." It was best to stay logical in these situations.

I hated the miscommunication trope in books, and there was no way I planned to fall into that trap.

Lochlan laughed and leaned forward to squeeze the woman's hand.

My stomach twisted in knots, and my mind spun as I tried to come up with any reason that this wasn't what it looked like—a date.

I watched as the couple continued to laugh and chat, my heart aching more with each excruciating minute that passed. Lochlan grabbed a gift bag from beside his seat and held it out to her.

In response, the woman leaped from her seat and threw her arms around his neck. When his arms tightened around her, I couldn't watch anymore and dropped down into my seat.

It was a good thing I was a ghost who didn't eat, because I'd have thrown up all over the library's polished floor.

How could Lochlan have done the things he'd done to my body, and claim he was mine, and then go on a date not even two days later? He didn't even try to be sneaky about it, and had picked a cafe across from where I lived. It was unnecessarily cruel.

Had Rhodes and Evander lied as well? Were all four men just telling me what I wanted to hear?

Maybe romance was just as dead as me.

Viciously wiping at the wet streaks running down my face, I stood. It seemed like the best thing I could do was to figure out what was going on with the ghosts. The sooner that whole business was finished, the collectors would leave and hopefully the reapers would go back to their regularly scheduled programs as well.

No more men. No more heartache. No more distractions.

Soft fur brushed my ankle, and I glanced down to find Wasabi looking up at me as though waiting for orders.

I knew exactly what I needed to do first. "Wasabi, I'm going back to the scene of the crime. Zacharias was willing to kill because we got too close to whatever he was working on. Are you coming along?"

With a squeak, he took off toward the storeroom, his chubby backside jiggling with each step. At least there was one being I could count on to always have my back.

To my dismay, the tunnels were just as creepy the second time around.

"If I never have to come down here again, it will be too soon," I whispered to my pint-sized companion.

It was weird, but I felt safer having him at my side, even though he was no match for anything that might be lurking in the shadows. Except for maybe the spiders. A shiver trailed down my spine.

It didn't matter that I was a ghost, I was also a scaredy-cat. Nowhere in the rules did it say I had to be one or the other.

The trip to the chamber where we'd been attacked seemed to take twice as long as it had the first time.

"Maybe because you were more focused on the guys being in danger?" I mumbled, eyeing a particularly menacing-looking shadow.

By the time I pushed open the door to the room, I was

floating two feet off the ground, and jumping at every misshapen stone and gust of wind. There seemed to be an almost cruel irony to the fact that the girl who'd been terrified of scary movies had been cursed to live forever as one of the very things that went bump in the night.

In my humble opinion, Fate was a douche who enjoyed screwing with other people's lives. If I ever had the chance to meet him, I was going to tell him exactly what I thought, and then I would tell him to stick his meddling dick where the sun didn't shine.

"*Ahhhhh!*" I screamed as the door closed behind me with a loud creak.

Wasabi tilted his head, eyeing me as though making sure I hadn't completely lost it.

"I'm fine," I mumbled. "Help me look for clues."

The room wasn't large, probably less than twenty feet long and ten feet wide. Other than a decrepit-looking desk that sat against the far wall, the chamber was empty.

If this was some kind of secret villain's lair, it sucked hellhound balls. I'd expected something more grand. So why would Zacharias defend it with such violence?

Moving to the nearest wall, I ran my fingers along it as I walked. Inch-by-inch, I looked for a loose stone or hidden lever, but the walls were as boring as the room.

"What am I missing?" I asked the chubby rodent that followed my every step.

Moving to the desk, I bent and studied the worn wooden desktop. A thick layer of dust covered the wood, except for two perfect rectangles. I'd recognize the sexy shape of a book anywhere.

Well, now I knew he'd had books in here, but not what those books were about, which would have been far more helpful in my covert mission. I slid open the top drawer of the desk, unsurprised to find it empty. The second and third drawers were harder to open, but were equally barren.

Floating to my feet, I sighed and looked around for my tiny sidekick. "I think this was a bust, Wasabi. Let's head back."

He gave a muffled squeak in response. Spinning toward the noise, I watched as Wasabi slowly backed out of the tiny crack behind the desk.

"What are you doing back there?" I dropped to the floor beside him just as he tugged a single sheet of paper out from where it must have fallen. "Wasabi! You're the best!"

He released the paper and accepted a quick chin scratch as a reward.

The paper looked like regular printer paper, but most of what was written on it appeared ancient, like the stuff you would find carved on Viking artifacts. There were a few scribbled lines in English, but they only added to my confusion.

Pepperoni, mushrooms, anchovies, onions, hold the cheese.

"If this is his pizza order, he is a monster. Who orders pizza without cheese?" I shivered in disgust and giggled when Wasabi covered his face with his paws and mimicked my shiver.

Forget diamonds or dogs. Rats were a ghoul's best friend.

Turning the page in my hands, I squinted at the sloppy scribble on the side of the page.

Tiny Tank. Low inventory. Expensive. Best distiller in the UG.

"Okay, so he wants something to drink with his nasty pizza. That doesn't really help us," I grumbled, growing frustrated at not being able to decipher anything more from the paper.

Flipping it over, I practically shouted in relief when I discovered more English scribbles on the back.

Philetus' Scythe: unknown.

Epolir: located.

"Well, that's about as useful as a grave robber in a crematorium," I complained. "Who is Philetus? Do you think reapers lose their scythes often?"

Wasabi's only response was a huff that stirred the dust from the floor into the air and caused him to sneeze. Scooping him up in my hand, I deposited the gray ball of fur on my shoulder. Usually, I would have needed to concentrate to perform a physical task, but it seemed being hyped up on reaper juice had its perks.

Scanning the page, I finally found what I was looking for. Someone had written the initials UG, along with tomorrow's date and a time.

"It looks like I have a date tomorrow, Wasabi! I just need to figure out where UG is."

As I raced through the darkness toward the library, I

174

TBR: DEAD BUT WELL READ

tried to puzzle out what it could stand for, but I kept coming up blank.

Like it or not, I was going to have to visit the guys. Hopefully, I could avoid Lochlan long enough to get the information I needed from Rhodes or Evander.

CHAPTER 16

AXELLE

I materialized in the guys' living room, coming face-to-face with the one person on Earth I didn't want to see.

"Are we being haunted?" Lochlan asked, a teasing smile spreading across his lips.

"In your dreams," I snorted, glancing around the room in search of Rhodes or Evander.

"Boo, I dream about you every time I close my eyes." Lochlan stood from his seat and took a step toward me, only to stop when I took a panicked step away.

He frowned. "Everything okay?"

"Uh. Yeah. Fine." I couldn't bring myself to meet his piercing green eyes. "Is Evander around?"

Of the four men in my life, Evander was the least intimidating, and right now, that made him the most approachable.

"Evander is out with Rhodes on an errand. Is it something I can help you with?" Loch took a single step forward, which I countered by stepping to the side.

"No," I answered a little too quickly.

Why did it hurt so much to be in the same room with him? I'd gone my entire adult life without falling in love, and somehow, I'd given up my heart to four guys in about a week's time. A stranger shouldn't have been able to hurt me so much.

I was saved from any further awkwardness by the front door swinging opening. To my relief, Rhodes strode in with Evander behind him.

"Axelle!" the pair shouted in unison.

The relief and joy on their faces had bats banging around in my stomach. I'd convinced myself they were just having some fun with me while in town, and I'd come to their house fully prepared to treat this as a cold, hard fact-finding mission. But seeing the affection shining in their eyes, I questioned if I'd been wrong.

Lochlan had looked like a kicked puppy when I stepped away from him, and now Rhodes and Evander were looking at me as though they'd just been handed the lottery. Unsure of how to react, I remained frozen in the middle of the room, like a terrified rabbit that didn't know whether to run or hide.

In two long strides, Rhodes closed the gap between us. Gathering me in his arms, he held me against his chest as though he thought he'd never see me again.

"We were so worried about you." My hair muffled Rhodes' words. "Is everything okay?"

"I... I'm fine." My voice wobbled, but I held it together.

Lochlan gave a harsh bark of laughter. "That's a lie. She's nervous and practically shaking with anxiety. She's acting like I'm going to eat her, but not in the fun way this time."

"What happened? Did someone hurt you? Threaten you?" Rhodes' voice vibrated with the type of growl I didn't think humans were supposed to make.

In my romance books, I'd always questioned how I'd react if a man growled at me. It was a tossup between squirting him with a water bottle until he stopped acting like a naughty dog, or throwing myself at him and begging him to mark me as his mate.

It turned out both were the wrong answer, and I was the one who ended up getting a little wet.

"Yes, please," I whispered, then realizing I'd spoken out loud, I added, "No one has threatened me."

Unless you count Saul threatening me with a good time.

"You disappeared. We searched the library and the tunnels, but couldn't find a trace of you." Evander stepped close, brushing the back of his fingers along my cheek. "Are you up to telling us what happened? Was it something we did to scare you?"

If he'd ordered me to tell him, I would've shown him my shiny new spine and my two middle fingers. It was his gentle touch and willingness to let me decide that was nearly my undoing.

Nope, I'm definitely not going to break down into tears. Why? Because I'm a monster-freaking bad-apparition on a mission.

I had a catch phrase, now all I needed was a theme song, and I could have my own TV show.

Bad ghouls, bad ghouls, whatcha gonna do?

Whatcha gonna do when they exorcize you?

Hmm. I'd need to circle back to the song later. Right now, my priority was getting control of my tumultuous emotions. Knowing I couldn't concentrate as long as he was holding me, I pushed away from Rhodes' chest and moved to sit on the couch.

Not quite trusting myself with small talk, I got straight to the reason I'd come. "Do you guys know someone named Philetus?"

Rhodes' eyes widened slightly. "Yes, I do. All the collectors know the names of the reapers."

It was my turn to be surprised. "You know the name of every single reaper?"

Lochlan chuckled. "Don't look impressed. They are a dying species, so it isn't like we have to memorize thousands, or even millions, of names."

Leaning back against the sofa cushion, I stared at the three men. "I don't understand. Aren't reapers immortal?"

"They are immortal, but not invincible," Evander explained, moving to sit beside me. "Over the centuries, there have been accidents where reapers have died. This, and the last female reaper dying, has caused their numbers to dwindle."

Lochlan scoffed. "Maybe if the reapers weren't so stuck up about the purity of their bloodlines and took a partner from another species, they could turn things around. But that isn't going to happen."

"Lochlan, show some compassion," Rhodes snapped. "Not all reapers are arrogant pricks. Many are simply solitary by nature and prefer to avoid interacting, even with their own kind."

"Well, introvert or not, if my species was about to go extinct, I think I'd get out and do some mingling." My stomach churned at the disdain for reapers that was etched across Loch's face.

He wasn't going to like it if he found out I'd spent the night in a reaper's bed.

Evander leaned forward. "Philetus was pushing for that change. Remember? He even took a collector as his wife."

"A lot of good that did since he disappeared before they could produce a child," Loch shot back.

Rhodes scrubbed a hand down his face and sat in the armchair across from me. "Philetus didn't leave. He was murdered."

Fear trickled down my spine like ice water. "Someone is murdering reapers? Who would do something like that?"

Evander shook his head. "Either the reapers don't know, or they aren't telling."

We sat in silence for several minutes, which was good because my brain had a lot to process. Why did Zacharias care where Philetus' scythe was?

Rhodes was the first to speak. "Evander, did you figure out the name of the reaper who attacked us?"

My forehead creased in confusion. "I thought you knew all the reapers?"

"We know all their names, but we wouldn't recognize them all in person. Some we know because we've bumped into them more often than others, and there are others we know by reputation," Evander, ever patient, explained. "The one who attacked us is named Zacharias, and we only know him through rumors."

"Zacharias?" Loch sat up. "Are you sure?"

Evander nodded. "He matches the description on file and the inscription on his scythe matched the records as well."

"If Zacharias is in town, then Saul is close by as well," Rhodes murmured, exchanging a dark look with the other two collectors.

Saul.

An invisible hand seemed to squeeze my throat closed, making it impossible to speak. Which was fine, because I was afraid if I spoke, the guys would catch a tremble of emotion in my words.

"I'm not surprised they're involved in whatever shady business is going down in Amberwood." Lochlan stood and began pacing in front of the window.

"How do you know?" I tried to act nonchalant, shifting positions and tucking my leg under me in an effort to avoid eye contact.

"Saul, Philetus and Zacharias were close for as far back as their records go. If you bumped into one, the other two were nearby. Since Philetus' death, Saul and Zacharias are usually spotted in the same vicinity, at least from the gossip I've heard." Evander grabbed a notebook from the coffee table and flipped idly through the pages.

"Yeah, well, according to some collector friends, Saul went off the deep end in the past few years and Zacharias has been forced to pick up the pieces." Lochlan turned from the window and crossed his arms over his chest. "Even the reaper court is fed up with Saul and his unwillingness to follow protocol. If it weren't for Zacharias' dedication to keeping his friend out of trouble, Saul would have gone dark."

A memory of glittering purple eyes with cat-like slits leaped into my mind, followed by the memory of the inky shadows that had wrapped us in a protective cocoon while we slept.

Those were normal traits for all reapers, right? I didn't have a clue, and this didn't seem like the best time to ask.

"Then it's possible Zacharias attacked us to protect Saul," Evander mused aloud.

"Do we know who the second reaper was?" Loch asked.

Evander and Rhodes shook their heads. My fingers drummed against my thigh as my anxiety spiked. Saul said he hadn't attacked us, but could I trust him?

"None of us got a good enough look. It would make sense if it were Saul, though. Maybe he showed up and Zacharias gave up fighting us to focus on getting Saul away from there?" Evander laced his fingers through mine, and gave them a gentle squeeze.

"I think that's the theory we go with right now." Rhodes

sighed. "If any of us encounter any reapers while alone, back away and do not engage. Is that understood?"

Clearing my throat, I clarified, "By engage, do you mean don't start battling it out?"

Rhodes nodded his head. "Yes, that's exactly what I mean."

"Okay, got it." I gave him a little salute.

Rhodes' dark eyebrows drew together. "What else did you think I could be talking about?"

Trying to look innocent, I shrugged. "Oh, nothing in particular."

I had no plans to battle a reaper, but despite my irritation with Saul, I was still intrigued by the idea of engaging with him… in bed.

Rhodes kneeled in front of me, taking my hands in his. "Please be careful, Axelle. I'd prefer to keep you hidden away here in the house until this whole mess is over, but I know you're too independent to go along with it. You need to understand that a reaper has never attacked a collector before. We are in uncharted waters and I don't know what kind of danger that could put you in."

I leaned in and placed a soft kiss on his check. "Don't look so worried. I'll be careful. Besides, I spend most of my day hiding in the archive room reading. How much trouble could one ghost actually get into?"

My laugh was met with three grim expressions.

"By the time you see Saul, you are already in grave danger." Rhodes' grip tightened on my fingers. "Do whatever you must in order to escape, but do not antagonize him."

I thought back over my time with Saul and winced. Too late.

His warning had come a little late. But were we even talking about the same Saul? I was having trouble reconciling the man who'd danced for me, healed my injuries, gave me his energy, rocked my world, and then held me while I'd slept with the unstable, violent man the collectors seemed to fear.

I was going to have some questions for the sexy reaper the next time I found him.

"Okay, I think that's enough depressing talk for the evening. Let's watch a movie. I'll get the popcorn!" Evander winked and headed into the kitchen.

"I have some reports I need to read first. If anyone needs me, I'll be in my room." Rhodes grabbed his laptop from the kitchen counter and disappeared up the stairs.

Evander returned less than four minutes later, plopping down on the couch beside me.

I peeked at Lochlan from beneath my lashes, hoping he was going to excuse himself, too. The arrogant man knew I was watching him. Raising a brow in challenge, he grabbed the remote and sat down on the couch.

The heat of his body seeped into my left arm and hip, instantly sending a sense of reassuring calm through me as it always did when the men touched me. Not in the mood for catching any feelings off him, I scooted closer to Evander, pressing myself against his side.

"Hey. Don't fret, Axe. I know you've had a rough few days, but you're safe here with us. Relax and enjoy the movie." Evander dropped a soft kiss on my forehead.

My heart melted at the faint blush spreading across his face. Saul, Rhodes, and Lochlan were all alpha men who walked with confidence and sucked the oxygen from every room they were in. Evander wasn't a small man, but there was a gentleness to him that was equally attractive.

Lochlan flicked through the streaming menu, hitting the play button on a brand-new horror movie. I'd rather have watched a ten-hour marathon of the worst sequels of all time than a scary movie, but I kept my mouth closed.

I was a ghost. Scary stuff was our bread and butter. Besides, how bad could it be?

Within five minutes, I was clinging to Evander's arm so tightly I was cutting off the blood flow.

Thirty minutes in, I was shrieking louder than the poltergeist who kept jumping at the screen every five seconds.

I made it forty-five minutes before clambering onto Evander's lap and clinging to him with the ferocity Rose should've used to hold on to Jack.

"We can turn it off if you're scared, boo," Lochlan teased.

"No need," I said between clenched teeth. "I love horror movies."

It probably would've been more convincing if I hadn't been stuck to Evander's chest like an octopus. I expected Lochlan to call me out on my boo-crap, but when I peeked in his direction, I was surprised to find all his usual mischievousness had been replaced by sadness.

He'd seemed happy this morning at the café, so what had changed?

Turning back toward the television, I watched as the blonde who hadn't died yet arrived on a college campus. The campus' initials were UT, and a flash of inspiration hit me.

I'd just figured out how to ask my second question without raising suspicion.

"That's funny! I saw something with the initials UG recently. I wonder which college it stands for."

"Not a university. UG is the UnderGrave." Evander popped a piece of buttery popcorn in my mouth.

Food hadn't tasted good since my demise, and since I hadn't needed to eat for survival, I'd opted to skip it all together. But those fluffy pieces of popcorn tasted incredible when they were being fed to me.

"What's that? A funeral service?" I giggled, trying to act as though I didn't really care about the answer.

Evander smiled at me. "No. It's a club in the wildest city in the US. Someone enchanted it to keep the humans from accidentally stumbling inside, which is good since that place caters to the underbelly of the paranormal world."

"That sounds horrible!" I shivered, not needing to fake it thanks to the creature on the screen contorting itself as it crawled across the ceiling.

Resting my head against Evander's chest, I tried to ignore the screams coming from the TV and focused on the steady rhythm of his heart. I tilted my head back and took my time tracing the lines of his face. He had more boyish good looks, while Rhodes had a ruggedness about him and Lochlan was, well, beautiful.

I darted a glance at Lochlan to find him scowling. Was he… jealous?

Deciding I sucked at reading men's facial expressions, I turned my attention back to Evander, the movie completely forgotten at this point. His left arm wrapped around my waist, holding me to him while he gently massaged my scalp with his right hand. Everything about this man was soothing and reassuring.

Unlike the explosive personalities of the other men, Evander was steady as a rock. Saul, Lochlan, and Rhodes would hunt down anyone who caused me to shed a tear. Evander would be there to hold me as I cried.

Flattening my palm against Evander's cheek, I guided his face down to mine. "Are you sure you're not a ghost?"

Evander's eyebrows drew together. "I think I'd know if I were a ghost. Why do you ask?"

I grinned. "Because it's spooky how good you look."

Both guys groaned, but Evander's groan quickly shifted to something far deeper when my lips brushed his. I'd been prepared for him to take charge like Saul and Lochlan, but Evander didn't push for control. Instead, he let me lead. It was intoxicating, and it didn't take long for the familiar heat of desire to stir in my belly.

Shifting positions, I straddled his lap so I could bury the fingers of both my hands into his hair. Evander was enjoying our make-out session if the hard length pressing against me was anything to go by.

His hands moved to my waist, then slid just under the hem of my shirt. I whimpered as his fingers brushed against my bare skin, fanning my desire. When he made no move to continue exploring, I rested my hands on top of his and slid them up my stomach and ribs.

Thankfully, that was all the encouragement he needed to touch me. Our slow kisses became hungry, and his thumbs had just brushed against the sides of my breasts when a snarl shook the room.

I'd been so lost in Evander's touch and taste that I hadn't been aware of my surroundings, and the sudden noise caused me to jump nearly a foot off Ev's lap.

Scanning the room, I found Rhodes standing over us like a hangry grizzly. What in the Samhain was he so mad about?

"Dude! You scared her!" Evander snapped, rubbing reassuring circles on my back.

"That's not difficult. She's afraid of everything," Lochlan piped up.

Yeah, well, I wasn't scared of the big bad reaper who had them crapping their pants. Sadly, I had to keep my retort to myself to avoid unwanted questions.

"Here." Rhodes held out a file. "I got a report about some odd deaths in the neighboring city. It seems people on the street started dropping dead, but no ghosts emerged from the bodies. You two go check it out. Now."

Lochlan rose. "I'm going to grab my gear. Ev, I'll meet you at the car in two minutes."

A muscle ticked in Evander's jaw, and for a moment, I thought he was going to argue with Rhodes. With a frustrated sigh, Evander broke their glaring match and focused on me.

"Let's continue this later." He kissed my forehead and the tip of my nose.

"Your grave or mine?" I teased, trying to lighten the mood.

"Enough." A steel band circled my waist, lifting me off Evander's lap and into the air.

"What in the apple-bobbin' goblins—" I yelped, my words getting cut off as Rhodes tossed me over his shoulder. "Put me down!"

"Oh, I plan to." Rhodes took the stairs three at a time. "In my bed."

CHAPTER 17

AXELLE

F or the second time in as many days, I found myself being tossed onto a bed. Before my butt had stopped bouncing, Rhodes was on top of me, caging me in with his body.

His lips captured mine, kissing me with a passion that set my body on fire. Before I'd met these men, I'd been perpetually cold. Not comfy, but not really uncomfortable either. Now, thanks to being showered with so much touch and affection, I was toasty warm as long as I was with them. It was nice.

When Rhodes broke the kiss, his breathing was harsh and his eyes glittered. "I need to say something to you, and then you can either stay or walk out that door."

"Okay. I'm listening." That was only half true.

I was finding it difficult to focus with his spicy scent in my nose, his taste on my lips, and his muscular body pressing me into the bed. The men were great at turning me on, but their follow through reminded me of my mini golf games as a human. The first putt always went great, but no matter how close to the edge I got, or how many strokes I used, I could never get the ball in the hole.

He pressed a kiss to the hollow of my throat. "Axelle, I want to make love to you. I want to make you mine."

"Wh-what?" I asked, voice cracking.

This man wasn't playing around.

Lifting his head, Rhodes caught my gaze and held it. He'd dropped any pretense of being the tough, confident leader and was letting me see his raw desire for me.

There was something else in his eyes, though. Fear. What would a powerful man like Rhodes have to be afraid of?

The same thing I was afraid of. Rejection.

"I wanted to be patient and give you time to sort through your feelings. And if you decided to accept us as your circle, I wanted to let you figure out who you wanted to be with first." Rhodes looked away, and his mouth tightened. "But it feels like I have a wild dog shredding my insides every waking minute. I found you in the library that first day we were in town, and you do not know how hard it was to keep from kissing you."

He was wrong. I knew how hard it was because I'd desperately wanted to kiss him, too.

"Hades! It makes me sound like a creep, but if you had let me, I would've wrapped your legs around me and buried myself inside you right there on the spot." His head dropped to rest against my chest. "I swear I've never been like this. It's you. Since meeting you, I've felt as though my blood is gasoline and you've set me on fire."

Lifting a trembling hand, I brushed my fingers through his hair. The truth was that I wanted him too, but the moment I said those words, there would be no going back. Was I ready for my world to change forever?

"I'm selfish and stubborn," Rhodes continued. "It should be your decision who you want to bond with first, but it's making me crazy. When Lochlan came back from the library and talked about his time with you, I wanted to rip him apart. In the tunnels, when you healed us, I was too weak to do anything. Hearing you climax with Evander was more painful than being attacked by the reaper. Trying to remain in control while watching Lochlan taste you was a special kind of torture. When I came downstairs to find Evander kissing you, touching you, I couldn't take it anymore."

Rhodes began kissing his way up my neck. "I am going out of my mind. It is still your choice, and I will respect whatever you desire, but I can't remain quiet any longer. Axelle, I want to make love to you."

I hesitated, struggling to voice what I needed to say before things went any further. "Rhodes, if we do this, you know it will change things. I don't think this pull between us will be a one-night-stand."

"This isn't a one-night stand. This is forever." His lips brushed across mine. "We'll belong to each other. Heart and body."

Swallowing hard, I whispered, "I keep hearing that I'm

supposed to fade away. What if that happens and I leave you?"

His fingers curled in my hair, tilting my head back so I could see the hard set of his face. "I will not let that happen."

"But what if it does?"

Rhodes dipped his head to kiss my chin. "Then I will be thankful for every minute of heaven I spent with you." He trailed slow, erotic kisses down the column of my neck.

"Oooh," I moaned, my vision blurring. "Rhodes? I know you guys said you were okay with sharing, but there is another man—"

Rhodes' fingers tightened in my hair, turning my head to the side as his teeth pressed against my neck. "I won't let him take you from me." His deep, guttural growl caused the window panes to rattle.

"It's not that. He knows about you guys—" I tried to explain, but I wasn't sure Rhodes was even listening.

"Is that where you went the night you ghosted us?" Rhodes' arm snaked beneath me, pulling my body hard against his.

As though they had a mind of their own, my legs hooked around his waist. "Yes, but it was an accident."

"Did he touch you?" Rhodes asked harshly.

I wrapped my arms around his neck, clinging to him. "Yes."

Rhodes' hand slid from my waist to cup my butt. "Did he make you come?"

TBR: DEAD BUT WELL READ

"Yes." The room was becoming unbearably hot. Had someone turned on the heat?

"Did he claim your body with his?" Rhodes snarled, grinding his hard length against my aching core.

"No," I whimpered.

Rolling his hips in a way that had me seeing double, Rhodes asked, "Did he keep you safe?"

"He did." If they were right about Saul being dangerous, I probably couldn't have been any safer than I'd been in his bed. It didn't seem like many people would dare attack him.

"If you want this man to join our circle, I have no argument. But if he hurts you, I will kill him," Rhodes swore.

"His name is—"

"Right now, you are in my bed, and I don't want to hear another man's name on your lips. Not even if he's the devil himself." Rhodes captured my mouth in a possessive kiss.

Pulling away, I pressed my fingers against his lips. "There's one more thing I need to tell you."

"You better hurry," Rhodes grumbled before sucking my fingertips into his mouth.

"I, uh..." With his tongue swirling across my skin, he was making it impossible for a girl to remember her name, let alone what she wanted to say. "I read a lot of books."

Rhodes' eyebrows lifted. "That's what you needed to tell me?" The words were barely intelligible, but I understood most of it.

"Yes. Just because we're a thing doesn't mean I'm going

to give up reading. I made a commitment to my TBRs first, and I'll need uninterrupted time to meet those obligations."

"Evander spends most of the day with his nose in a book. You two will get along great. I think I can survive a few hours without your attention." His deep laugh was unexpected and had my stomach quivering at the sheer masculinity of it.

Hexes! The man was sexy... and he wanted to be mine. It was time to stop messing around and tie him down tighter than a straightjacket.

Silencing the last of my fears, I threw my arms around his neck and kissed him with the passion I'd been too terrified to give in to.

I focused on my energy just long enough to make my clothing waver and vanish. Rhodes groaned as his hand slid over my bare skin.

My fingers fumbled with the fly of his jeans, struggling to undo them. "Grrr!"

Why couldn't he wear gray sweatpants like all the good book boyfriends? Those would've been a lot less frustrating to get off.

He had the audacity to chuckle. "Let me help, sugar."

Rolling off the bed in the kind of smooth move wet dreams were made of, Rhodes stood and shed his pants. I'd expected him to be a boxer guy, but I wasn't disappointed to see the tight pair of black briefs that clung to his bulge and butt.

Why hadn't I jumped his bone—I mean, bones—right from the start?

His fingers hooked the band of his underwear, and when his briefs went down, something else went up... and I'm not just talking about the temperature in the room.

Rhodes didn't try to hide himself, nor did he do a cheesy pose. He stood tall and motionless, letting me drink in the sight of him in all his naked glory.

"Am I satisfactory?"

His answer came when the lightbulb in his bedside lamp exploded, and the overhead light flickered wildly.

"I'll take that as a yes." Rhodes grinned and retook his position on the bed.

Once more, I was pinned beneath him, but this time it was skin-to-skin. His erection seemed far too hot, and I wondered if I'd simply forgotten that fact, or if he had lava pumping into it.

Our lips met in a tender kiss that went from PG to R faster than I could say boo. And after being promised a good time repeatedly over the past few days, my body was more than ready for him.

Slipping my hand between us, my fingers brushed against the velvety steel that was stabbing my belly. His hips bucked reflexively toward my touch as I gripped his length.

"Sugar, you're driving me insane," Rhodes hissed.

Lining him up with my soaked entrance, I guided the rounded tip inside, causing us to groan in unison. Rhodes gave a tentative push, burying himself deeper in my tight heat. I'd expected some pain, but my ghostly form seemed to adjust itself so that he fit inside me like a hand in a glove

—or a cock in a condom. Which thankfully I didn't need since ghosts couldn't get sick, or pregnant.

"Am I hurting you?" Rhodes asked, his voice strained.

"Not at all." I moved against him, quivering as tiny shocks of pleasure shot through me. "You feel perfect."

Bracing his left forearm on the bed to support his weight, Rhodes' hand pressed against my lower back just above my butt, holding me to him.

"My turn," he whispered, playfully nipping my neck just beneath my ear.

His turn to what? "Oooh!"

Rhodes undulated his hips in a smooth body roll that only mermaids and a few gifted dancers could pull off. Was there some kind of afterlife stripper certification men had to go through or something?

Finding the perfect rhythm, Rhodes' hard length slid back and plunged forward as he continued rolling his body. With each forward thrust, he watched my face, figuring out which angles gave me the most pleasure and adjusting his movements in response.

I'd experienced two types of sex when I was alive. Fast and hard—which usually ended up with me faking things during the climatic scene. And the second type was lackluster and boring—which also required me to brush up on my acting skills just to get it over with.

Rhodes' body was taut with tension and his own need, but he was in complete control. Every move of his body was purposeful, yet unhurried.

This was a different kind of sex, and it was intoxicating.

Tilting my head back, I looked up into Rhodes' face and saw the answer shimmering in his eyes.

It's different because he's making love to me.

Lacing my arms around his neck, I pressed my cheek to his chest. "Don't freak out, but I think I'm falling in love with you."

For the first time, Rhodes' movements faltered and his breathing hitched, but he quickly steadied both. "That's good, since I'm already in love with you."

Squeezing my eyes closed, I tried to keep the tears from falling. I'd never heard those words from a man. Heck, the last time anyone had even bothered to care about me, I'd been in kindergarten.

I mattered to Rhodes.

I was loved.

Clinging to his sweat-soaked body, I came apart as white-hot pleasure hit me with the force of a runaway train. Rhodes thrust twice more, then stiffened as he followed me into mind-numbing bliss. Rolling to his side, he pulled me into the shelter of his body and held my trembling body as tears of happiness slid down my cheeks.

I LAY ON THE BED, watching the minutes of the bedside alarm clock slowly tick by. It was 1:20 in the morning, which meant I needed to make my escape if I wanted to make it to the UnderGrave in time for the mystery meeting at 2:30.

That was assuming I could even find my way there. I'd been directionally challenged when alive, and that hadn't changed in death.

Before I worried about finding the club, I needed to get away from Rhodes without him knowing—something that was easier said than done, since the giant of a man was cradling me against his chest like I was his personal teddy.

I needed to shift to the reaper realm, but that would take finesse. If I vanished too fast, Rhodes' arm would drop and it might wake him. And worse, what if I screwed this up and ended up in Saul's bedroom? I had questions I wanted him to answer, but tonight was not the night.

With painstaking slowness, I let my body turn to shadows. It took almost ten minutes, but by 1:30, I was on the street outside of the house. A cool breeze drifted lazily down the street, tossing bits of debris and leaves along its path.

Closing my eyes, I built a mental image of the sin city with its extravagant dinner shows, restaurants, and pretty much every other type of entertainment on Earth. I'd teleported myself halfway around the world to a place I'd never been. This had to be easier.

When my mental picture was as good as it was going to get, I steadied my nerves and forced myself to relax.

"Branson, Missouri, here I come."

CHAPTER 18

AXELLE

S tanding outside the club, I sighed in relief. It turned out, teleporting was a breeze… as long as I didn't count my detours through a cow field, a movie theater, and someone's sweet sixteen birthday party.

Watching the ghosts drift in and out through the walls, I decided this had to be the place. Plus, where else would you expect to see two guys with scythes smoking cigarettes, a green-skinned woman vomiting on the sidewalk outside, and three women parking their brooms next to a line of Harleys? Forget electric cars, brooms had to be the cleanest mode of transport.

Glancing down at my go-to shirt and sweats, I decided I needed to give myself a makeover if I wanted to blend in. Closing my eyes, I thought about the red silk dress I'd bought but never had the chance to wear.

In the front, the silk fabric draped loosely over my breasts, before dipping low enough to nearly show my belly button. Thin straps held up the front of the dress and tied in a bow at the back of my neck, creating a halter top that left my back bare.

The dress wasn't as short as what some girls going into the club were wearing and fell a few inches above my knee. But thanks to the slits that ran from the hemline almost to the top of my hips on either side of the dress, I was flashing a lot more skin.

I gave up my fuzzy socks for a pair of black strappy heels and replaced my lop-sided, messy-hair-don't-care bun for dark curls that fell halfway down my back. My makeup skills veered more toward a birthday party clown, so I opted for a simple smokey-eye and a crimson lip. I needed to blend in, not stand out.

Satisfied I'd done the best I could, I headed toward the front door of the club. The bouncer blocking the door gave me the once-over from head to toe, licked his protruding tusks, and let me inside without a word.

Stepping into the dark interior, I blew out a relieved sigh. The first part of my mission was complete. I'd made it to the UnderGrave with time to spare before the meeting.

Next, I needed to make my way around the club and see if I could spot Zacharias. Discreetly, of course.

There was a circular bar area set up in the middle of the room, and deciding that would be the best place to scope out the place, I made my way over and slid onto a bar stool. Sitting down in my dress was a challenge I hadn't antici-pated, and the slits in the side showed a lot more thigh than I was comfortable with.

Maybe I should imagine some glue and stick the skirt to

my thighs. I was a ghost who conjured clothes out of thin air. Getting those clothes to stay in place seemed like something I should be able to figure out.

A warm hand pressed against my lower back. "Hey… sexy. I'm buying. Whatcha drinking?" the owner of the hand slurred.

I squinted, trying to figure out what type of paranormal he was since he could see me and touch me. Although I suspected the reason Wasabi had been able to touch me was due to the massive energy dump Saul had poured into me.

"No need. I like to buy my own drinks." I scooted forward in my seat, staring straight ahead and hoping he would get the hint.

"Don't be like that, sweetie." His breath stank of liquor and tooth decay, and I nearly gagged as he leaned in closer. "Just because your date didn't show up, doesn't mean you have to be nasty to all guys. I'll watch out for you."

This was exactly why I hadn't gone out when I'd been alive. And apparently, being dead didn't exempt you from being hit on either.

"Mister, you're wasting your time. I'm here for the *booze*, not the boys." Angling my body away from him, I hoped he would finally get the hint.

"That's just because you haven't given me a chance. Let's go to the booth in the corner over there and get to know each other." He wiggled his eyebrows when he said the word *know*, leaving me with zero doubts about his intentions.

Before I could tell him to go take a long bubble bath in a

witch's cauldron, his clammy fingers curled around my elbow. With a hard jerk, he yanked me forward, causing both the stool and me to topple sideways.

It happened so fast that I forgot I could simply have floated away. Instead, I braced for an impact that didn't come.

An arm circled my waist, catching me mid-air and pulling me back against a hard chest. My rescuer gripped the creepy dude's elbow, and an instant later, there were two sickening cracks and the man dropped to his knees.

"When a lady tells you no, listen the first time." My rescuer's voice was eerily calm.

It was the kind of calm that had warning bells clanging in my mind, telling me I was in peril. But I didn't need the alarm. I'd known I was in danger from the moment the newcomer touched me.

Saul.

The last person I wanted to deal with at that moment.

"What's your problem, man? There are plenty of great tits here tonight. I saw this one first." The guy on the floor shrieked up at Saul. If he'd been sober, I doubted he would've been so bold. "I think you broke my arm!"

He'd reduced me to a pair of boobs and tried to call dibs? Oh no, he didn't!

I tried to free myself from Saul's hold. "Let go of me!" I hissed. "I'm going to go ghost and bust his—"

Saul's arm might as well have been made from granite because it wasn't moving. Ignoring my futile efforts to escape his hold, the reaper focused his full attention on the man who'd staggered to his feet and swayed unsteadily in front of us.

"You're wrong. I broke your arm in two places." With the speed of a striking viper, Saul's fingers wrapped around the man's uninjured arm. There was another sharp crack, and the man roared in pain. "And now you have two broken arms. Since your arms are out of commission, it looks like you're going to be celibate for a while. Use that time to think about how you treat women. You should appreciate the mercy I've shown you."

"All this because of her?" the man wailed, his face turning a mottled maroon from either pain or rage... or maybe a mix of both.

Shadows leaked out from around Saul as he tucked me against his left side and stepped forward. Before the man could blink, Saul's right hand gripped his throat. The guy had to weigh well over two hundred pounds, but Saul lifted him as though he weighed nothing.

This time when Saul spoke, his voice had lost its polished elegance and raw malevolence seeped from every word. "Remember this warning. Death will come for you if you so much as look at her again. And I won't be merciful the next time we meet."

Saul dropped the man to the floor as though he were a sack of potatoes. Then, giving me a slight bow, he offered me his arm and led me away from the man who lay broken and cursing on the floor.

As soon as we were away from the man and the small

crowd of spectators who thought they were getting drinks and a show, I tried to pull away.

"Thanks for the help, but I didn't come here to see you. I'm here to have a night off and enjoy myself." The lie didn't roll off my tongue the way I hoped, and Saul's smirk told me he wasn't buying what I was selling, either.

"You're going to come sit with me so I can keep you out of trouble," he stated, clearly expecting me to fall in line and behave.

Wrapping an arm around my waist, he guided me toward a velvet booth at the back of the bar.

I gritted my teeth. "You aren't the boss of me, Saul."

"Tonight is not the night to try me, pet." He smiled at me, but his tone carried a warning.

"Listen, just because I have a soft spot for you and I go weak in the knees every time you touch me…" I trailed off, realizing I'd gone off track. Wrangling my free-ranging brain cells, I tried again. "Just because you're hot doesn't mean I'm going to be your toy."

Not as powerful as I'd hoped, but he should still get the point.

One minute, I was digging my heels in and staring up at him defiantly, and the next, I was on his lap in the booth at the back of the bar. His lips captured mine in a panty-melting kiss, and his fingers trailed up my leg and exposed hip.

When the kiss ended, he leaned back against the booth and twirled one of my curls around his finger. "You've got things backwards, beautiful. I'm your toy to use however you desire."

Heat rushed between my thighs and I tried to think about anything except how much I wanted this man.

Centipedes. Tampons. Pea-green baby food.

It didn't work. I'd been drawn to him the first time I saw him, but with each encounter and soft touch, my attraction to him grew and my desire to have him as mine became more demanding.

What had started as fate screwing with me had turned to something more. Could it be that I was falling for him?

"You aren't going to like what I'm about to say, but I need you to listen to me." Saul's teasing expression was gone and an expressionless mask was fixed firmly in its place. "I need you to remember that things aren't as they seem. To keep you safe, I'm going to ask you to obey me without argument until I can get you away without drawing suspicion."

The urgency in his words had my stomach flopping around like a fish out of water. "What's going on?"

"I will tell you everything later, but right now, I need you to do as I say." Gripping my hips, he shifted me on his lap so that I was straddling him instead of sitting across his thighs.

He tugged down my dress as best as he could and used one of his hands to hold it in place over my butt.

Leaning forward, his lips brushed my ear as he whispered, "Pet, I need you to remember that nothing I say or do in the next few minutes is how I feel about you."

"I don't understand." Leaning away from him, I searched his eyes for answers.

"Trust me. Please," he whispered.

"Saul! You got here early!" a male voice boomed from behind me.

I started to turn, but Saul caught my chin between his fingers and held me in place.

"I'm always early, Zacharias." Saul rolled his eyes at the other reaper. "You have always been chronically late."

"Truer words have never been spoken," Zacharias laughed. "Although, I wish I'd been a few minutes earlier tonight. I heard chatter as I came in that you caused a scene among the other paranormals."

Saul lifted one shoulder in a half-hearted shrug. "A drunk was acting up, and I dealt with it."

"Now I'm even more intrigued. You never dirty your hands by getting involved in matters that aren't reaper related." Zacharias wasn't going to let it go, and I caught the slight twitch of annoyance at the corner of Saul's right eye. "They are saying it was over a woman. Is it this one?"

"Yes," Saul answered in a bored tone. "Did you invite me out to quiz me about my love life? If so, I'm going to head home because I have better things to do."

"Of course not. I just find it funny that you finally lowered your standards to have sex for the first time, and you're already looking for your next lay. I never thought I'd see the day when Death would be gathering broken hearts instead of souls."

Saul scoffed. "I think you've confused me with someone

who cares about hearts and emotions. We both know that's not me. Sex was entertaining, that's all. Tonight, I grew bored while waiting, and I decided to try a different flavor."

Sitting on Saul's lap, mere feet from Zacharias, my mission as a spy was going better than expected. So why did I feel like someone was stomping on my grave and grinding my soul to dust? My heart ached at his callousness. Is that why he was at the club? To find someone to get him off because I'd ghosted him and left him with a bad case of boo-balls?

Saul still held my face, and his thumb brushed my cheek with what felt like tenderness. Was he trying to remind me he wasn't the cruel, cold man his friend thought him to be?

He told Zacharias we'd had sex, which was a lie. So maybe it was all a lie.

"Well, was this one worth the fuss?" Zacharias asked. "If you want to stick around until I wrap up my business, I can make it worth your while, hun."

Saul's hand on my butt tightened, and the muscles of his thighs flexed beneath me. "Go get your own plaything. This one is mine."

Saul's fingers sank into my hair, holding me in place as he kissed my mouth and neck. I couldn't figure out if he was proving a point to Zacharias, or needing to let off some steam before he attacked another man for making a pass at me.

Whatever the reason, my body eagerly responded to his touch. It didn't matter that we were in public, or that I could feel Zacharias' gaze burning my back. All that mattered was that Saul was mine, and he wanted me.

Which was a problem, since I still didn't know who he really was. Hex! I didn't even know if he was a good guy or a villain. My heart said he was a good man, but my track record for picking guys when I was alive worked better as a cautionary guide. I think my brain saw red flags and thought it had to catch them all.

And now I was sitting in the lap of an arrogant reaper who may or may not have tried to kill the collectors, and who may or may not be doing some sketchy stuff with the ghosts in town, and who may or may not actually care about me.

Stop it, Axe. That isn't fair. He's shown you nothing but care. And so far, you haven't caught him lying to you.

Zacharias was making small talk, and Saul listened with his hand wrapped around my throat, and his thumb absently brushing my skin.

He was wearing a mask, but he'd let me see the real him when I showed up in his room. Saul had teased me, made me laugh, listened to every word I'd said, fed me, healed me, touched me, and had given me several hours of the best sleep ever while cuddled in his arms. I didn't care what the rest of the world thought about him. I knew the real Saul.

My Saul.

Joy bubbled up in my chest and I forgot where we were. Leaning forward, I pressed myself against him, capturing his face between my hands and kissing him as though I were starving and he was dessert.

He started to groan but caught himself just in time.

"Tiny Tank will be here any minute. You need to get her under control so you can focus," Zacharias snapped.

Saul's fingers dug every-so-slightly into my derriere, but his face remained impassive as though he were unbothered by the other reaper's words.

"She'll behave," Saul assured him. "And if she doesn't, I will handle it."

It was like the man didn't even know me...

CHAPTER 19

SAUL

"S he'll behave. And if she doesn't, I will handle it."

I realized I'd made a grave error the moment the words left my mouth.

Axelle's beautiful face was expressive, making it easy to know what she was thinking.

When Zacharias had arrived, a delighted relief darted across her features. Had she come to UG looking for him? Jealousy unfurled in my chest, twisting around my lungs and making it hard to breathe.

I needed a little more time to figure out if I'd been blinded to Zacharias' true motives, or if he was simply following through with the plan we'd put so much time into. But seeing the confusion and hurt that filled her eyes and caused her pouty lips to droop had me ready to stop the charade. I was trying to keep her safe by hiding her identity from the man who had once been like a brother but who I now suspected was my enemy.

There was another way I could keep her safe: by

claiming her as mine. She would be untouchable, because no one would risk my wrath. Which was wise, since I yanked the soul out of anyone who dared to cross me, and rather than helping them to the beyond, I'd let her collectors devour their energy. We hadn't officially met, but I had a feeling we were going to see eye-to-eye on anything related to Axelle's safety.

I'd never been great with emotions, but in the wake of my brother's death, I'd found it impossible to work up the mental energy to care about what happened in the world around me. I did my job, but I'd grown quiet, allowing Zacharias to take a leadership position. He'd grown bold and bossy, something he wouldn't have dared to pull on the old me.

Watching him in the club, I realized he'd forgotten who he was dealing with—*what* he was dealing with. He continued aiming barbed insults at me, stirring up the thing inside me that had gone quiet in recent years.

I kept my composure, acting as if nothing had changed between us, even as a storm built inside me. This was a game, one that would be over in less than two days. Then I'd make him bow in front of my woman and apologize for his disrespect.

It had been difficult, but I played my role well... right up until the moment I saw the anger and betrayal in her eyes morph into trust. No matter that I was hardly more than a stranger to her, she'd decided to trust that I wasn't the man treating her like little more than arm candy.

She'd thrown herself against me, showering my cheeks,

forehead, eyelids and mouth with exuberant kisses. Her kisses were overflowing with love, rather than just carnal lust. I desperately craved more, wanting to soak in the affection I could see swimming in the depths of her soulful brown eyes.

For the first time in my very long life, I was drowning in a sea of warring emotions and I didn't know how to act. I wanted to get on my knees and beg her to forget every word I'd said that had pierced her heart. My cock had been painfully hard since she'd left my bed, and my skull pounded with the primal urge to take her somewhere private and claim her body until she was screaming in ecstasy.

As if I wasn't confused enough, my need to avenge my brother's death and get him justice demanded I put aside my desires and stick to the logical course of action. I was a master of self-control; denying my body for two days shouldn't be this hard.

With my world turned upside down, I clung to the mask that had served me well for decades and said, "She'll behave. And if she doesn't, I will handle it."

I would've laughed at my stupidity if not for the fear that seeped into my soul. A golden ring that lined the outside edge of her irises glowed to life as her eyes glinted with mischievous glee.

Her crimson lips curved into the wicked smile of a siren, luring sailors to certain death. And just like those doomed sailors, I was hooked. My mouth went dry and my erection strained against the seam of my pants.

Whatever she was planning, I knew I was in for the absolute best-worst time of my life. I'd won the last game we'd played, but the odds weren't in my favor this time.

"I'm sorry." Axelle dropped her chin, looking up at me through her thick lashes.

She clasped her hands together and dropped them to her lap, appearing repentant—which we both knew was a lie. "I forgot where we were and you looked good enough to eat."

"It's fine." The words came out harsh as her knuckles brushed against the bulge barely hidden by my dark slacks.

"Tiny Tank!" Zacharias called.

Glancing over Axelle's shoulder, I watched as the warlock's head turned in our direction and he lumbered through the crowd toward us.

Zacharias stood, offering his right hand for the warlock to shake, only to have the other man give him a weird fist pump. It was painfully awkward, and I enjoyed it.

Tiny Tank was tall—well over seven feet—but his frame was too thin. His skin hung loose from his body, giving his eyes a slightly too-large and protruding appearance. Greasy strands of hair hung around his face, and if it weren't for his height, I would've asked if he'd ever found his precious ring.

I'd dealt with warlocks over the years, and they'd taken meticulous pride in their hygiene. That, combined with the fact that they wouldn't have been caught dead—or alive—in the UnderGrave, was enough to make me suspicious of this man.

Unlike Zacharias, I remained seated and waited for Tiny to extend his hand before I leaned forward and shook it. The movement caused the devil on my lap to be pressed against me, something she took immediate advantage of.

I'd opened my mouth to give my name just as she gripped my erection through my pants and slid her fingers along the length. Just her touch had pleasure surging through me. To my horror, I barely managed to clamp my mouth shut before I dazzled everyone within earshot with my impression of an anime girl moaning.

Axelle took advantage of her hands being hidden between our bodies to massage along my length a second time. This time, my ears rang and my pulse jumped from the delicious torture.

Still sitting upright, I ran my fingers through her dark curls until I cupped the back of her head.

Angling her so that our cheeks touched, and her hair hid my mouth, I whispered a single word, "Behave."

The brat had the audacity to hum, as though thinking about it. "I want to be good, but I'm really, really bad at it."

Her voice was low and slightly husky, as though she'd been screaming my name all night long. My brain struggled to reconcile the sex kitten on my lap with the gorgeous bookworm who'd barely been able to maintain eye contact with me while I'd danced for her.

Was her stubbornness and desire to win canceling out her embarrassment when it came to sex?

"Don't push me, pet. I'm not above taking you right

now and making sure every man here knows you are mine."

"Is that the truth, though? Because technically, only one man has followed through with claiming my body"—turning her head a fraction, her tongue traced an intricate line up my neck—"and it wasn't you."

My snarl was loud enough to catch the attention of everyone sitting nearby, but I didn't care. I knew the collectors were part of the deal if I wanted her. She'd been open about that. But knowing another man had been inside her, while I'd stood in a cold shower for hours and stroked myself raw in a futile effort to rid myself of my erection, was enough to make me insane.

I focused on my breathing and keeping the shadows from escaping my control and causing a scene. Zacharias and Tiny Tank fell silent, their small talk forgotten as they studied me.

"Everything okay?" Zacharias asked, raising an eyebrow in question.

Clinging to my mask, I rolled my eyes and drawled, "Of course it is. My pet is struggling with being patient, and needs a reminder of who's in control."

I'd half-expected Axelle to get mad and storm away, but she didn't.

"For a man who's cold as ice, you are hot as Hades." Her soft, breathy laugh was like a caress. "And there must be something wrong with me because I shouldn't be this turned on by you."

Her words repeated over and over in my mind.

She wanted me.

My cock strained against my slacks, eager to do her bidding.

Sagging back against the booth, my vision flicked back and forth at a rapid-fire pace. My control was hanging on by a thread. Not wanting anyone to see my unusual cat-like pupils, I pulled my sunglasses from my pocket and slipped them on. Axelle and my brother were the only two I'd allowed to see my eyes in their natural form.

Grabbing my drink from the black cloth-covered table, I focused on not-so-Tiny Tank and tried not to think about the gorgeous ghost sitting on my lap.

"I've had my ear to the ground, but no one has tried to pawn it or sell it in the Dark Faire." Tiny Tank took a long drink of his foamy beer. When he finished, he used the back of his hand to wipe across his mouth.

The mention of Philetus' missing scythe stabbed through my heart like the blade of a knife. When a reaper passed, their scythe absorbed their energy. The scythe then passed to an heir, or the next in the bloodline.

It should've been mine.

If it hadn't been stolen, the moment I touched it, I would have been recognized as the scythe's new vessel. The energy stored inside it would've poured into me, and our reaper magic would have merged my brother's scythe with mine, forging a new weapon that combined our unique abilities and the intricate art that adorned each curved blade.

I didn't care about the power. As far as I was concerned,

I already possessed more power than the reaper court was aware of, and far more than I was permitted to use. But I would've loved to hold my brother's scythe one final time, and have its markings on my blade to honor Philetus' life.

In the recorded history of scythes, this was the only one to have been stolen. Reapers' blades stayed in the reaper plane after death and remained untouched until the nearest family member arrived to claim it.

Only a reaper could have seen his fallen weapon and taken it. And the court was shielding them.

Without realizing it, I'd rested my hand on Axelle's thigh, unconsciously seeking comfort.

"The moment you hear even a whisper, I want to know." I sipped my drink, studying the shady warlock. "Find the scythe and I will pay ten times your normal fee."

The warlock's eyes gleamed. "Of course, Reaper."

"If I find out you have lied to me, I will take your soul and wipe all evidence of your existence from the face of the Earth." I delivered the promise of reward and the threat in the same bored tone, wanting him to think I didn't care which option he picked.

"Ignore his rudeness. Saul's been on edge lately, but he's a good guy." As always, Zacharias hurried to apologize for my behavior.

It was an odd habit he'd picked up in the last few years. I was blunt, but Zacharias was only charming in person. Behind closed doors, he had a harsh sense of humor and was far more vindictive than me. Yet, he enjoyed playing good cop to my bad cop.

I zoned out as Zacharias pulled out the grocery list of potions he needed to restock his shelf. Magic was finicky, and I wasn't interested in touching anything this warlock had cooked up.

Unable to resist, I cupped Axelle's face and brushed my thumb across her bottom lip. She sucked the digit into her mouth and her tongue swirled over my skin. Her eyes glittered and her fingers brushed featherlight along my pants, making sure I knew what other part of my body she was imagining was in her mouth.

She was chaos on a level I hadn't encountered before, an anomaly that didn't fit in with anyone, but stood out as her own unique being. How would I do my work as a reaper and keep her out of mischief? Perhaps I could lock her inside a room filled with books and that rodent she spoke to as though it were a friend. Yes, that plan had potential.

A bartender walked up and held out a tray with a drink on it. "Miss, this is for you, from the gentleman in black at the end of the bar."

"She doesn't drink anything unless I buy it and watch you make it." I waved him away, scowling at the man who dared to make a move on my woman.

Couldn't the fool see she was sitting on my lap? I didn't recognize his face, but power leaked from him despite his efforts to hide it. He was powerful by paranormal standards, but if he decided to make a move on Axelle, he'd find himself seriously outmatched.

"I can answer for myself, Saul. And I can buy my own drinks." She looked up at the waiter and with a sweet smile.

"Tell the gentleman I said thank you, but I'm not interested."

"Yes, miss." The waiter's face had taken on a starstruck look and he grinned goofily back at her.

He had five seconds to walk away, or I was going to make it so he couldn't walk away without help. Finally, the server made his way back to the bar, carrying the drink back with him.

"Stop acting like an insecure manbaby. Imagine if your face gets stuck like that." Axelle rearranged her face, trying to mimic me. It didn't last long before she burst into laughter.

"Saul! We are trying to work here. If your hooker is going to keep getting gifts from her clients and interrupting us, maybe she needs to leave until we're finished." Zacharias glared at her back with far more anger than the situation warranted.

Axelle bristled, and before I could stop her, she shot back, "So what if he is a client? It sounds like you're just jealous no one likes your bedside manner enough to use your services a second time."

"I'm a reaper! People only die once, so they can't use me again!" Zacharias snapped. "First a drunk one, now a stupid one. I'm going to help you pick your next date."

Axelle wasn't stupid, and a satisfied smirk spread across her face at getting him riled up and defensive.

"Insult my date again, and you won't have a place to sleep tonight, Zacharias." It was a far cry from snapping his

TBR: DEAD BUT WELL READ

neck and tossing him around the bar like my every instinct told me to, but it was a blow meant to hurt him.

The sprawling mansion was owned by me, but Philetus and Zacharias had lived in it since the day I'd purchased it. It had been just as much their home as it was mine. And I'd threatened to kick him out.

"You wouldn't!" Zacharias' jaw dropped.

"Don't test me. Let's finish the business so I can leave." The pulsing beat of the bass and drunken shouts were getting on my nerves.

When Zacharias resumed his negotiations with the warlock, I caught Axelle's chin and brought her lips to mine. "Don't contradict me, pet. What I say goes when we're in public. In private, you can enjoy your games, but outside the safety of our home, you have to trust me to protect you."

"Mr. Grim, with all due respect, I'm a woman. Not all men are douches, but being harassed or disrespected by pushy men is a common occurrence in every woman's life. Tonight has been a pretty chill night, actually."

"My name isn't Grim," I growled, irritated at how blase she was acting about men being creeps.

If she was correct, and this happened every time we went out, I was going to end up leaving a trail of dead bodies in her wake.

"If the name fits." She shrugged. "You've been grumpy all night."

"Well, maybe it has something to do with the fact you're the hottest woman who has ever walked through those doors. The men in here haven't stopped staring in this direction and salivating like rabid dogs."

Axelle dropped her sex kitten persona and blushed. There was no denying she was gorgeous in her slinky red dress, crimson lips, smoky just-had-sex eyes, and the sexy heels that practically screamed she wanted to be taken to bed and ride her man all night long. She pulled off the look with a seductive classiness that set her apart from every other woman.

But I'd loved seeing that flash of the woman I'd fallen in love with. The one who wore orc-sized shirts that swallowed her body, ridiculous fuzzy socks, and her hair in a precarious pile on her head. The woman who trusted books more than people because they'd never let her down, and used a ridiculous amount of energy protecting the creature most of the world looked at with disgust.

I worshiped the female who'd attacked a reaper to save those she loved and who'd done what no one had dared to before by showing up uninvited inside my house, but had been too embarrassed by her body's reaction to me to maintain eye contact.

That was the Axelle I wanted to hold in my arms as she slept each night. Fierce and loyal, but also sensitive and sassy.

"They can only see my back, right?" Axelle asked, the mischief in her eyes making my pulse quicken.

"Yes." I narrowed my eyes, bracing myself for whatever new torture she'd thought up for me.

"So they can't see me do this?" she whispered so low only I could hear.

Axelle slid the front of her dress against her waist, and rolled her hips slightly, giving me a glimpse of the black thong she wore.

I tried to breathe, but I'd forgotten how.

"Only you can see me do this, right?" She slid a finger under the edge of the fabric.

I couldn't have answered even if I wanted to.

"Is it better if I do it this way so you can see?" she asked, keeping her voice too low for anyone else to hear.

Using her right hand, she pulled the scrap of fabric to the side, allowing me to drink in the sight of her.

I was in serious trouble.

Axelle sounded confident as she did her best to seduce me, but I caught the slight tremble in her fingers as she moved the fabric, and the light flickered overhead.

She was being naughty and pushing for me to react. But she was also being incredibly vulnerable with me. Axelle wanted to win this round, but it was written all over her face that she was trying to please me—even if that pushed her outside of her comfort zone.

With her right fingers still holding the thong, she used her left pointer finger to trace her entrance.

My erection jerked, sending a spasm of pain rippling through me. I was too engorged, but I hadn't been able to get it to go down no matter what technique I tried.

She slipped a finger inside herself and began to stroke. Her movements were tiny, and she was careful not to call attention to what she was doing. Biting her lip, she slipped a second finger into her tight heat.

She closed her eyes and mouthed my name. "Saul."

My soulmate was wet with need, and imagining my touch. I was still trying to listen to Tiny Tank describe the properties of the various potions, but it was a battle I was quickly losing.

Remembering how her body had reacted to my commands, I leaned in and kissed her. "Let me taste you," I whispered against her mouth.

Axelle's eyes widened, and she froze.

"Why are you wet?" I purred against her throat, loving the way her body responded to even the pitch of my voice.

"That's your fault, not mine!" she hissed, summoning a bit of defiance.

"If I caused you to be aroused, then the sweetness between your thighs belongs to me. Bring your finger to my mouth and let me taste you." I kept my voice low and spoke against her neck so only she would hear.

It wouldn't have bothered me the slightest for the world to know she was mine and I was obsessed with everything about her. But for all her bravado, I knew Axelle would be horrified to have attention on her during such an intimate moment.

Her finger trembled as she discreetly brought it to my lips, but didn't touch me. My eyes met hers, daring her to look away as I curled my tongue around the slick finger and sucked it into my mouth to continue licking away every drop of my prize.

Her eyelids grew heavy with lust, then she whimpered, "Oh no."

I couldn't speak with her finger in my mouth, so I raised an eyebrow.

"Saul, I think I just soaked my thong. I need to move before I get your pants wet again—if it's not too late." Her eyes shimmered with unshed tears and her playfulness vanished. "I'm sorry. I didn't think this through, and you have to wear these pants until you get home. It's just... I want you so much it hurts."

She was hurting and upset, and it was my fault.

Change of plans. I was going to show her she had nothing to apologize for and then I would make sure the world knew she was mine and they needed to think twice before they crossed Death. Now and until the end of time. If this meant my plans to avenge my brother's death were blown, so be it.

I loved my brother, but he was gone. He would have been proud to meet a spitfire like my soulmate.

Axelle had shown me affection, and I'd been cold and had told her to behave.

Never again.

CHAPTER 20

AXELLE

G

athering me in his arms, Saul strode away from the table.

"What are you doing? We're in the middle of something," Zacharias snapped.

Saul didn't even slow. "This is more important. You can wait or finish the meeting without me. It makes no difference."

I peeked over Saul's shoulder to see Zacharias opening and closing his mouth. He wanted to lash out, but there was hesitation in his eyes. I scanned the room, studying the expressions of the paranormals we walked by. Every single person dropped their heads, pinning their eyes to the floor as Saul passed.

"They are afraid of you," I whispered against his neck.

"As they should be."

I didn't want to hurt him, but I needed answers. "People say you gave yourself to the dark and you're unstable.

Some people say Zacharias is your long-suffering babysitter who keeps you from hurting people."

He was silent for several seconds, then asked, "And what do you believe, Axelle?"

"I think Zacharias is an evil man who has purposely manipulated situations to make you appear unreasonable or demanding while he comes out smelling like roses. You seem to care for him, but he is not your friend. And I wish I would have bitten him harder." I muttered the last sentence against his skin and jumped when he barked a laugh.

"Now, now, pet. You can't go around biting people just because you don't like them." The teasing note shifted to a somber one as he stepped into the bathroom, locking the door behind us.

Sitting me on the copper trough-style sink that ran the length of one wall, Saul asked, "What do you think about the darkness? Are you afraid of me?"

His eyes searched my face, needing to see if I would tell him the truth.

"I don't think you gave yourself to the darkness. Honestly, I don't even feel like darkness is the right word. Each time I've seen the shadows, and your eyes have shifted, your emotions were heightened, or you were protecting me."

Reaching up, I slipped off the dark glasses that hid his beautiful eyes from me. "Saul, it's not wrong to feel emotions. You're allowed to be angry and protective of those you love."

His irises glowed a brilliant violet, and his pupils expanded and contracted. "Are you afraid of me?"

I lifted my chin. "No."

"What if I told you I'm thinking about hunting down the man at the bar and reaping his soul for touching you?"

"But you won't. Because you're a good man."

"What if I told you I could kill half the people in this club before they even knew Death was coming for them?" he growled.

I brushed my fingertips along his stubbled jaw. "Then I'd say they had it coming, and you handed out fair judgment."

Faster than the speed of light, he spun me around to face the mirror. The hard edge of the sink dug into my stomach as his right hand wrapped around my throat and his shadows whipped across my skin. He ground his erection against my butt, and his left hand slid down my stomach to press against my aching core.

His movements were purposely rough, as though he wanted to scare me away. "Are you afraid of me, Axelle?"

"No." I rolled my eyes. "But I am getting turned on." I wiggled my butt against him.

Our eyes locked in the mirror, and I watched as his hands moved down my body, then shoved my slinky dress over my hips. With a flick of his wrist, his scythe appeared in his hand. Never breaking eye contact, he slid the flat edge of the blade up my arm and down my bare back.

My adorable reaper. He was trying so hard to get me to run, but he only proved I was safe with him. The man wasn't even willing to risk accidentally cutting me with the sharpened edge of the blade.

The cool steel of the blade felt good against my burning skin. I sighed in delight and nearly burst out laughing at the befuddled look on Saul's face.

He hooked my thong strap with the curved tip of the scythe's blade, slicing the fabric with ease. Unbuckling his belt, he pulled it free with a snap and let it drop to the floor. "What if I took you hard and fast right here in this bathroom?"

I narrowed my eyes at him in the mirror. "Stop promising me a good time if you aren't going to follow through."

"You deserve so much more than this." His mouth trailed hot kisses down my spine. "Why don't you fear me? Nothing I did made you so much as flinch."

"Because you said I'm yours and I know you'd never hurt me." I caught his hand and kissed it.

"But what if I do?" His voice had gone from commanding to unsure.

"You want me to be afraid, because you're afraid you might lose control and hurt me," I murmured as realization slapped me in the face. "Saul, I've fallen in love with you— all the parts of you."

"Axelle, what if I hurt you?" he repeated the question.

"If you walk away out of fear, you are going to hurt me." Pushing aside my pride, I asked him for what I wanted. "Love me. Please?"

The atmosphere in the room changed so fast my ears

popped. Saul's hands moved to cradle my body against his, and the shadows brushed softly against my skin.

"I love you," Saul purred between kisses. "I know things moved fast, but I've never felt attracted to anyone until I saw you."

My jaw went slack. "So Zacharias wasn't joking about the V-card thing? I thought he was messing with you."

Saul shrugged. "I've witnessed plenty of sex while reaping souls. But nothing about the ordeal seemed appealing."

I wiggled my butt against the stiff length in his pants. "Clearly you've changed your mind."

"Yes, but that has led to a new issue." He gripped his length through his pants and hissed between his teeth. "I've been erect since you were in my bed."

"Wh-what?" Surely I'd misheard him.

"It's been inconvenient," Saul said as though this were a normal thing.

"Shouldn't you go to the doctor? Do reapers even have doctors?" I asked. What if his bat and balls died and fell off?

"I don't need a doctor." His eyes glinted in the mirror. "I need you."

"Did you... you know? Try taking care of things yourself?" I asked, getting wet just imagining him stroking himself while thinking of me.

"I may not have experience with sex, but I've been around for a while and I'm not an idiot." Saul snorted. "I spent hours in the shower trying to deal with it, and all it did was make me more sensitive. In the past, I didn't pay attention when other reapers spoke about their sexual escapades. But I remember hearing a rumor that once a reaper met his soulmate, they were the only person who could arouse him, and the only one who could get him off. In my case, I never experienced attraction to anyone or sexual desire until I met you."

How did you respond to something like that?

"So we really are true soulmates? And I'm not just imagining the way I feel drawn to you?" My eyes widened as a new thought occurred to me. "Which means only I can turn you on and off?"

"Pet, I recognize that naughty look in your eyes." Saul growled a playful warning and gently smacked my butt. "Yes, we're true soulmates. But I knew that before my cock confirmed it. I believe it was nature's way to ensure the perfectly matched reaper couples produce offspring. Since the male reaper is only attracted to his soulmate, all his attention is focused on her, ensuring she is well satisfied and bred before his erection subsides."

"That's kinda hot, but I'm sorry you were left hanging. Well, not hanging, more like— Oh, nevermind!" I bit my lip. "You hissed when I stroked you in the bar. I didn't mean to hurt you."

"Everything is painful right now because of how sensitive I am. But your touch was intensely pleasurable." His voice was husky as he placed soft kisses on my shoulders. "You are the only one whose touch I ever want to feel on my body."

"Tell that to Zacharias." I whimpered with every brush

of his fingers against my overly sensitive skin. "He seems really into you trying different women out."

"And I want to rip out his soul every time he says it. I'm sorry I have hidden the truth about what you mean to me. My goal was to protect you while I stayed close enough to Zacharias to uncover what he's been hiding. I worried he would recognize you from the tunnels and seek vengeance for biting him. Worse, when he realizes I am no longer on his side, he will likely seek to use you as a pawn to control me."

"I understand why you did what you did, Saul. It's okay." My heart soared with happiness at his admission. He was a good man with a protective streak a country mile wide.

Saul slipped two fingers inside me and groaned. "I love that you get so wet for me."

Without thinking, I blurted out the truth, "Because you're freaking hot and my body tries to turn my insides to ectoplasm or something every time I look at you. I still can't believe a guy like you is actually kissing and touching me. You are way out of my league."

"We'll need to work on how you see yourself, pet. Because from where I'm standing, I have the sexiest woman on Earth soaked and smelling of desire, telling me she loves me. If you could see the way your body looks bent over in front of me, you'd know why every man in that bar was thinking about risking my wrath for the chance to approach you." Saul was back to his silky purr as his hands traced every curve of my body.

There were so many questions I wanted to ask, but they would have to wait. "Saul," I whimpered. "I need you. Now."

Still, the frustrating man took his time stroking and stretching my tight channel as he undid his pants. By the time his erection sprung free, my knees were wobbling and barely holding me up.

I was thankful the man didn't have one of the long dongs described in my favorite romance books. While I'd never *ew* someone else's *yum*, the idea of a penis so long it could plunge inside me and reach my tonsils wasn't exactly a turn on.

Where we might have a problem was his current girth. Let's just say the scythe in his pants was pumped up and ready to jam… and by that, I mean jam inside me and never come back out.

I licked my suddenly dry lips. "You're going to have to go slow, Saul. Give me time to adjust."

"Just tell me what you need from me and I will do it," Saul assured me. "If it hurts, tell me and we'll stop."

I leaned forward on the sink, lifting my butt to give him better access to my soaked entrance. Saul lined himself up, gently rubbing the rounded head against me. Even that little bit of friction had shivers racing along my skin.

Saul pushed the tip in, and we both moaned.

"You feel like paradise," he whispered in awe.

"Wait. It gets better," I promised.

Just like it had with Rhodes, my ghostly body shifted

and adjusted my insides, creating a perfect fit for his cock. "I'm ready."

With unbelievable control for a man who'd lived with a hard-on for two days, he slowly stretched and filled me. My eyes crossed and my legs gave out. Saul's hand slipped under me to rest against my belly, holding me up with ease.

When he'd buried himself as deep as he could go, I smiled at him in the mirror. "Now the fun part. Slide out and thrust in faster this time."

Saul did as I instructed and gasped, "My love!"

"Saul? My body is too sensitive and worked up from the teasing in the bar and your touch. I'm not going to last long." I struggled to speak as he plunged inside me a little faster each time, causing my desire to coil tighter and tighter as he drove us toward release.

"Why do you sound like that's a bad thing? It means you're receptive to my touch." His hands moved to grip my hips, holding me in place as he grew rougher with each thrust.

"I don't mind, but when I climax, my muscles are going to clamp down on you. It might hurt." My warning fell on deaf ears.

"It will be fine. Don't fight your release because of me." His mouth sucked and kissed every inch of my skin he could reach. "I want to feel you come while I'm inside you."

He shifted his hips a fraction and drove himself inside me, causing my coiled desire to spring free, tossing me into a body-convulsing orgasm. I screamed his name as my muscles tightened around his scorching length, quivering with each wave of pleasure that washed through me.

Saul didn't stand a chance.

He roared my name as his muscles went stiff and my tight walls milked the orgasm from him. Saul used one hand to brace himself on the sink, and the other to keep me upright as our bodies jerked and trembled with pleasure.

Just when I thought it was over, my hip began to burn beneath his hand. "Ow, ow, ow! I think you're setting me on fire."

Saul jerked his hand away. "I don't have that ability, pet."

Standing on wobbly tiptoes, I twisted my hip toward the mirror and gasped.

"Did you tattoo me?"

Saul didn't respond, and I glanced up to find him staring at the mark with shock and awe. "It's the mark of a soulmate."

"Where's yours?" I huffed, eyeing the exposed skin along his hips. "If I'm going to be branded, you should have one too!"

"Wherever you want it. But Axelle? It might not work, since you aren't a reaper." Saul traced his fingers along the four-inch purple scythe on my hip. "Reaper marks have only been recorded in couples where both partners are reapers. I was able to mark you because I'm a reaper."

"Do you want me to try?" I asked hesitantly.

"Yes. I'd love to be marked by you."

"Okay..." I dragged out the word. "How does this work, and where am I supposed to put it?"

"Wherever you want," he answered, then laughed when I shot a look between his legs and wiggled my eyebrows. "If that's what you want, but I'd prefer a place where I could show it off. Maybe my arm, chest, or neck?"

My insides went all gooey with love. He wanted everyone to know he was mine.

"I love the idea of it being on your neck so I can kiss it even when you're wearing a shirt." Even though we'd just had sex, I felt shy admitting it, and the bathroom lights flickered above us.

Saul slipped out of his shirt and kneeled in front of me.

"If it doesn't work, I will get a tattoo that matches your mark here." Catching my right hand in his, he placed a gentle kiss on my palm before pressing my hand against the side of his neck. "Think about how I belong to you. If the reaper magic is going to work, the mark will come naturally since we just claimed each other for the first time."

Keeping my hand on his neck, I leaned in and kissed him. He was mine, just as Rhodes was mine.

How did I get so lucky?

My hand warmed, then burned, and I fought the urge to yank it away from his skin.

Saul covered my hand with his. "Be still, pet. It will be over in a minute."

When the burn faded, I let my hand drop from his skin. There on his neck was a purple scythe, exactly like the one on my hip.

Saul stood and looked into the mirror. "It's perfect."

BANG. BANG. BANG.

I jumped, floating upward until I could cling to Saul's neck like a terrified cat.

Saul shook his head in disbelief. "I couldn't even make you blink, but someone knocking on the door has you leaping three feet off the ground?"

BANG. BANG. BANG.

"Reaper, your presence is required immediately."

Saul slid up his pants as though he had all the time in the world, and as though I weren't still clinging to his back like a koala. "By whose order?"

"The Reaper Court!" the male voice shouted through the door.

Saul's lips curved into a smile as he took his time dressing.

"Why are you smiling? It doesn't sound like they're here for a social call."

My handsome reaper's chest rumbled with amusement. "The court avoids me, so if they want to see me, it means I've found a new way to upset their rules and get under their skin. I can't wait to find out what it was this time. Our species is slowly going extinct, but they are too set in the old ways to consider changes that might benefit the reapers."

"What if they punish you?" I struggled to even say the words. "Can they hurt you? Kill you?"

Saul finished buttoning his shirt and caught my face between his palms. "My love, stop fretting. I've already told

TBR: DEAD BUT WELL READ

you, no one messes with Death. Now, let me help you fix your dress."

"No need." I winked, then focused on the energy wavering and bending around my body.

When I finished, I looked exactly as I had when I'd walked into the bar early this morning.

Saul caught my hand and spun me in a slow circle, inspecting my body with open appreciation. "That was impressive, pet. I haven't heard of ghosts being able to manipulate energy with such finesse."

I glowed beneath his praise. "Thank you."

"Let's go introduce you to my fan club," Saul teased, looping my arm through his and leading me toward the door.

CHAPTER 21

AXELLE

Saul paused, glancing down at me. "One more thing, pet."

"Yes?" I asked, trepidation in my voice.

He lifted me in his arms so that we were at eye level. "Ignore everything I said when we were in the bar earlier. I don't want you to behave."

My stomach fluttered as he leaned in and brushed his lips against mine. "But—"

"No buts. I enjoy maintaining control of everything in my life. That isn't likely to change, and I will always be bossy." Saul caught my bottom lip between his teeth and gently nipped before releasing it. "But you, my love, drive me wild when you don't behave. When you push back and challenge me. I've never tolerated that behavior in others, but with you, it's different. Don't let anyone out there treat you with disrespect."

Laughing, I shook my head and teased, "That's easy for you to say, Mister One-Touch-And-RIP."

"I'm not that bad," Saul huffed. "I'm a reasonable reaper. They'll get one chance to apologize to you before I drop them at your feet."

Circling my arms around his neck, I clarified, "Alive?"

"Mostly." Saul's lips twitched as he fought to appear serious.

"So you're saying I can do as I please and they'll deal with it because the grimmest of reapers is standing right behind me, watching and waiting?" Like a cat, I rubbed my cheek against his, savoring the heat that washed through me from the skin-to-skin contact... and enjoying the way his scent clung to my skin afterwards. "This is like the touch-her-and-die trope in my books."

Saul chuckled. "Yes. If they touch you, I'm going to touch them—"

"Which means they'll die!"

"It seems fair to me." He shrugged. "If they keep their hands to themselves, they won't have a problem."

Burying my face against his neck, I kissed his soulmate mark. "I love you, Saul."

"And I love you." His thumb brushed across the mark on my hip. "You know, we could just teleport somewhere else and not waste our time here."

"No, we're going to get this over with." I wiggled in his arms, forcing him to set me on my feet.

Saul tucked me against his side and wrapped his arm around me. His face showed no signs of stress or worry. If anything, he seemed amused. Still, he was taking precautions to ensure I was protected.

Which was adorable since I was already dead.

I might have lived if Saul had been there the night I died. But I wasn't complaining. Death had given me the freedom to read to my heart's content, and it had brought Rhodes, Saul, and Evander into my life... and Lochlan. I was still mad at him.

Saul flicked the lock, swung the door open, and strode out into the hall as if he owned the world.

To my undead horror, five reapers stood against the wall on either side of the hallway, their scythes touching and creating an arch above our heads. My hand had been resting on the small of Saul's back, but as we exited the grim gauntlet, I twisted my shaking fingers into his shirt and clung to him.

"They're watching us." And by they, I mean every freaking patron of the bar had given up all pretenses of doing something and were staring directly at us.

If anyone ever complained about the walk of shame again, I was going to ask if they had to walk under instantaneous death blades held by stoney-faced reapers, all while a drunken crowd of random paranormals watched.

"Yeah, I just had sex. And it felt so right," I whispered, humming the melody of a song I couldn't even remember the lyrics for.

My lips had barely moved, so I didn't think anyone could have heard me, but Saul made a noise that sounded like a cough and sneeze had a baby. And the last reaper on my right snickered. I shot a look at his face, but it was an emotionless mask again... until he winked.

It was good to know at least one reaper had a sense of humor.

Zacharias pushed his way through the crowd and headed straight toward Saul. "What have you done now? Drawing the attention of the court isn't wise when you have so much to deal with already." Little drops of spit flew from his mouth, showing just how close he was to losing his grip on the long-suffering friend persona he'd crafted.

I'd gathered enough from his chat with the giant warlock with crappy parents who'd stuck him with the name *Tiny Tank* to know Zacharias was trying to create something that could bond with energy. What he would do with that creation was lost on me, although he'd mentioned planes several times, which had raised my suspicions.

Still, how could a device that sent energy into a plane cause issues? Saul was a powder keg of energy and he moved between the planes with ease, as did my collectors, and although I wasn't supposed to, I somehow managed to as well.

I needed to think through all I'd heard, and research a few of the ingredients Tank had mentioned. But that wouldn't happen as long as I was near Saul—or any of the guys. They were distracting as hex!

"Back up." Saul's voice was calm, too calm, and it sent a chill down my back.

Fire burned in Zacharias' eyes, and he opened his mouth to say something, but wisely closed it. He took a half step back, not wanting to give into an order, but too afraid to ignore it.

"I'm looking forward to finding out what I've done." Saul smiled at the ancient-looking reaper who stood behind Zacharias. "It's been far too long since I disrupted their day."

The fact that not a single reaper reacted to Saul's taunting jab, and the ancient reaper only responded with a sigh, spoke volumes about who held the power in the room.

Zacharias dropped his tone and tried to convince Saul he needed to tuck his tail and be an obedient dog. Not in those words, but that was the gist. He was going to milk this opportunity for all it was worth, making sure the group of reapers saw he was a long-suffering friend who kept them all safe from the big bad wolf's mood swings.

Needing to distract myself before I either vomited on him or bit him again, I let my gaze drift around the club. The place had been buzzing and unbearably loud just an hour ago, but now was as silent as a church, even though it was just as packed. Every patron was leaning in, as eager to hear every word as if this were their favorite telenovela.

Huh. Starring in a romance drama about my love life hadn't been on my bucket list, but I would've devoured a book with a plot exactly like this.

Just as that thought crossed my mind, my eyes locked with a pair of familiar green ones.

Son of a witch! What was he doing here?

If I weren't so rattled, and it wasn't my life that had just taken a sharp turn off a tall cliff, I might've appreciated how juicy this moment was.

The entire club would eat it up if they figured out that

I'd just been banged in the bathroom by the raven-haired reaper who'd broken a man's arms for speaking to me... and also belonged to the pale-haired, fae-prince-looking collector who sat with his boots up on a table. And to make it worse, it had been less than twelve hours since Lochlan had warned me to run if I ever encountered Saul.

Lochlan's eyes tracked every movement Saul made—every place on my body that he touched. Gone was his lighthearted, take-nothing-too-seriously attitude. It had been replaced by hard lines and a grim set to his jaw.

His eyes met mine again, and he mouthed the words, *Are you okay?*

I was still mad about him going on a date and rubbing it in my face by taking her to the cafe across from the library, but it felt nice to know he was worried about me.

Not wanting to draw attention to myself, I nodded. Lochlan's eyes narrowed, scanning my face before turning his attention to Saul.

The lights above me hummed and flickered as I realized Lochlan didn't believe me. He thought I was being held against my will. If he suspected what had happened in the bathroom, did he think I hadn't been a willing participant? No wonder he looked like he was counting how many people he was going to kill.

I needed to talk to him and explain things, but Saul wasn't going to let me walk around the club alone, especially with so many ticked off reapers lurking about. If I waved him over, it was going to stir the hornets' nest even more.

Zacharias was still droning on, growing more annoyed with each quick-witted jab Saul tossed at him.

I wracked my brain, trying to come up with a way to reassure Lochlan. Maybe the best way to prove Saul wasn't holding me captive was to show Saul affection that clearly hadn't been coerced. I didn't want Lochlan to be killed by trying to save me, and this seemed like the least disruptive way of making sure he got the message.

Slipping from under Saul's arm, I moved to stand in front of him. My hands slid up his abs and chest as I went up on tip-toe. Reaching up, I caught his face between my hands and gently tugged him down so I could kiss him.

What I'd intended to be a sweet kiss that I initiated, without prompting from Saul, took a different turn when Saul responded with gusto. His hand moved to my butt, and I couldn't help but notice the way his fingertips brushed the hem to make sure my dress hadn't ridden up.

The fingers of his free hand sank into my hair, cupping the back of my head as he provided such incredible mouth-to-mouth, I thought he was on the verge of getting my heartbeat back.

When we finally broke apart, Saul brushed his fingers across my cheek. He wasn't trying to convince the room I was his plaything; he was letting them witness how he felt about me.

"Saul! I'm glad you figured out how your dick works, but pay her for her time and send her on her way. This mess could turn into a crap-storm that disrupts both of us if you don't grow a pair and deal with it." Zacharias finished his rant by grabbing my arm and trying to yank me away from Saul.

That was the moment I realized my plan to be non-disruptive had a huge flaw.

Saul was still high on sex and he'd decided that only one thing in the world mattered to him anymore. Me.

The only reason Zacharias had managed to touch me was because Saul had been so focused on stroking my face. Zacharias probably viewed Saul's gentleness toward me as weakness and a sign his friend was no longer the man the world feared.

I was sure Zacharias had a brain in there somewhere... he just chose not to use it.

And Saul was about to show him just how badly he'd miscalculated.

CHAPTER 22

AXELLE

When Zacharias jerked my arm, he'd pulled me off balance and I teetered backward on my high heels. Before I had the chance to shake off the hand still jerking me back or attempt to right myself, Saul reacted with the same predatory grace he'd shown me the night I'd dropped into his bedroom. Only this time, his movements were inhumanely fast and fueled by rage.

Zacharias howled in pain as his hand was removed from my arm with several stomach-churning cracks. Saul caught me with his right arm, and used my momentum to spin me, guiding me so that I was pressed against his right side again. He kept his arm over me, holding me to him as he lunged forward.

Saul's fingers were around the other reaper's throat before Zacharias even realized Saul had made a move. He tried to speak, but with Saul crushing his windpipe and vocal cords, his efforts were in vain.

Shadows spread out around us, thin tendrils seeping into the air, reminding me of the way ink spread when spilled on paper. Twisting my neck, I caught the brilliant glow of my soulmate's eyes. This time, he didn't hide behind dark glasses. He wanted Zacharias to see.

POP!

At the unexpected crack of a gun being fired, I screamed and threw my arms around Saul's waist. The weight of his right arm vanished, and opening my eyes, I stared in disbelief at the bullet he rolled between his index finger and thumb.

My terror had the lights in the club flickering wildly, and one by one, the lightbulbs in the wall sconces lining the hallway exploded. It was clear from the pale faces and wide eyes that everyone believed Saul was using the lights to amplify their fear, and I couldn't blame them.

I loved this man and trusted him with my life, but even I felt a chill of fear watching him use the bullet he'd caught mid-air as a fidget toy, while also holding Zacharias off the ground with so much ease that his muscles hadn't even flexed.

With a flick of his fingers, Saul sent the bullet traveling back across the room where it embedded itself between the eyes of a man I guessed was an orc and who still held the gun it had been fired from. He was dead before he hit the ground.

From the corner of my eye, I noticed movement from a reaper behind Saul as he adjusted his grip on his scythe. His muscles bunched, and he rolled his weight to the balls of his feet, preparing to attack.

Letting go of Saul's waist, I turned to face the reaper whose balls clearly weighed more than his brain.

"Don't even think about it," I hissed, keeping my back close to Saul's, prepared to fight if needed.

"Are you joking?" the reaper blurted out. "You're a ghost."

"Yeah, so?" I snapped, my irritation rising.

"Ghosts can't fight! I can end you with a single touch." His fingers flexed on his scythe.

"Go ahead and try it! You'll change your tune after you feel my wraith!" Lifting my hands, I shifted my weight to run at him if he came for Saul.

But the reaper didn't run at me. He did the opposite, taking several steps away and letting his scythe disappear. I knew why an instant later when Saul's arms wrapped around me, pulling me into the heat of his body.

"Feel your wraith?" He leaned down, nuzzling my neck as though we were the only two in the room and he hadn't been shot at or very nearly attacked. "What were you going to do, pet? Bite him?"

"No," I huffed. "Maybe. I'm more of a think-on-my-feet person."

Saul's chest vibrated with laughter. "But you know martial arts?"

"What? No! Why would you think that?" It was my turn to laugh.

"Because instead of making fists, you flattened your hands when you brought them up to fight."

I shrugged. "That's what they do on TV."

"That's probably why you lost the boxing match with the Easter bunny." Saul swept me up into his arms and spun around just in time to catch the scythe aimed for his back.

"You remembered?" It was a ridiculously trivial thing, but he hadn't forgotten.

Saul yanked the scythe from the reaper's hand, spun it around and slammed the handle into the man's stomach, knocking the wind out of him. "Of course I remembered." He turned to the gathered audience. "Does anyone else want to take a swing or a shot at me?"

"Attacking a fellow reaper is a punishable crime. It is natural that these two would come to Zacharias' defense when you were strangling him." The ancient reaper sniffed.

"But Saul wasn't holding Zacharias when goon number two tried to stab him in the back, literally," I pointed out.

Saul pinched my butt. "Such a naughty pet."

The ancient one turned a strange eggplant color and hissed, "You are not a reaper, so you have no voice to be heard in this matter, ghost."

"Do not insult her," Saul warned. "I have something to say, and when I finish, I want you to pass my message to the rest of the paranormal world."

Hooking two fingers in the collar of his shirt, he pulled it to the side and angled his head so the purple scythe on his neck was visible.

"A soulmate mark?" the ancient reaper barked. "That's impossible!"

I searched the room for Lochlan, wondering how I was going to explain this to the collectors. They'd been the ones to encourage me to follow my heart, but I doubted they wanted me to follow it in this direction.

"Yes, it's a soulmate mark." Saul's eyes glowed and pride practically radiated from him.

"But there are no female reapers alive! Unless you both bear the mark, it is a false bond," the ancient reaper who I decided to nickname Rip Van Reaper protested.

"Maybe it's a tattoo," another reaper suggested.

"He's a showman who has mastered tricks. That's all this is," Zacharias croaked from the floor.

"I suggest you remain quiet so I forget you're still alive," Saul responded, his voice reverting to his icy, calm tone that was scarier than if he were shouting threats.

Saul leveled a stern look in Rip's direction. "She bears a matching soulmate mark, etched on her skin during our claiming."

"Prove it. Present this female and let us judge the mark for ourselves," Rip demanded, and the rest of the gathered reapers slammed the handles of their scythes on the floor in what seemed to be the reaper way of agreeing.

Alright then, it was my time to shine. I dematerialized and teleported myself a few feet from Rip. Soft gasps rippled around the room.

Rip's brow creased. "I don't understand. You're a ghost. You can't disappear from the ghost realm."

Since I didn't have answers, I didn't respond. Angling my body to the side, so Rip could see the mark, I pushed the fabric upward until the slit in my dress reached the top of my hipbone.

I could've used some energy to make my skirt longer, but my nerves were frazzled and I was afraid I'd end up making it shorter—or worse, vanish. That meant I had to fight with the two flaps of fabric as I tried to keep my important bits covered.

I'd wanted to appear strong in front of the reapers, rather than hiding behind Saul, but there was no denying I was relieved when Saul stepped behind me. His frame blocked anyone from catching an accidental peek of my bare butt.

Saul rested his hand against my stomach, moving it slowly south until his large palm held the fabric in place and covered me. Even though I was as nervous as a porcupine in a balloon factory, and strangers were staring daggers at me, the heat radiating from his skin had desire bubbling in my belly.

It was pathetic the way the four men could drive me crazy without even putting in effort.

Lifting my chin, I stared up at Rip. "I am Saul's soulmate, and I bear the mark to prove it."

Thanks to our height difference, Saul's hard length pressed against my back. Poor guy had just taken care of that problem, and now he'd gotten aroused by this?

"This can't be." Rip reached out a hand as though intending to touch the mark, but snatched his hand back when Saul growled and shadows swirled around me like snakes ready to strike.

"Are you a reaper?" Rip asked.

"No, I'm a ghost." There was no reason to lie.

Rip looked at Saul with disgust. "If you possess the ability to mark other species, why waste it on a ghost who will be gone within weeks? At most, you have a few months."

"I possess the ability to mark only my soulmate. No different from any other reaper," Saul answered coldly. "She is mine, and I am hers. We are bonded and marked under reaper law."

"Do you hear this?" Rip threw up his hands. "Saul wishes for us to accept that this specter is his bride!"

His what?

Several of the reapers laughed, but I stood frozen. I knew soulmates were a for life sort of deal, thanks to all the shifter romance—I mean, research books—I read. But marriage?

When I died, I'd grieved the fact I'd never be a bride or a wife. And now I find out I'd gotten married in the bathroom of a club?

Way to keep it classy, Axelle.

"We are married by the laws of our species and you dare to mock my bride?" Saul's voice shook with rage.

Instead of stopping while he was ahead and not dead, Rip decided to do the equivalent of dropping a handful of Mentos in a soda bottle and shaking it. "Why are you like this? You take perverse pleasure in choosing the path that brings shame and disgust upon your species. No other paranormal species would lower themselves to take a ghost for a bride."

The loud, overly dramatic and drawn out clearing of a throat drew everyone's attention.

"Actually, you're mistaken." Lochlan pushed away from the wall where he'd been hidden in the shadows only a few feet away from Zacharias.

The reapers closest to him jumped in surprise. He'd moved so quietly, they hadn't even realized he'd been lurking in the shadows, ready to join in the fray if things went further south.

Lochlan made his way to stand in front of me, a reckless glint in his eyes. "Hey, boo."

Ignoring that things were still stiff between us, that a reaper had just told the world I was his wife, and that he was surrounded by reapers who were twitchy and looking for reasons to attack, Lochlan pulled me away from Saul.

Holding me against his chest, Lochlan whispered, "May I kiss you?"

I hesitated for a fraction of a second, then nodded and Lochlan's mouth immediately captured mine. He didn't just give me a quick peck, either. No, he took his time, kissing me with a passion that made sure everyone in the room got the impression we were lovers.

When he finally released me, my lips were red and puffy and I struggled to clear the haze from my vision. The man knew how to work magic with his mouth.

Turning to face Saul, Loch stretched out his hand. Saul

accepted the offered hand, and the men clasped forearms in a warrior's greeting.

"Welcome to our circle, bro." Lochlan's eyes glinted with mischief as he spoke, knowing the effect his words would have on the gathered reapers.

I'd overheard enough talk between the collectors to know reapers didn't join collector circles, they didn't share their partners, and they'd never view a collector as family. And Lochlan had pushed things further by calling Saul *bro.*

"Thank you. I am pleased to be part of Axelle's family," Saul responded with sincerity.

The room was silent except for the ragged breathing of several livid reapers.

"Who are you?!" Rip demanded, glaring daggers at Lochlan.

Lochlan spun on his heel to face him and immediately took the stiff stance of a commanding military officer. "Lochlan of the Knights Baudelaire. And proud member of Axelle's circle."

I didn't know who the Knights Baudelaire were, but the rest of the room did, judging by the gasps and excited murmurs.

"You expect me to believe a Baudelaire has a ghost as a partner?" Rip's voice rose in disbelief.

"No, I expect you to believe the truth. All three Knights Baudelaire have chosen to be part of Axelle's circle."

"This is unnatural! She is an abomination who has already begun the work of tearing down paranormal society!" Rip shouted and several reapers banged their scythes against the floor in agreement.

"Before you travel a path that will lead to your demise, I suggest you listen." Saul's voice boomed like thunder. "I am Saul, the last heir of the Olothreuo bloodline."

Saul paused and leaned down to whisper in my ear, "My love, close your eyes and cover your ears for a moment. I don't want to frighten you."

I straightened my spine. "You don't scare me."

"That's a lie, pet." Saul's hand moved across my skin as he spoke. "You know what happens when you lie to me." His laughter was positively wicked.

Something brushed against my legs and I looked down to find an inky black, floor-length gown formed of shadows hugging my body. It was absolutely beautiful in an oh-by-the-way-you-definitely-accidentally-married-the-darkness sort of way. But hey, at least I didn't have to worry about flashing anyone.

Saul pressed a kiss to the top of my head, then turned to the reapers. "My bloodline has been called by many names over countless centuries. I claim those names and my role as the last of my line." He opened his hand and his scythe appeared.

"I am Saul Olothreuo." The scythe's handle banged the ground.

"I am Saul Thanatos." He banged the ground with the handle a second time and the reapers shifted, their eyes darting to Rip's pale face.

"I am Saul Nekros." Bang.

Rip stepped toward Saul. "Saul, I think I was too hasty."

My reaper ignored him. "I am the Destroyer."

The ground trembled.

"Hades! He isn't messing around." Lochlan wrapped an arm around my waist. "Hold on. If he's doing what I think he is, things are going to get wild."

"I am the Death Bringer." Bang.

Saul's glowing violet eyes found mine, searching my face for signs of disgust or fear.

Lifting my hand to my lips, I blew him a kiss and laughed in surprise when he pretended to catch it.

Lochlan groaned and dropped his face into his hand. "Boo, everyone in this room is wetting their pants in terror and you are seriously blowing kisses?"

Between Saul's raw power and Lochlan's kiss, my panties were already wet. I really knew how to pick them. It seemed all the *research* I'd done the past three years had paid off in a big way.

Saul raised his voice and roared, "I am Death."

BANG!

The lights went out, his scythe turned to fire, and shadows poured into the room. Wind ripped around us, shrieking as it picked up everything that wasn't nailed down, throwing it against the walls. People screamed and scrambled over each other as they tried to find the doors.

Saul stood tall, his hair not even moving as he let them see who he was... and what he was capable of. Catching my gaze, he made his way to me and brushed a soft kiss against my lips.

"Quiet!" The wind disappeared, and the shrieks stopped instantly.

"Let me introduce my wife, Axelle Olothreuo. I will lead fairly and with an open mind. But if you disrespect my soulmate, you better hope I'm in a good mood and make your death swift. I will ignore the disrespect shown previously, so make your decision now. Will you acknowledge her as my wife and give her the respect she is entitled to?"

I watched in shock as reapers dropped to the ground, bowing in front of Saul. Then patrons of the bar began to drop to their knees. Even Lochlan dropped to his knees in front of Saul.

"Stand up, Lochlan of the Knights Baudelaire," Saul ordered. "You will not bow to me, brother."

What exactly had Saul done? Why were they treating him like some kind of royalty? I really should have spent more time doing research in my romantasy books.

Not everyone seemed ready to embrace what had just happened. Zacharias and two other reapers disappeared, and a handful of club patrons made their escape. Several reapers moved to stand behind Rip.

Saul sighed. "It doesn't have to be like that."

The reapers raised their scythes and ran at Saul.

Terror clawed at my throat and I tried to get to him, but Loch held me back. "You can't help him! He's got this."

Glancing over his shoulder at me, Saul winked. "Lochlan, keep her safe. I'll be home soon."

With a snap of his fingers, the floor dropped out from beneath our feet, sending Lochlan and me plunging into absolute darkness.

CHAPTER 23

LOCHLAN

A s we fell through the darkness, I held Axelle against me, waiting to see where the reaper was sending us. To my surprise, we were vomited out onto the living room floor of the house Rhodes had rented for our stay here.

How did the reaper know where we lived? And how long had he been stalking her like some kind of creeper reaper?

"Ugh!" Axelle was on her hands and knees on the floor beside me, her body trembling as she dry heaved and tried not to be sick. "It's never like this when I teleport."

"I bet it has something to do with the fact normal reapers can't teleport someone without physically going with them, and your boy-toy just did the impossible. It's a miracle we aren't lost and tumbling in the darkness for the rest of eternity." I rubbed gentle circles on her back, wanting to soothe her, but also wanting to demand answers about everything she'd been hiding.

265

Evander appeared on her other side. "What is going on? Where did you two come from? What do you mean *when you teleport?*"

"Give me a minute. The room won't stop spinning," Axelle groaned.

"Where is Rhodes?" I asked Evander. "We need to have a family meeting. Now."

Evander's glasses kept slipping forward as he bent over Axelle, so he pulled them off and tossed them on the side table. "Chatter came through the collector network that something huge was going down at the UG and it was likely there would be mass casualties. I was supposed to make sure Axelle was safe and then find you so we could join him there."

"I have to go back," Axelle choked on a sob, and although I knew she was likely the catalyst for changing the balance of the entire paranormal world, my heart ached to see her in distress.

"Hey, it will be okay," I assured her, reaching out to pull her onto my lap, only to have her scoot away from me, her red-rimmed eyes flashing with hurt.

"You cannot be serious right now," I snarled, shoving to my feet.

"Calm down. There's no reason to get angry." Evander held out a hand in a gesture that reminded me of the one humans used when trapped with a wild animal that was about to attack.

"No reason to get angry?" My laugh was harsh and

bitter. "Dearest brother, let me count the reasons I have to be furious."

Inwardly, I hated myself for the flash of hurt that crossed Evander's face, and I watched as he immediately retreated into his protective shell. But then he looked down at Axelle and a change came over him.

Evander stood tall, squaring his shoulders as he stepped in front of Axelle. "Loose the attitude or walk away until you can find a new one."

I was lost for words as I took in his blazing eyes and newfound confidence. Rhodes and I had waited years to watch him bloom into the beautiful flower we knew he could be. But why did Evander have to pick today of all days?

"I think I'm entitled to throw a bit of a tantrum after everything she's put me through," I vented, with more whine than rage. "I also think I deserve a drink."

Evander crossed his arms. "Since you're pitching a fit like a toddler, you obviously aren't old enough to drink. Sit down so we can talk like adults."

My jaw went slack. "Who are you?"

He didn't answer and simply waited for me to take a seat.

Which I did... but only because my muscles ached and I was exhausted thanks to the massive amounts of adrenaline that had pumped through my veins for the past two hours.

"Good." Evander tilted his head in approval, as though I were a naughty student who'd been put in time out.

I really couldn't wait to see him pull this bossy crap on Rhodes.

"Let me help you, Axe." Evander bent, helped her to her feet, then guided her to the sofa across from me.

"I can't stay! There were too many of them! They'll kill him!" She tried to pull away, but Evander firmly held onto her.

That wasn't going to work if she decided to teleport herself like a freaking reaper.

"Who is going to be killed? I need you to tell me what's going on so I can help." Evander was impressively calm.

Axelle sat, her gaze darting around the room and her fingers twisting in her lap.

Squeak!

A gray ball of fur tumbled from Evander's pocket and scurried into Axelle's lap.

"Wasabi?" She stroked his head with a trembling finger. "How'd you get here?"

As expected, the gray rat didn't respond, which I appreciated, since with the way things were going, I wouldn't have been surprised if he had. At least *some* things were still as they seemed.

"I went looking for you at the library and found Wasabi sleeping in your blankets. Rhodes and Lochlan had talked about your rat friend, and I didn't want him to be alone. He's been hanging out here with me while I tried to figure out where you two had gone," Evander explained.

As Axelle continued to pet the rodent, the tremors in her hands eased.

I sighed. Not only had our circle grown to include a reaper, we'd added a rat, too. And from where I was sitting, she seemed to prefer the rat to me.

What had I done to make her go from desiring my touch, to shying away from me? I knew I could be a dick, but I'd gone over and over my actions and words and couldn't figure it out.

Unless she had been uncomfortable with the intimacy we shared, but hadn't been brave enough to say so. She'd seemed into it, but maybe she regretted it?

But it seemed like more than embarrassment or shyness. No, she was angry at me. Besides, she'd proven she wasn't shy with her reaper make-out session in front of the entire club.

"Who are you worried about?" Evander repeated his question now that she had calmed down enough to speak.

"Saul." Axelle dropped her chin to her chest and her lips quivered.

"Saul? The reaper, Saul?" Evander shot me a quick look that I returned with a smirk. He had no idea what was coming.

Axelle whispered a watery, "Yes."

"You were supposed to run if you saw him!" Evander's voice rose slightly.

I laughed. "Oh, she did. She ran straight onto his cock."

"Lochlan! Don't be crude," Evander hissed.

"Don't get your boxers in a bunch, bro. It's cool. They're allowed to have sex since they're married." I was being harsh, but I was too hurt to care.

269

"Married?" Evander grasped Axe's chin, tilting her head back so he could see her face. "Is that true?"

"Yes. I felt the bond with him, just like with you guys. He's my soulmate." Her eyes shimmered with tears. "I followed my heart, but things got out of hand and…"

"Had you met him before we told you about him?" Evander asked.

She nodded. "Twice. The first time, we didn't speak, but I saw him watching me in the library. I hadn't known he was a reaper. Then I accidentally ended up in his house when I tried to hide from you guys."

"Did he hurt you or try to make you do anything you weren't comfortable with?" Evander's tone echoed the same fear I was feeling.

She'd been alone. In his home. What kind of torture could he have inflicted on her?

Axelle's large doe-like eyes went soft, the same way she used to look at me. "No. He was sweet."

I snorted. "No one has ever used that word for Saul."

Fury burned in her gaze as she turned her wrath on me. "You saw the way he treated me tonight! When I was in his house, he healed my injuries, fed me his energy, and held me while I slept."

My stomach dropped to the floor, and I pushed to my feet. "You were hurt? Why didn't you tell us?"

"Because you guys were hurt worse. And it doesn't matter, you couldn't have done anything except worry. I didn't tell him either. He figured it out." She angrily swiped at the stray tears on her cheeks.

I kneeled in front of her, but not wanting to be rejected again or make her feel uncomfortable, I didn't touch her. "And then you gave us too much of your energy?"

"I was fine. Tired, but my energy would have bounced back. It always does. Saul is just overly protective." A tiny smile flitted across her face for a moment. "It felt great to sleep, though. I've missed that."

He should have sent her into the beyond the moment he saw her wandering around—it was what any other reaper would have done. But the dark reaper had taken better care of her than we had. Maybe we had misjudged him.

"I want to be honest, things happened that night in his house. Not sex, but other things. I really wanted to tell you guys, and I told Rhodes. But when I tried to tell him Saul's name, he didn't want to hear it because we were in the middle of... well, you know." The table lamp hummed and flickered.

How could she exude sexual energy like a succubus, wrap four men around her pinky, have every guy in that club sporting a hard-on, and yet get bashful talking about sex?

"Are you sure Saul hasn't tricked you into letting him claim you?" I pressed.

My gut knew the answer. I'd watched every move he made in the club, and there was no way he could fake the way he felt about her. The man was in love and wanted the world to know it. It was unnerving to watch him switch between death personified as he toyed with the reapers, to a besotted, lovesick puppy with her. He'd called Axelle his pet, but from what I'd seen, he was the one who was ready to sit, stay, and roll over at her command.

Maybe I'd buy him a collar and leash... once I was sure he wouldn't risk upsetting Axelle by murdering me.

"Saul would never! Hexes! After he performed his strip-tease dance for me, I would've done anything he wanted. But he focused on taking care of my needs and then held me while I slept."

I was still struggling to process the idea of Death dirty dancing, when Axelle added, "So, yes! He's made mistakes, but at least he owned up to them and apologized!"

That last bit felt directed at me, but I couldn't figure out what she meant.

"Enough of this. I want you to be straight with me. No more dodging questions and avoiding me!" I growled in frustration.

Axelle clenched her jaw and stared over my shoulder at the wall behind me. This ended now.

"Don't ice me out," I pleaded. Cupping her face between my palms, I gently forced her to look at me. "If you won't talk, then you can listen to what I have to say. I saw the look in your eye when you casually asked about the Under-Grave, and I knew you were hiding something. So when we got back from our mission, and you weren't in bed with Rhodes, I tracked you down.

"When I got there, you were nowhere to be found. The club was buzzing with excitement over something, so I grabbed a beer and sat down to eavesdrop. It seemed a ghost chick no one knew had shown up dressed to kill, and every man in the bar had planned to shoot their shot with her."

I paused, swallowing back the possessive jealousy that lodged itself in my throat. "But the dark reaper appeared out of nowhere, wrecked a collector who'd hit on the ghost, and then whisked her to the private area of the club out of everyone's reach."

The corner of Axelle's mouth turned down in a small frown, but she remained silent.

"I'll be honest, at that point, I was terrified they were talking about you, even though it was hard to imagine my adorable sweatpants-loving boo in the risqué, red mini-dress and heels they couldn't stop talking about. But then the orc behind me started talking about how the ghost chick had sat on Saul's lap, enjoying his touch, and returning his kiss with enthusiasm. I decided it couldn't be you.

"So imagine my surprise when the reapers showed up demanding to see Saul, and he strolled out of the bathroom with you at his side." I brushed my thumb against Axelle's bottom lip. "I had my blades out, and I was prepared to kill him or die trying. He'd die for daring to use your body for his pleasure. And then I saw your eyes. Those gorgeous, sleepy, bedroom eyes I saw when I licked you until you came. You looked happy, content, and well-loved."

I stopped, needing a moment to steady my breathing, and Axelle whispered, "Lochlan—"

"No, let me finish." I had to get this out now. "I saw the fear in your eyes when you spotted me, and I caught the flash of disgust. It hurt because I still don't know why you went from sharing yourself with me to hating me. I knew you were afraid I would attack and hurt Saul. Then you threw yourself at him, rubbing it in my face that another man got to touch you."

"That wasn't why!" Axelle protested, but I pressed a finger against her lips.

"Please let me finish. You may never accept me as your partner, but I need you to know how I feel. I wanted to leave, to not see another man have what I wanted most, but I couldn't. Not while you were in danger. Saul is impressive, but he was outnumbered, and he'd nearly killed his only ally for touching you.

"So I began making my way closer. I knew if a battle broke out between the reapers, I wasn't going to make it out unscathed. But I wasn't leaving until you did."

Her eyes shone with tears, and I blinked hard to stave off my own. "When that old-as-dirt reaper laid into Saul for dirtying his species name by marking you, I couldn't stay quiet while anyone spoke about you like that. Axelle, I risked my life and sacrificed my reputation to contradict the reaper and defend your honor... and the honor of the reaper you'd hidden from us but clearly loved. I felt the way your body stiffened when I kissed you in front of them. But you were desperate enough to protect your precious reaper that you were willing to act out your part and kiss me back."

My voice broke, but I pushed to finish. "It nearly broke me to hold the woman I love more than life itself and know she may never feel that way about me." My hands dropped from where I held her face to land limp at my sides. "I will treasure that bittersweet kiss for the rest of my time on this earth, but I never wanted to make you uncomfortable, boo. From now on, I will no longer try to touch you or get in your personal space."

"Why did you do it?" Tears slid down her cheeks. "Why did you stay when it hurt you so much?"

That was easy to answer. "Because I love you and your happiness matters more than mine! I'll always be there to protect you and your circle, even if I'm not one of your claimed."

"If you love me so much, why would you whisper all those promises and be intimate with me, and then take another woman on a date less than a day later?" Axelle dropped her head into her hands and her shoulders shook with her sobs.

"What?!" I rocked back on my heels as though she'd struck me.

I had forgotten other women even existed the moment I'd laid eyes on my beautiful little ghost. Where had she gotten the idea I was seeing other women?

"I saw you at the cafe across the street from the library. Giving her gifts and hugging her. You were rubbing it in my face!"

An icy hand squeezed my heart, twisting and crushing. Such an innocent thing had cost me the love of my life. I'd never thought about how it looked, and because of my idiocy, I'd been forced to see the distrust and hurt in her face. I doubted I would ever recover from the memory of her putting the chair between us, as though afraid to let me get close.

"Are you talking about his sister?" Evander asked, speaking up for the first time.

"His... sister?" Axelle's energy dimmed so fast I thought she was fading in front of us.

"Hey! Don't fade! Take my energy if you need it." Breaking the promise I'd only just made, I grabbed her hand and pushed my energy into her.

"Stop! I'm not fading." She yanked her hand away from me, sending another knife through my heart. But then she touched my cheek and asked, "That was your sister?"

"Yes. I called her to get some information about reapers since her husband was close to Philetus. But then she started prying about why I was glowing and I spent the whole meal talking about you. And the gift was for my niece."

"Oh, Loch!" Axelle cried, throwing her arms around me and burying her face against my skin.

I swept her into my arms, finally feeling like I could breathe again. I knew I should say something, but I couldn't speak. My eyes burned, and I quickly closed them, not wanting her to see me cry. I'd caused her enough pain and sadness.

My heart was hers and hers only... whether she chose to keep it or not.

CHAPTER 24

AXELLE

I 'd done exactly what I said I wouldn't do. Instead of asking Lochlan, I'd jumped to conclusions and hurt both of us.

The raw pain and despair in his eyes as he poured out his heart to me was something I'd never be able to forget. Even now, he was clinging to me with a desperation that shredded my heart.

"You're a better man than I deserve," I cried against his neck.

He'd been willing to stand—and die, if needed—by my side. All the while believing I hated him.

Evander scoffed from behind us. "That's taking things a bit too far. You two had a misunderstanding and now you can have make-up sex. It's what couples do."

POP! POP! POP! One by one, the lightbulbs in the room exploded.

"You don't need to be embarrassed, Axelle. He's already seen you naked. Besides, it's inevitable. And I'm sick of him hogging the shower while he polishes his dick and thinks about you."

"Evander!" Lochlan shouted.

"What?" Evander asked innocently, then burst into a deep laugh that was positively wicked. "After the years of razzing you've put me through, it's my turn for some fun."

Lochlan groaned into my hair. "Don't listen to him."

Leaning back, I met his eyes, "I'm sorry—"

"Shhh. No more sadness, boo. Next time, just talk to me when I've been an idiot, okay?" He kissed my cheek. "And I'm sorry I didn't think about how things might look. I'll try to think things through better in the future, but I can be thick-headed and impulsive, so I'm probably going to mess up again."

"He definitely will," Evander agreed, earning him a deadly glare from Loch.

"Book boyfriends are so much easier to figure out," I mumbled.

"What's a book boyfriend?" Evander asked.

"The male characters in romance books that girls fall in love with and think about while muffin' buffin'," Lochlan answered before I could.

"No, we don't!" I wheezed.

Lochlan gave me a look that said, *Really? You expect me to believe that?*

Wasabi chose that moment to grunt, which I was sure was just a coincidence.

"I'd like to read about your book boyfriends." Evander

grabbed a notebook and sat on the floor next to us. "What are their names?"

"You can't be serious!" My entire body flushed just thinking about him reading some of my favorite books.

"I'm completely serious. Research is my hobby, and if they are providing something you enjoy, I'd like to take notes." Evander slid his glasses back on and clicked his pen as though he truly thought I'd start naming names.

"Don't worry, Ev. I've got that covered. When I couldn't find her, I spent time in the archive room and found a stack of books and a Kindle. I took down some names, and I've already read through two of them." Lochlan's eyes sparkled, and he grinned. "Your highlighted portions were particularly enlightening. You're a naughty girl, boo."

Someone please kill me. Again.

Lochlan looked back at Evander. "I'll email you my notes. I made a list of a few scenes we could have some fun performing for her. If we get Rhodes and Saul involved, we'd have enough bodies to really drive her wild."

I couldn't tell if I was burning alive from mortification, or if I was so turned on that I was on the verge of cremating myself.

Evander was scribbling notes. "Good idea. We could also each pick a different book boyfriend from her favorite series and create a date night where she gets to have all of them at the same time."

"I have four sexy guys who drive me wild just by touching me. I don't need you guys to go through so much effort," I protested, trying not to squirm on Lochlan's lap.

"But if we can make your wildest imaginings come true, why wouldn't we do it?" Evander's brow creased in confusion. "Isn't that the point of having partners who love you?"

Leaning to the side, I kissed Evander. Lochlan's hand moved to support my back and keep me from toppling over. With my body sideways, the loosely draped fabric that made up the low-cut bodice of my dress fell to the side, something I didn't realize until my nipple was sucked into the heat of Lochlan's mouth.

With a gasp of surprise, I tried to twist back into a sitting position on his lap, but the men weren't having it. Lochlan shifted me on his lap so I was straddling him and I arched backward, allowing Evander to sink his fingers into my hair and cradle my head as his mouth captured mine in a nearly upside-down kiss.

Lochlan licked and sucked first one breast and then the other. The palm of his right hand was flat against the curve of my back, supporting me so my muscles weren't strained. His left hand explored my body as though reassuring himself I was truly there and that I wanted his touch.

"Guys," I murmured between kisses, "we need to make sure Saul and Rhodes are safe. They might need us."

"Rhodes texted ten minutes ago that he will be headed back soon." Evander placed soft kisses all over my face.

"And Saul told me to protect you and he would be home soon. That means I'm not allowed to let you go running back into the fray," Lochlan breathed, flicking his tongue across the hardened peak of my nipple. "And when Basileus Death tells you to do something, you do it."

Evander's head snapped up to stare at Lochlan. "We don't have a Basileus. No heir was willing to take on that role."

"We do now." Lochlan continued to swirl his tongue over the sensitive skin of my breast. His breath teased my skin as he gave a low laugh. "And you're kissing his wife."

"You can't be serious," Evander whispered.

"Deadly serious." Lochlan's mouth left heated kisses between my breasts as he moved south.

"Why now?" Evander's fingers massaged my head as he tried to make sense of what Lochlan was telling him.

I didn't have a clue what a Basileus was, but Evander's expression worried me.

"They insulted his bride." Lochlan's hand slid to my neck, undoing the ribbon so that the top of my dress fell around my waist. "You should have seen it, Evander. Saul claimed the role just so he could force them to bow to his wife. Some refused, which gave him the right to destroy the threat they posed to him, and by extension, his bride."

I sat up, crossing my arms over my chest to hide my exposed breasts. "Hang on. What is a Basileus? What role are you two talking about?"

Lochlan grinned. "Saul is the king, ruler, sovereign, emperor, czar, or whatever title you want to use, over death. Didn't you know you married into royalty, boo?"

"No. That can't be right." But as Saul's words and the

banging of his scythe replayed in my mind, I became light-headed. "So he's the head of the reapers?"

"No, he's head over all of death, and both the reapers and collectors answer to him. That means no more free agents or the reaper court trying to impose their rules. We're under a monarchy again," Evander explained.

My ears rang, and my vision blurred. "He did that because a few reapers didn't think I was worthy of wearing a soulmate mark?"

Lochlan threw back his head and laughed, the sound deep and rich. "Boo, he did more than that. He declared war, and they don't have a ghost of a chance of winning."

They had to be teasing me. Most guys just punched someone for insulting their girl.

Evander whistled. "Hades. I think I'm going to like him."

"Now, how about we focus on comforting our queen while she waits for the victor's return?" Lochlan pressed a kiss to the hollow of my throat.

I opened my mouth to protest, but Lochlan's fingers brushed against my thong and Evander's mouth captured my moan.

"Let us love you," Lochlan pleaded, undisguised need in his words.

We both needed this. "Claim my body, Lochlan. Make me yours."

"Um, should I leave? Or is it cool if I stay?" Evander scratched his neck.

"Stay." I forced myself to look at them while I confessed, "I want both of you. Unless you both prefer our first time together to be more private—"

They didn't answer and instead just carried me to Evander's room.

"Ev, sit on the bed," Lochlan ordered, setting me on my heels, and stepping behind me.

I didn't know what he was doing until he whispered, "I'm going to finish undressing you and Evander's going to watch."

His fingers traced the curves of my breasts and down my ribs to my waist. Gripping the skirt part of my dress, he slowly worked it down my hips until the silk slipped to the floor and I was left standing in my black thong.

Evander swallowed hard. "Axelle, you're breathtaking."

Loch's fingers hooked under my thong strap on each hip and repeated the slow process of slipping it down, while his mouth sucked and kissed along my neck and shoulder.

When I was in nothing but my strappy heels, Lochlan's right hand brushed against my stomach, then lower until he cupped me between my thighs. "Are you wet for us, boo?"

"Y-Yes," I answered hoarsely.

"How wet?" Lochlan asked, using his left hand to move my hair out of the way so he could nip and kiss the back of my neck.

I didn't even know that was a sensitive spot on my body, and my knees went weak. Lochlan held me up with his hand pressed against my heat.

"Lochlan, what are you doing to me?" I whimpered.

"Making you so needy that you're going to beg for us."

He wanted me to beg? I could save us all time and start begging now. I was already on fire.

"Let's see how wet you are, my love." Lochlan slipped a finger inside my heat. "Mmm. So tight."

Evander rubbed the front of his pants, then quickly moved his hand away.

My body clenched around Lochlan's finger.

"Something just excited our girl." Lochlan ground his palm against me. "What was it?"

"Evander," I croaked, my mouth dry thanks to all my fluid rushing south.

"What did you do, Ev?" Loch asked, moving his left hand to my breast.

They were going to kill me.

Evander's brow furrowed. "I don't know. All I did was adjust myself in my pants—"

My muscles clenched, and Lochlan's chest rumbled with amusement. "I think our ghost likes to watch her men. Undress for her."

Evander stood, unbuckled his pants, and let them drop to the floor. He wasn't wearing anything under them and his erection sprung upright.

It was a good thing I didn't need to breathe, because I wouldn't have been able to with the lust clogging my throat.

"Oh yes, she likes what she sees." Lochlan slipped a second finger in my tight heat.

A new voice came from the doorway. "Then maybe you two should do it properly."

Our necks snapped around to see Saul making his way toward us.

"Saul! You're okay!" I cried in relief.

"Of course I am." He stopped in front of me and lifted my chin. "I can't stay long, but I wanted to make sure you weren't upset."

"I'm so glad." Tears blurred my eyes.

"No tears, pet. You're in the middle of something." Saul brushed a soft kiss against my lips, then focused on Evander. "If you really want to drive her wild, come get on your knees in front of her. I'm Saul, by the way."

"Nice to meet you. I've heard a lot about you," Evander responded, trying to cover his crotch with his hands. "I would shake hands, but, yeah..."

I would have laughed at the weirdness of my husband introducing himself to a member of my circle while he was naked and we were getting it on, but my belly was heavy with need and all I could think about was having their hands all over me, and their bodies stretching and filling me.

"We'll have time to meet properly later. Right now, you two have my mate worked up, and it's only fair you take care of it." Saul brushed his fingertips across my stomach as he moved behind me. "Lochlan, go stand where Evander was. It's your turn to strip for her."

Saul took Lochlan's place behind me, his left hand resting on my hip. Evander kneeled in front of me.

"Hook your leg over his shoulder," Saul purred.

My eyes snapped to Evander, unsure how he would feel about it. I enjoyed teasing Saul, but this position was more dominating than anything I'd experienced before.

Evander leaned in, placing slow, erotic kisses up my inner thigh, clearly into whatever Saul had planned.

Saul nipped my neck. "Pet, I told you to put your leg over his shoulder."

Using the reaper to balance myself, I obeyed and lifted my leg over Evander's shoulder. The moment I was in position, Evander's hand wrapped around my leg, and his tongue stroked my slit.

"Oooh!" I yelped, overwhelmed by a rush of pleasure I hadn't been prepared for.

Unable to hold still, I wiggled, but with Evander's arm locked around my leg, and Saul pressed against my back, I wasn't going anywhere.

Saul's fingers trailed across my breasts, moving upward until they curled around my throat. He gently angled my head so that I looked up and at Lochlan, who stood naked and very aroused just behind Evander.

"I'm going to die," I whimpered as heat rushed between my thighs and raw lust awakened inside me.

"No, you're not. Because I'm Death, and you aren't going anywhere, sweet little pet." Saul's thumb rubbed gentle circles on my neck. "Here's what's going to happen. Lochlan's going to stroke himself, while Evander laps up your sweetness."

This was a different level of torturous bliss, and my

muscles quivered at the thought. Evander's tongue dipped inside my heat, eagerly licking and thrusting. Lochlan gripped his erection; a sexy smirk curved his lips as he began to slide his hand along his length. The man didn't even break eye contact as he stroked himself.

Evander's mouth disappeared from between my thighs. "She got so wet after you started, Loch."

"Tell them why." Saul traced the scythe on my hip.

"Because they're hot," I muttered.

"I think that's only part of it." Saul massaged his way down my back as Evander delved his tongue inside me again. "You don't see yourself the way we see you. I've seen the way you look at each of us, and I think somewhere in that pretty head of yours, you can't believe that you turn us on."

"Is he right?" Lochlan asked, his eyebrows nearly touching his hairline.

"Well, yeah." I sounded defensive, but I couldn't help it. "Loch, you look like a freaking fae prince. Evander is a heartthrob, and I wouldn't be surprised if every girl in the country had a poster of his face on her wall. Rhodes looks like the tough guy they describe in every motorcycle romance. And Saul, he's like that sexy demon you know you should be scared of, but you just can't resist his sweet talk. So forgive me if I struggle to accept that you four are obsessed with me."

I paused, then added, "You guys are perfect, and it's a challenge being around you when the slightest touch makes me all needy. When I get to see how turned on you guys are, and know it's because of me, it's exciting."

"And here I've been trying to hide my boner every time I'm around you, so you wouldn't think I was a pervert," Evander joked.

"Same here," Lochlan huffed. "Boo, we're yours, and we aren't going anywhere. Why would we when the most gorgeous and exciting woman on earth belongs to us? It's nice to know you like what you see, too." He winked at me, his eyes sparkling. "Does this mean I get to be the fae book boyfriend?"

"Book boyfriend?" Saul growled. "I like your collectors, but I really don't think my jealousy can handle you taking any more mates."

"I don't think my body can handle any more." I moaned as Evander's tongue flicked across my clit, sending shock-waves of pleasure through me.

"We'll explain later," Lochlan assured Saul.

Evander's hand gripped his cock, stroking it in time with the thrusts of his tongue. Saul was still fully dressed, but I could feel the evidence of his arousal grinding against my lower back. His hands trailed across my skin to cup my breasts.

Lochlan had slowed his pace, his gaze fixed on my face as Evander pushed me faster and faster toward my release. When I came, I would've collapsed to the floor if the two men hadn't held my limp body upright.

"I've got to go. There are things I need to settle and I need to find Zacharias. I will be back in two days." Saul nuzzled my neck, breathing deep.

Was he smelling me? Reapers were weird.

"Two days?" My stomach pitched like a ship at sea.

"I hate to leave you, but I know you're in good hands. Once I deal with these loose ends, you'll be safe." Saul tilted my head back against his chest so he could kiss my lips.

"Saul?" I asked when he pulled away.

"Yes, my love?"

"Next time someone is rude to me, could you please not start a war over it?"

Saul laughed and smacked me lightly on the butt. "No promises."

Lochlan shrugged. "Personally, I thought his reaction was perfectly reasonable."

"That's because you enjoy violence and revenge," Evander pointed out.

Saul gave me a final kiss, then disappeared.

"Okay, enough playing." My body ached with the need to be filled. "Evander, go sit on the bed."

He did as I asked, and his eyes widened as I kneeled between his legs.

"I want to return the favor." Twisting around to look at Lochlan, I wiggled my finger in a *come here* motion. "Sit behind me."

Lochlan did as I asked, then waited to see what I would do next.

Raising myself to my knees, I leaned forward slightly and licked the tip of Evander's erection.

"Axelle," he hissed, his fingers reflexively burying themselves in my hair.

I was practically presenting myself to Lochlan, but he hadn't moved other than to grip himself.

"Are you going to do something about it or just look?" I grumbled, wiggling my butt a bit to get my point across.

Lochlan didn't need to be told twice. He shifted positions until he pressed against my entrance. At the same time I took Evander into my mouth, Lochlan buried himself inside me.

Unlike Rhodes and Saul, who had tried to take things slowly at first, Lochlan threw himself into claiming my body with wild abandon. With each thrust of his hips, Loch plunged deeper and shoved me forward onto Evander's length.

Both men were breathing hard, as Ev used his fingers in my hair to guide my mouth and Lochlan rocked my body faster with each pump of his hips. My pleasure built until I ached with the need for release, but still I couldn't quite get there.

Lochlan's fingers found my clit, and that friction was all it took to send an orgasm tearing through me. As my muscles spasmed around his cock, Lochlan buried himself deep one last time, growling my name as he came.

Thanks to Evander's length filling my mouth, my moans were muffled, but their vibrations were the catalyst that sent him over the edge. He tried to pull away, but I wouldn't let him and continued to suck and lick as he joined me in bliss.

When it was over, Lochlan scooped me up and dropped me on the bed between them. Rhodes came in a few minutes later, utterly exhausted and too tired to talk. He collapsed across the foot of the bed and curled his fingers around my calf. Within minutes, all three men had drifted to sleep, leaving me to wonder how I'd gotten so freaking lucky.

CHAPTER 25

AXELLE

I lay in bed for several hours, wishing the entire time that I had my Kindle with me. Someone had donated it to the library, but since it was an older model with deep scratches on the screen, Bertha had tossed it in the trash.

My reading streak was broken since I'd been caught up in what was going on with Zacharias and investigating the tunnels.

Slacker. This is why I wasn't going to get involved or play with the cute boys.

I dismissed those thoughts. Sure, things had gotten a little crazy, but I didn't regret my decision to claim these men as mine. I just needed to make sure I had my books ready to be read when the guys went to sleep.

I was a modern ghost who could haunt by day and read by night. Who said women couldn't do it all?

Teleporting myself from the bed so I didn't wake the men by crawling over them, I floated to the couch and sat down. Wasabi squeaked, and after a moment of searching, I found him curled up in a tiny cat bed. Had Evander bought that for him?

Wasabi yawned, pulled a piece of paper from his bed, and made his way to me.

"What do you have there?" I asked, scooping him up from the floor and setting him in my lap.

He didn't respond, just waited for me to pick up the paper.

Leaning back against the couch cushions, I squinted at the tiny, old English font. The paper was a warm sepia hue but felt different from normal papers. It felt more like leather, or what you'd expect a scroll to be made of.

This wasn't just old, it was ancient. Where had he found it? And what priceless volume had he ripped it from?

Wasabi rolled to his back, hinting he wanted me to scratch his tummy. He was clearly unconcerned about crimes he may have committed.

Giving in, I petted his tummy, still slightly amazed at how much easier it was to interact with him since Saul had given me energy.

I lifted the paper and began slogging through the off spellings and strange terms. It took several minutes, but I finally deciphered enough to realize it was a journal entry summarizing the results various herbs and poultices had on an injured reaper. A reaper he was keeping on the edge of death and trapped in his cellar.

Talk about nightmare fuel. Torturing and holding a reaper hostage counted as medical science and advancement?

My stomach churned, and I was about to put the paper on the table when a word caught my attention. *Epolir.*

Bringing the paper closer to my face, I read the next few lines with mounting horror and trepidation. The wannabe scientist was drugging the reaper with Epolir to keep him weak. That allowed him to cut the reaper and take notes on which injuries were too deep for the reaper to heal. Instead of trying to help the reaper, he was only worried the reaper was going to die before he could conclude all his tests.

At the UnderGrave, Zacharias had confirmed my suspicions that he was the one who'd set up the meeting with Tiny Tank, so it would make sense that he had scribbled all the notes on the paper Wasabi and I had found behind the desk in the tunnels. But why would he need Epolir?

Did Saul know what it was used for? My soulmate had seemed bored out of his mind when Zacharias and Tank had talked about herbs and potions, so I was guessing the answer was no.

And Saul had gone to hunt Zacharias down. He could be in danger and not have a clue.

I had to get to him! Quickly plopping Wasabi on the seat beside me, I rose and prepared to teleport to Saul's side. Then stopped.

Was I a complete idiot?

I had three mates who were trained in all things battle asleep in a bed upstairs. Meanwhile, the only discipline I'd trained in before my death was the art of marathon reading, where I could binge an entire series in one go without feeling the strain of fatigue or pangs of hunger.

Which meant going after Zacharias alone was a dumb plan.

Don't be that chick in the horror movie everyone is screaming at for hiding from the killer in a butcher shop.

Teleporting upstairs, I shook Rhodes' shoulder.

"Hmm? Everything okay, sugar?" His sleep-laden voice was all sexy gravel, but this was not the time to be admiring it.

"No, I think Saul's in danger. Will you guys come with me?"

"Death in danger?" Lochlan huffed a laugh and stretched. "Boo, he *is* the danger. You gotta stop worrying about him."

"Lochlan's right. After what I saw at the club, there is no question that Saul can handle himself. He doesn't need backup." Rhodes kissed my cheek, then stood and pulled on his pants.

Confused, I watched as Lochlan and Evander did the same. Each man put on their boots and dropped knives in various hidden sheaths.

"You just said Saul wasn't in danger, so why are you gearing up?"

All three collectors stopped and looked at me as though I'd missed something.

"Love, you asked us to come with you. It doesn't matter if Saul needs us or not." Rhodes caught my face in his hand and brushed his thumb over my lips. "We will always go with you."

Don't cry, Axelle. Don't do it, I warned myself.

"I'm just glad you asked us to come along," Evander commented, sliding his belt through the loops of his pants.

"Right? I love you, boo, but you have a habit of finding trouble, so I'm pleasantly surprised you didn't try to sneak off and save the world on your own." Lochlan spun a knife in his hand and winked at me.

"Do you know where you want to go?" Rhodes asked, his tone all business.

"I can teleport to Saul's side; I've accidentally done it before. But I can't take you guys with me." I caught my bottom lip between my teeth. "I think whatever Zacharias is planning is going down somewhere in the tunnels. Maybe we should all go there and check it out?"

The guys nodded.

"Let's go find Death." Rhodes led the way out of the room.

"Yeah, I'm not loving how that sounds. The context is confusing. How about we go find Saul and stay alive?" Lochlan swept me into his arms and followed Rhodes down the stairs.

"I can't wait to see his face when Axelle tells him we're there to rescue him." Evander grinned at me.

My stomach twisted itself into knots. If Saul was fine, he was going to be ticked that I didn't stay safely out of danger.

I was going to be in trouble, but I was willing to risk it. Besides, Saul was sinfully sexy when he was angry, so it was worth it.

#

"It's just as empty as it was the last time I came down here," I groaned.

Lochlan shot me a suspicious look. "Investigating on your own?"

"I thought I'd help. Plus, I was getting cranky about how much of my reading time all this ghost drama was distracting me from, and I thought I could get you out of my hair faster if I solved it."

Lochlan grabbed his chest. "I'm hurt. And here I thought you couldn't get enough of us."

"You're growing on me." I bit my cheek to keep from laughing.

"So once this is over, are you going to travel with us?" Evander asked, leaning against the wall as he waited for my answer.

I opened my mouth, then closed it. We'd never talked about how our future would work, only that we wanted to be together.

"How would that even work? Maybe it would be best to leave me here to read while you guys go do your thing, and then come home to me. I wouldn't be an asset to the team."

Rhodes shook his head. "We are sometimes gone for weeks or even months on complicated cases. I can't be away from you that long."

Evander rubbed his jaw. "If you're worried about being an asset—which you shouldn't be—remember that you saved our lives. You'd be like traveling with a portable battery pack just in case there was an emergency."

I thought about Saul's warning that there would be

Hades to pay if I fed the guys without him there to make sure I didn't give too much. He wasn't going to like this plan, but I wanted to be near the guys just in case they needed me.

"How about we figure it out case by case?" Lochlan offered. "I snooped on Rhodes' laptop, and one case he's considering is a supposedly haunted cruise ship. You could come along and enjoy the cruise and read to your heart's content while we work. And when we're not working…"

"Stop going through my laptop!" Rhodes snarled.

"Why? Are you afraid I'll tell Axelle about the poetry you started writing for her? Don't worry, your secret is safe, bro." Lochlan pretended to zip his lips and throw away the key.

"Are you sure you're attached to him? There would be more room in the bed if I make him disappear." Rhodes asked me, a knife appearing in his hand out of nowhere.

"Yes, I'd very much like to keep all four of my men. Now let's focus and find my reaper."

"I wonder what said reaper will have to say about us taking Axelle with us? He might want to lock her up for safekeeping," Evander mused out loud.

Squeak!

Wasabi's head appeared from a pocket in Evander's rucksack.

"What is he doing here?"

"He looked sad, and I didn't want to leave him alone, so I brought him with us," Evander answered sheepishly.

Wasabi scampered down Ev's back and leg to the floor.

As though he were a rat on a mission, he ran straight to the far wall of the chamber. He leaped up onto a small stone near the floor.

It stuck out just enough that he could sit on it, which he did, and stared up at us as the tunnel trembled and a piece of the floor slid to the side, revealing a set of stairs.

"Why does it feel like he's judging us?" Evander whispered.

"That was the most thug life thing I've ever witnessed! He didn't even break eye contact while he made us look like idiots!" Lochlan laughed, bending down and holding out his fist for Wasabi to bump.

I knew Wasabi was smart, but Lochlan was giving him a little too much credit. "Loch, he doesn't know what that means—"

Wasabi rested his tiny front paw on Lochlan's knuckles.

"That was just a coincidence. Now let's focus on finding Saul." I watched Rhodes head down the stairs into another creepy tunnel.

Thankfully, this one was far shorter and led straight to a large room packed with various types of modern lab equipment. Was this Zacharias' evil laboratory?

Nothing appeared particularly menacing, but a sense of heaviness permeated the air.

While Evander stood slightly in front of me, Rhodes and Lochlan moved around the room, checking beneath cabinets and behind the sparse furniture for anyone who might be hiding.

"It's clear," Lochlan told us.

Evander relaxed and shifted to stand beside me now that he wasn't worried about an immediate threat. There had to be some irony in the fact that they were trying so hard to keep me alive, when I was technically already dead.

"We've found our ghosts," Rhodes called from where he stood in front of a small door with a viewing window.

We squeezed in around him and peered through the window. A chamber that was the size of an ice-skating rink stretched out in front of us. It was empty except for the ghosts packed inside it. They barely had room to move without bumping against another ghost.

"How long do you think he's kept them down here?" My chest tightened. Why had Saul agreed to this?

"Not more than a few weeks to months. Otherwise, they would have faded, and I assume he wants their energy for something. The better question is, how is he keeping them confined?" Rhodes shook his head in disgust.

"I'm guessing it has something to do with the metal pipes wrapping around the walls and the roof. Those pipes hook to the large vats in here. I bet he's feeding one of his concoctions through those pipes and the ghosts can't cross them." Evander's ability to problem solve on the fly was nothing short of impressive.

It would've taken me far longer to put those pieces together.

"You have to get them out of here." I turned to look at the guys. "I know you can't walk through walls and stuff, but if you led them back out the way we came in, could you get them to one of the vortexes and help them get to the beyond?"

"Yes, but we aren't leaving you here. It will take too long leading this many ghosts out and getting them to safety. Collectors can't teleport wherever they want, like a reaper, or a certain ghost we all know and adore, but we can teleport them directly to a vortex and return to our previous location. It will take a while, but we will get them all to safety," Rhodes answered, his face grim.

"It might not take as long as we think." Evander pulled several papers from his bag and spread them on the table. "This place isn't on the map, but we should be right in this area. I think the back wall of that room is probably hiding another door that leads to the old mine entrance. If we find that door, it would be easy to get them out of here as a group and then get them to the nearest vortex."

"You're amazing!" I squealed, throwing my arms around his neck and kissing his cheek.

"Let's move fast. We'll need to cut off the stuff flowing into the pipes, then find the door." Rhodes turned the handle, and headed into the room, calling over his shoulder, "Axelle, stay in there until we're sure the containment system is down and you won't be hurt."

I stepped out of the way and watched as my men moved like a well-oiled machine as they worked to free the trapped ghosts. Within ten minutes, they'd found the door, broken it down, and had the last of the sludge draining from the pipes.

"Come on, Axelle! It's safe," Lochlan called as he started

wrangling the ghosts toward the back of the room, where Evander and Rhodes waited in the old mine to make sure none of the ghosts wandered off again.

When they got the last ghost into the mine and I couldn't see them, I decided I didn't need to guard the hall anymore and headed toward the containment room.

"What have you done? I'll kill you for this!" The shout came from behind me and, spinning around, I came face-to-face with a livid Zacharias.

Glancing over my shoulder at the mine entrance, I prayed the guys wouldn't realize right away that I hadn't followed them. I threw myself at the button with the label that read *Lockdown*.

A metal panel slid down from the ceiling to block anyone in the confinement area from getting back into the lab. Good.

Now my guys would have to get the ghosts to safety. I could have teleported myself out of the lab, but that would have left my collectors, and the ghosts, open to an attack by Zacharias.

No, I had to stay here and distract him long enough for them to get out of the mine.

Zacharias raised his scythe and rushed at me.

All I had to do was dodge and weave faster than he could swing. It was just like elementary school dodgeball, only deadlier.

CHAPTER 26

AXELLE

Zacharias swung at me as though he were a baseball player trying for a home-run. "You are dead! Matters involving the living are none of your business!"

The whistle of his scythe slicing through the air accompanied his shout, and the black cloak he was wearing spun around him. He looked every bit an avenging reaper.

I teleported across the room before his blade had the chance to slice into my skin. It hadn't killed me when I'd grabbed onto it while trying to save my men in the tunnels, but it wasn't something I was eager to experience again.

The moment I re-materialized directly behind him, I grabbed the hem of his cloak and yanked it over his head. Thrown off balance, he stumbled to the side, crashing through a glass-fronted cabinet and sending trays of vials to the floor. A few rolled away unscathed, but most shattered on impact.

Hex, yeah! That's what I'm talking about!

I might not have known proper fighting techniques, but I knew how to pants a bully.

There was no time to celebrate, because the moment he extricated himself from the cabinet, the moment he got his wits back, he was going to come twice as hard for me.

"Why won't you die?" he snarled, stepping on an unbroken vial and nearly falling backward.

"I can't until I see how your story ends. Book girls are downright feral when it comes to finishing our books." Taunting him was a bad idea, but it was the only one I had at the moment.

If he stayed distracted, he wouldn't be thinking about the ghosts who'd just ghosted his toxic flat arse.

Zacharias teleported so fast I didn't have a chance to do more than raise my arms to cover my face before he reappeared in front of me, and his scythe sliced across my forearms.

I refused to give him the satisfaction of hearing me scream. Dropping to the floor, I teleported myself to the other side of the room and crouched behind the cabinets. But the moment I re-materialized, Zacharias was looming over me.

His scythe sliced across my back, cutting through my shirt as though it were made of tissue paper, and leaving a deep slash from my right shoulder blade to my left hip. Man, I sucked just as badly at Sidestep the Reaper as I had at dodgeball.

"Are you a witch? Is that how you turned Saul against me?" he snarled, lifting his blade.

I stumbled to my feet, trying not to slip in the ecto-plasmic energy that had dripped like blood from my arms to the floor. Using my ghost speed, I blurred across the room, but it was no match for the speed of a reaper.

The flat side of the blade slammed into my side, hurtling me into a metal filing cabinet. I crumpled to the floor, thankful I didn't need to breathe since it felt like he'd broken several of my ribs and the agony was making it hard to not pass out.

If he'd been a collector, I could have escaped to the reaper plane and he couldn't have caused me physical pain. Just like a human couldn't hurt my ghostly body. But there was nowhere I could go that Zacharias couldn't follow.

"I was so close and you just had to come in here and screw me again." His fingers grabbed my hair and used it to lift me from the ground.

The searing pain had my eyes burning with unshed tears, but I stubbornly blinked them away. He would never see me cry or hear me scream. Even if he killed me, he'd know he hadn't broken me.

"Why can't you be a normal ghost and follow the rules? And why didn't you vanish the moment my scythe touched you? A slice by a reaper's scythe is fatal for every living being. Only a reaper can survive the cut of a scythe. Ghosts go *poof* when touched by a scythe." He held me in front of him, narrowing his eyes and studying me as if he'd find the answers written on my face. "So what makes you different?"

Relaxing my throat so he wouldn't hear the anguish I

was experiencing on the inside, I borrowed Lochlan's lazy smirk. "I'm a free spirit."

Zacharias wasn't amused and spun around to shove me onto the countertop. Stars sparkled in my vision as my cheek connected with the unforgiving surface and I nearly vomited from the edge of the counter punching me in the gut.

I could teleport far away, but I wasn't sure if the ghosts and my collectors were far enough away yet. Zacharias couldn't kill me with his scythe, but my men weren't immune. And they couldn't teleport away from him. If I teleported to Saul, there was a chance I could get him back here before Zacharias mowed down hundreds of innocent ghosts and my circle. They would be sitting ducks.

No, I would give them as long as possible before I teleported away from here. Assuming I could still summon the energy to do it.

"You haven't won," he hissed against my ear, crushing my battered body into the counter. "I have a backup plan to destroy the reapers because I knew if Saul figured out we weren't going to help the ghosts into the beyond all at once, like he believed, he'd shut it down. No, for my plan to work, I needed to drain them dry, and Saul wouldn't have liked that. He was broken and so set on getting justice for his brother that he trusted me without asking questions. Until you showed up and his entire focus changed. It's amazing what a guy will do for a girl if she knows how to suck a dick."

Despite my dire situation, my heart soared with happiness. Saul hadn't known Zacharias' true plans. My husband might have been the grimmest of reapers on the outside, but he was gooey goodness on the inside. I smiled just thinking about how much he would hate to hear me to say that out loud.

"You think this is amusing?" Zacharias used his grip on my hair to twist my neck to the side with a hard jerk. "You're not walking or floating out of here alive."

"Duh. I'm already dead." I forced out a harsh laugh. "What's funny is I'm dead, but you're the one who needs to get a life."

Zacharias shouted in fury and yanked my head back. I braced myself for the blow I knew was coming. How long had it been since the fight started? How much more could my body take?

The tremors in my muscles, my waning energy, and the sticky fluid that was leaking from my body to pool on the floor answered my question.

I'd underestimated my injuries.

I'd waited too long.

But I didn't regret my decision. I'd trade myself for the lives of my circle and hundreds of innocent captive ghosts every single time.

If it was my time—again—I couldn't help but be thankful for the incredible death I'd been given the chance to live.

Zacharias' eyes were wild and his grin had that unhinged edge that made for the most terrifying horror movies. "The best part of this is knowing your death will destroy Saul. The reaper who could have had it all, but never appreciated it. He lost his brother, he's about to lose his species, and now he'll lose his soulmate."

"You think by bringing Death to his knees, you will prove you're superior?" I lifted my chin and locked eyes with Zacharias. "Even on his knees, my husband towers above a pathetic, sniveling, butt-munching leech like you. I bet you hide your own Easter eggs and still can't find them!"

His chest was heaving, and the vein on his temple pulsed. Pressing his scythe against my throat hard enough that it cut a thin line in my skin, he hissed, "Are you finished?"

"Actually, no. There's one last thing." This time I was the one wearing the unhinged grin. "You might be faster than me, but you can't outrun Death."

I didn't even get to see his reaction to my Oscar-worthy last words before he vanished.

No, not vanished. Just tossed through space and time faster than any being had traveled before.

I would have collapsed on the floor if not for the arms that caught me mid-air. "Boo!"

"That's my line, idiot," I croaked, my throat tightening with unshed tears at seeing Lochlan's face.

I turned to see Saul's scythe clash against Zacharias'. Both men were powerful, but Zacharias' arms and legs trembled from the impact of each blow he blocked.

"I tried to warn him Saul wasn't going to be happy," I

told Lochlan, wanting to see him smile, rather than look at me with such sorrow in his eyes.

"We'll be lucky if Saul doesn't accidentally lose it and reap all of Amberwood with a click of his polished leather loafers." Lochlan clamped his hands around my forearms, trying to slow the flow of ectoplasm.

"That's because he really knows how to knock 'em dead. Get it?" I wiggled my eyebrows, then winced when my scalp screamed in protest.

Rhodes and Evander dropped to the floor beside us. "What can we do? How can we help you?"

"I'm fine, everything's fine," I lied reassuringly.

"Feed from us. Take all of my energy if it will help you heal!" Lochlan pleaded.

"So, funny story, but I don't know how to feed. I'm more of the feedee than the feeder."

"But you said Saul fed you. How did he do it?" Rhodes pushed.

"I don't know. He kissed me and then sort of poured it down my throat. A lot like funneling beer at a college party —not that I did that." A migraine began jack-hammering my skull, making it hard to think. There was something important I needed to tell Saul.

"Uh, guys?" Evander's whisper sounded like a scream, and I curled into the fetal position and covered my ears.

Why was everything so loud? And why did it feel like my skin was melting off my body?

Thud.

I'd come here because Saul was in danger. But why? It seemed like he was doing a lot better than me.

Thud.

There was something he needed to know.

Thud. Thud. Thud.

I felt hands on my body and screamed in pain. Something was wrong. This isn't what it felt like to die, and I would have known, since it wasn't my first rodeo.

"You were too weak and scared to take your position! I've spent years working to claim it as mine and you think you can just pick it up on a whim? You and Philetus were both weak and unworthy of your bloodline!"

Thud.

I've been in this moment before. No, I haven't. This is just déjà vu.

THUD.

"She's stopped bleeding." Rhodes' words seemed to come from a thousand miles away. "I think she's healing."

"But ghosts can't heal. They can't make their own energy, that's why they burn out," Evander reminded them.

Lochlan lifted me from the floor. "We need to get her out of here and somewhere safe before they cause the tunnel to collapse."

THUD.

"You don't deserve the power you have!"

Everything inside me went still.

This was the second time I'd heard that voice say those words.

The first time had been the night I died, and my murderer had been the one to say them.

Memories of that awful night flashed through my mind, and one after another, the pieces fell into place.

My death was something I tried to never think about because I was disgusted that it had been such a dumb, pointless one. While I hadn't been killed by Santa, the Easter Bunny, a Leprechaun, Cupid, or Sasquatch—I might as well have been.

That night, I'd decided to push myself to do something other than work, sleep, and read. An advertisement for an Amazonian art exhibit had caught my attention, and I'd attended.

The gallery was a large warehouse, and the team had outdone themselves, decorating the interior with various vines, flowers and giant leafed plants that could be found in the Amazon. It gave the viewer the feeling of walking through a jungle, and created the perfect backdrop for the pottery, jewelry, and paintings.

Everything had been fine until I'd decided to sit and rest my feet for a minute. I found a quiet corner and pulled out my phone to check the time and somehow clicked open my Kindle app.

I hadn't intended to read anything, but the next thing I knew, I'd been reading for an hour. If it weren't for the sensation of a bug crawling around under my shirt, it was possible I'd still be sitting in the corner of the gallery reading to this very day.

With an ear-piercing shriek, I'd scrambled to my feet,

desperate to get the bug out of my shirt. To anyone watching, I probably looked like I thought I was at a rave, and it was my mindless panic that had sent me running headlong into an early grave.

I'd rushed toward the bathroom, shoving open the door and trying to rip my shirt over my head.

"You don't deserve the power you have. It's wasted on you."

I froze with one arm out of my shirt, and the other stuck beside my head. "Is someone there?"

Had I run into the men's bathroom and started stripping? This was exactly why I stayed home—to avoid discovering how incredibly adept I was at coming up with new and creative ways to humiliate myself.

"She has nothing to do with this!" The second male's furious roar echoed around me, making it impossible to know which direction it was coming from.

Something slammed into me with enough force to send me hurtling backward. My back connected with cold, hard metal. I lay motionless, confused, and unable to suck in a breath.

"Don't! It's not her time!" The anguish in the man's voice had me wanting to comfort him. Which was weird, since I was pretty sure he was talking about me and I wasn't going to be going home tonight. Or ever again.

A sharp pain sliced across my stomach, followed by the sound of metal banging against metal and grunts. When silence fell, it was so absolute that I thought for a minute I'd gone deaf.

Why was I so cold?

The quiet was broken by a man's labored breathing.

Was it my attacker or the guy who felt bad for me? My arms felt like they were made of concrete, and by the time I freed my head from my shirt, I was gasping as though I'd just run up twenty flights of stairs.

I lay on the cold ground and took stock of my surroundings. Stars twinkled against a navy-blue background above me, and tall brick walls rose around me.

If my arms hadn't felt so impossibly heavy, I would have facepalmed. Thanks to my deep-seated terror of all things creepy crawly, I'd shoved open the wrong door. Instead of the bathroom, I'd rushed into the alley behind the gallery... and straight into the lead role in a future murder podcast episode.

Twisting my head to the side, I found a man lying on the asphalt a few feet from me. A pool of crimson was spreading out from beneath him. I couldn't feel my body below the deep gash across my stomach, but with effort, I dragged myself closer to him.

Using my shirt, I tried to put pressure on the worst of his stab wounds.

"You'll be okay. Just stay with me." I did my best to sound confident, not wanting him to panic. Scanning the alley, I searched for my phone to call for help, but I must've dropped it when I'd been sneak attacked by the bug.

"You are a terrible liar." He gave a weak laugh that turned into a wet cough. "I'm dying."

"No, you're not. I'm not going to let you." I had zero

medical skills, but I was going to do my best to pep talk him into surviving.

"Death is my area of expertise. I think I know what I'm talking about." His words were so soft I had to lean in to hear him.

A dizzying wave of pain rolled through me, and my muscles no longer obeyed the orders my brain gave them. I slumped on the ground beside him, and when I looked into his sad eyes, I knew that neither of us were making it out of that alley alive.

He grabbed my hand, squeezing it gently. Even though he was a stranger, I felt a sudden wave of comfort surrounding me. I wasn't going to die alone.

"I'm sorry I couldn't save you. You didn't deserve to die like this," he whispered.

My lips refused to form words, so all I could do was blink in response.

"I have something he wants, and when I die, he's going to come back looking for it." The man choked, each breath he took becoming harder to pull into his lungs.

Still, he was doing better than me. My lungs refused to inflate at all and my shallow gasps were coming further and further apart.

"I can't let him get his hands on it."

Well, duh. I didn't want him to get whatever he wanted if for no other reason than I was saltier than seawater over the whole being murdered thing.

His fingers tightened around my hand. "Wish I could tell my wife and brother that I love them. I guess you never know when it is your time, even when it's your job."

He wasn't making sense, or maybe the fog in my brain was muddling his words. Did he work at an ER? A mortuary? How did he think he could know when someone was going to die?

Were his eyes pink? No, it had to just be a reflection of the nearby streetlight.

"Is there someone you would say goodbye to?" he asked. His eyes searched my face, seeing the truth without me needing to say a word.

I had no one. Unless I wanted to call my boss and let him know I was calling out of work... forever.

There was only one thing I'd have liked to do: finish the last two chapters of the book I was reading. I was going to be left hanging on a cliffy, and there was no way a book girl could rest in peace when she was dangling like that.

"We're running out of time." The man's chest made an unsettling gurgling sound as he tried to get air into his lungs. "I should've healed, but he planned for that, too."

And I should've checked which door I was running through.

Catching a slight movement, I slid my eyes down to find a large beetle swaggering its way up my leg. A warrior who'd come to gloat over the body of his fallen enemy.

I didn't know enough about insects to know if the beetle had been a stowaway in the crates of art from the Amazon region, or if he was a local type of douchebug. All I was sure of was that this was the biggest beetle I'd seen in my life, and I was helpless to move as it sashayed its way up my leg.

"I'm supposed to help dying people, but my final act is using someone. Please forgive me," he rasped.

His words were making less and less sense, and the beetle was crawling faster and faster as he moved from my leg to my bare stomach.

PLEASE let me die before it gets to my face!

"I'm sorry." Those were the last words I heard before I saw the white light.

But instead of walking toward it and into peace, the light seemed to rush at me. It consumed me, burning my body from the inside out and outside in.

I screamed in agony, but of course, no sound came from my lips. As the light continued to taze the ever-loving-life out of me, my one consolation was seeing the beetle fall to the ground beside me, where he lay motionless.

Good. If I wasn't walking out of here, neither was he.

A moment later, the light won, and I was sucked into nothingness.

Thump.

The memories faded, and I was back in Lochlan's arms.

I knew who had killed me.

Thump.

I knew who had held my hand when I lay dying, and I now I understood what he was. Philetus. And Zacharias had killed him by using that herb to weaken him and keep him from healing.

Thump.

The same thing he planned to use on Saul.

THUMP.

Not a chance. I would not let Zacharias hurt any of my men. His murderous streak ended today. Forcing my eyes open, I teleported myself back to the secret laboratory.

I blinked in the blinding fluorescent lights, my migraine continuing with that annoying drum beat that pulsed in my ears. Dizziness washed over me and I grabbed the counter to catch myself.

My body still felt like I'd gone a few rounds inside a washing machine full of bowling balls, but my lacerations had closed so that my lifeforce was no longer leaking everywhere, and I considered that a definite plus.

I made my way down the hall and toward the sounds of fighting, and with every step, my energy flared a bit brighter. While I would've preferred a fast burn, I could settle for a slow burn as long as it eventually got us where we needed to go.

Watch out, Zacharias. I'm coming for you.

A shiver ran down my spine at my poor word choice. I was definitely not going to be doing any of that with him.

CHAPTER 27

AXELLE

S
tepping through a hole in the tunnel wall that was roughly the shape and size of the warring reapers, I stared at the scene in front of me.

Saul had Zacharias' body pinned against the tunnel wall. Zacharias' clothing was hanging in ripped tatters, while Saul had only a single rip in the sleeve of his black dress shirt.

Zacharias and his skin looked like Saul had replicated every injury that had been inflicted on me, and then some. I'd known Saul would be on the warpath when he saw what Zacharias had done, but this version of Saul was one I hadn't met. This was Avenging Death. He was judge, jury and executioner.

"I don't know if I want to kill you now, or if I want to keep you alive so I can make you relive the pain you inflicted on my soulmate over and over," Death snarled. His shadows writhed around him, like Medusa's serpents, as they ripped at Zacharias' clothing, skin, and hair.

"Are you sure you aren't just angry to realize I was always smarter, and you were too dumb to see what was under your nose?" Zacharias had balls to taunt Death, although with the way the shadows were lashing out, I wasn't sure how long he'd get to keep them.

"I am not weaker because I allowed myself to trust, grieve, and love. Those are the things that will make me a powerful and respected Basileus. I have my soulmate to thank for teaching me that." Death spun Zacharias around and pressed his scythe against the weaker reaper's throat. "My beautiful soulmate who would be uninjured if I'd followed my first impulse and crushed your throat at the club. I showed mercy because of our shared past. Thank you for this final lesson. In the future, I will show no mercy to anyone who even coughs in my queen's direction."

"She's a weakness! Why can't you see that as long as she can be used against you, it is impossible for you to reach your full power?" Zacharias spat.

"You fool. She isn't holding me back. She's making me more powerful than you can even imagine." Death laughed, the sound a haunting, melancholy sound that lured one's soul to their demise. "My soulmate is the anchor keeping me grounded. If I lose her, the darkness will be all that's left. I will torch the Earth—not because I want to punish innocents, but because I will be lost. Right now, I'm in control of the power, but if she dies, I will be helpless to stop it."

"Philetus and you were the crowning achievements of

your family line and the pride of the reaper court. You both threw it away for what?"

"Love." My voice was sharp enough to cut glass as I continued, "Don't mention Philetus. You aren't worthy to say his name."

"What do you know about Philetus? You didn't know him!" Zacharias' eyes burned with hatred as he glared at me.

I met Death's eyes as I answered. "Philetus held my hand as I died." My chin wobbled, and I swallowed hard, not wanting to lose control.

"You lying wraith!" Zacharias struggled against Death's grip, not caring that the scythe cut his skin.

"*You don't deserve the power you have. It's wasted on you.*" I repeated his words back to him. "That's what you said to Philetus before leaving us both to bleed out in that alley."

Death might as well have been carved from stone as he struggled to process the nuclear bomb I'd dropped in his lap.

"I couldn't see your face since I was struggling with my shirt, but I heard Philetus plead for you to spare my life. At the time, I didn't understand what I was hearing, but now I know that even though he was fatally wounded, he found the strength to protect me the best he could."

Zacharias shrugged. "He wasted his effort."

"He apologized that he couldn't heal me. He was dying and felt bad he couldn't do more for a human stranger." A tear slid down my cheek and I looked back toward Death. "He wished he could tell his wife and brother that he loved them just one more time. Until tonight, I didn't realize it was Philetus who had comforted me while I died. I'm sorry I couldn't have told you sooner."

Movement behind me caught my attention, and I glanced over my shoulder to find Rhodes, Evander, and Lochlan standing directly behind me. They held knives and stood ready to provide whatever backup I might have needed.

Zacharias used Death's distraction to grab something from his pocket and jab it into Death's chest.

"Saul!" I cried as he pulled the syringe from his chest, then staggered to the side and slid to the floor.

We rushed forward, but stopped when Zacharias held out his hand and his scythe appeared. He curved the blade around my soulmate's neck.

"The dose of Epolir I gave Philetus kept him too weak to fight or heal. Saul just got triple the dose. One well-placed, deep cut, and you'll get to watch Death as he dies in front of your eyes."

The pounding in my skull grew louder, like a drum calling me to war. It stirred that tiny flame of energy inside me until I could feel it doubling, then tripling with each steady drum beat.

I wanted to rush forward, but something held me back.

Patience.

Control.

The words had an eerie calm settling over me, as though I had a plan and the skill to execute it. All I had was the inability to stay down when I was knocked on my butt, and rapidly reproducing energy I wasn't sure what I was supposed to do with.

Wait.

Zacharias began to laugh. "This is so rich. You have been such a nuisance, it's truly satisfying to know I was the one who killed you." He kept his scythe on Saul's neck as he delivered a savage kick to my soulmate's ribs.

Thump. Thump. Thump.

The barometric pressure in the room plummeted, and the lights from the hallway exploded.

Now.

I didn't need to be told twice.

My foot connected with Zacharias' scythe, sending it clattering across the room before anyone realized I'd moved.

Oh, yeah! I could get used to running if it was easy like this.

I slammed my shoulder into Zacharias, knocking him backward. Pulling energy from the swirling orb inside me, I leaped onto Zacharias' falling body and released the energy straight into his chest.

Zacharias teleported away from me, clinging to the wall to stay upright. His chest had twin burn marks, and each breath he took was a struggle.

Good. He'd left Philetus to die gasping for air. Let him taste firsthand what that was like.

"I will not be beaten by a damaged ghost!" Digging deep, Zacharias called his scythe back to his hand and charged at me with the impressive speed only reapers could manage.

Until now.

I ran at him, reveling in the weightlessness and freedom of being a ghost, but equally enjoying the pure energy flowing through every molecule of what made me, well... me.

Zacharias grinned in anticipation as he lifted his scythe and swung it down, intending to slice me in half.

The clang of metal on metal as his scythe slammed into mine echoed around the room.

His eyes were wild as he stared at me. "How?"

"Philetus," I hissed. "You tried to steal his power so you could level up, but even as he lay dying, he found a way to keep it out of your hands so you couldn't hurt people with it."

"You are human! Reaper energy would have killed you instantly!" Zacharias protested, unable to accept that I, a defective ghost, had the thing he'd been willing to kill for.

"I guess it was a good thing you took care of killing me, huh? Philetus hung on long enough to time the energy transfer right as my heart beat its last and I began to separate from my humanity." I let the energy fighting to be released flow into my scythe, and watched in awe as it began to glow.

"What are you?" For the first time, I saw fear in his eyes.

"I don't know. Death's pet? Girlfriend to the Knights Baudelaire?" I mused.

"Will you marry us?" Lochlan shouted from where he was helping Saul to his feet.

"Yes!" I grinned and turned back to Zacharias. "Correction, Fiancé of the Knights Baudelaire, smut reader extraordinaire, library ghost, Saul's soulmate." I shrugged. "But those aren't the ones you need to worry about."

"I'm not scared of you." Zacharias' muscles flexed as he tried to force me to lower my blade.

"You should be, because today I'm fighting to avenge Philetus." I sent my energy pouring into the scythe, heating the weapon until it glowed hot.

Zacharias' blade groaned and cracked as his scythe shattered.

"You tried to take Philetus' scythe, so I've taken yours!" I shouted in victory, proud to have honored the man who'd unknowingly given me a second chance at life.

His power had merged with my ghost form, giving me the ability to produce new energy like a reaper. It was the reason I hadn't faded like every other ghost. I was guessing it had altered my body's makeup, allowing me to move in the reaper realm, and to give Saul a soulmate mark.

Who knew what else it had done? I was going to have a lot of questions for Saul.

But now I needed to finish this. I pressed my blade to Zacharias' neck and reminded myself of all the terrible things he had done and why he couldn't be allowed to escape again.

Zacharias curled his lip in disgust. "You saved the ghosts and you can kill me. But in five minutes, the reapers will be wiped out. You lose."

"What?" I asked, not understanding.

"Saul thought we were just creating a distraction with a

harmless explosion. But I wanted to make all the reapers pay for blocking my efforts to rise to positions of power within the court. But even after my allies accepted bribes to lock the file about Philetus' death, they refused to recommend me for a seat in court." He spat the words with such venom I wondered how he'd managed to hide his true self for so long.

"Our species has grown too soft, too lax. None are worthy of wielding a scythe. Right now, all the reapers are sitting down to eat the yearly feast, and my parting gift will go off and wipe the embarrassment we have become from the Earth."

"Where is it?" I moved to push my scythe at his throat, hoping it would encourage him to talk faster, but the scythe vanished.

"Axelle! You don't put down your weapons in the middle of a battle! Get it back out!" Lochlan and Rhodes ran toward me.

"I don't know where it is?" It came out sounding more like a question than a statement.

"What do you mean? Where did you put it?"

I threw up my hands. "If I knew, I'd get it back out. Maybe it went to the same place all my hair ties and favorite pens disappeared too."

"Well, find it!" Lochlan shouted, looking at me expectantly.

"I'm new to this! Cut me some slack!" I shouted back.

"I'd love to! Do you have a blade handy?" Lochlan quipped.

"You can't even wield your weapon like a proper reaper." Zacharias' cackle was cut short when Saul appeared behind him.

"I can though." With a swift swipe of Saul's scythe, it was over. "My soulmate doesn't have to lift a finger if she doesn't want to," he muttered, leaning against the wall, still fighting the effects of the drugs.

"I'll be right back." My announcement was met with a chorus of angry shouts.

Probably because they knew where I was going, and that I might not come back. But I wasn't ready to bet against myself. Hex! I was starting to think the bookworm might have been hiding a warrior's heart.

Still, I was beyond ready to get cozy with my sweat-pants and smut—I mean, my research on the effect hormones had on social behavior in forced proximity settings.

#

Ninety seconds after I hopped to the reaper plane, crashed their feast, and figured out how to absorb enough energy to power a theme park for several months, I re-mate-rialized in the exact spot I'd left.

The men were still in their same spots, alternating between arguing over what they could do to help and threatening to cuff me to the bed and keep me there if I was going to keep them stressed out.

Wasabi scampered over to greet me, but it took thirty more seconds for my circle to realize I was back.

They fell silent, their eyes slowly taking in my appearance.

"You guys look like you've seen a ghost—oh wait, you have!" I laughed, then hiccupped. "I think I have indigestion."

"You're glowing." Evander stepped forward and brushed his fingers down my glowing skin.

"Odd, right?" I turned my hands, mesmerized by the soft, moon-like glow of my skin. "I'm like a human glow stick, or those weird caterpillar dolls with the human face, and when you squeeze them, they light up from the inside."

"No wonder you hate scary movies if you slept with toys like that as a kid," Lochlan muttered.

Rhodes pulled me into his arms and kissed me. "I have no idea what happened here today, but you were awe-inspiring."

I hiccupped again, then turned away from him to cover my mouth and muffle my burp. "Maybe I should sit down. I'm not feeling so good."

Saul stepped forward and rested his forehead on mine. I knew what he was doing, and I saw the look of stark fear on his face when he reeled back.

"Get over here! She can't hold this much energy. If we don't get some of this drained from her, she will disintegrate from the strain on her body." Saul's mouth was already brushing mine. "I've never fed off someone's energy, but I want you to pour as much as you can into me."

"You're still too weak from the concoction Zacharias shot you up with!" I protested.

"Stop worrying. I've been handling reaper energy far longer than you have. I will redirect it to burn any traces of the injection from my blood and heal any damage it might have done."

His mouth captured mine, and I slowly pushed the energy into him like I had with Rhodes when he'd been injured in the tunnels. Saul was a fast learner, and it wasn't long before he was eagerly sucking it from me.

"We're going to undress you so we can use our mouths and hands to siphon energy as fast as possible." Rhodes explained.

At my nod, Lochlan, Evander and Rhodes removed my clothes, leaving me bare in front of them. This time, instead of the lights overhead flickering, I began flickering.

"Sugar, you have four men in your circle. You're going to need to get used to us wanting to see, touch, and taste your gorgeous naked body... because it's going to be hard keeping our hands off you." Rhodes' fingers trailed down my spine.

Saul broke the kiss, long enough to pant, "Grab onto Axelle. I'll take us home. Someone grab Wasabi."

All the guys had accepted that he was part of the family without me saying a word or needing to plead my case for why I should get to keep him. It made me fall in love all over again.

Saul teleported to his bedroom, the one I'd accidentally tumbled into when I'd been feeling overwhelmed.

"His bed works way better than ours," Evander commented.

He was right. Saul's bed took up as much space as two king-sized beds. "*Our* bed. I'll leave it up to Axelle, but if you're all comfortable here, we can make this our home when we aren't working. If you prefer something different, just find what you want and I'll have the money transferred to purchase it."

I laughed. "Just like that? You make it sound like it's as easy as buying a pair of pants."

"I spend more time with my tailor than I did with the agent while buying this house." He raised an eyebrow at my stunned expression. "Pet, I've walked this Earth for a while and I've amassed significant wealth, and that doesn't count the inheritances that were passed down to me from my parents' and grandparents' fortunes. If there's something you want, I'll have it here within hours."

I'd never been comfortable accepting gifts, but there was one thing I wanted.

Saul sat down and pulled me onto his lap. "I saw that look. What made you so excited? A boat? A plane? An island? A castle?"

"Not even close." Evander's soft chuckle quickly turned into a full belly laugh. My chest warmed, seeing him comfortable enough to laugh without trying to hide it.

Saul huffed. "Alright then, what has her practically drooling, and her eyes sparkling just thinking about it?"

"My coc—" Lochlan was cut off by the pillow Rhodes smashed in his face.

"A brand-new Kindle," Evander answered, wiping tears from the corners of his eyes.

"Done. I'll have it here by morning." Saul moved to kiss my lips, but I leaned back.

"But how will you know which one to get? There are different sizes, various colors, some are waterproof—"

"I was going to have my assistant send one of each color and style. Then you'd get the exact one you want." Saul's violet eyes glowed with so much love, it took my breath away. "Besides, I figured since we claimed a book girl, each of us should probably start reading more."

"I have a list!" Lochlan offered, shooting me a wicked grin.

"You read?" Rhodes gasped in exaggerated shock, then plucked Lochlan's knife from the air as it sailed by his head.

"Yes, I've found boo's favorite books are quite educational," Lochlan answered with a straight face. "I didn't realize reading could be so *up*lifting and really *raise* your spirit. A few have helped me to see things from a new *position* and enlightened me on how a group can really *come* together."

"He's reading romance books, isn't he?" Saul whispered loud enough for everyone to hear.

"Enough talk. We only siphoned off a little of the energy, and I'm starving." Rhodes pulled off his shirt, but left his pants on to my utter disappointment.

Saul traced his finger along my slit, then brought it to his mouth and licked it clean.

"So sweet," he purred, knowing the effect it had on me. "I think Rhodes would enjoy a snack."

Saul scooted back on the bed, setting me on the edge of the mattress between his legs. "Open your legs, pet."

When I opened them a few inches and stopped, Saul gently pulled them open, offering me to Rhodes. It was intoxicating, and a wave of slick heat rushed between my thighs, and I knew in my current position, all four of my men could see how soaked I was.

Rhodes dropped between my thighs and began to lick and feed as though I was the first meal he'd had in weeks.

"Ooh!" I gasped, struggling to keep my heart from bursting through my ribcage.

I froze.

"My heart is beating," I whispered in confusion.

It hadn't been a migraine pounding in my head.

Rhodes hummed his acknowledgement, but his mouth continued to lick and suck.

Lochlan, Evander, and Saul simply nodded in agreement.

"You knew? How? Why?" I gasped the last word thanks to Rhodes' skilled tongue.

Lochlan was the first to respond, "We're collectors and Saul is a reaper. Ghosts are our specialty, and we can feel them in a room before we see them. Plus, we are even more in tune with you, so when your heart started beating, it was hard to miss."

"We don't know why it happened, though. You still don't have a flesh and blood body on the human plane, so you're a ghost. We know that ghost organs don't really function, since they are no longer trying to keep the person alive. You're the only ghost to have a beating heart." Evander ran a hand through his hair. "It started trying to beat at the same time your body was struggling to heal from what Zacharias did to you. My guess is that you were only getting a trickle of the power Philetus hid inside you, and when your body was in crisis, you yanked a little harder and released the full power."

Evander gave me a smile. "Maybe one day we'll understand the details of how the reaper power blended with your ghost form, or maybe you're just a one-of-a-kind original."

"I've been thinking about that." Lochlan moved to kneel by my left side, then began to kiss his way up my ribs and toward my breasts. "Since you aren't exactly a ghost, and you aren't exactly a reaper, how about we call you a greaper?" Lochlan lifted his head to look at me, his lips twitching. "I can see by your expression you aren't feeling that one. Okay, how about rhost?"

I pulled his face up to mine and caught his bottom lip between my teeth, giving it a gentle nip. "I have learned to tolerate boo, but I will kick you out of the bed if you try to make either of those happen."

"But—" Lochlan began.

Rhodes cut him off. "No, you've lost your naming privileges."

The men fell quiet after that, Rhodes bringing me to the edge of release over and over, but denying me each time.

Lochlan's mouth and tongue were lavishing attention on my left breast, while Evander did the same to my right. Saul was massaging my back with his magic fingers while he kissed my neck and continued to feed from my energy. I'd occasionally feel him rock his hips, grinding his erection against me. It was a promise of what was to come, and I couldn't wait.

Surrounded by so much love, with my men draining the energy to levels I could handle and at the same time driving me wild with their every touch, I knew it wasn't possible for life—or death—to get any better than this.

And if I was totally honest, I wouldn't mind if all our missions ended this way.

ABOUT SEDONA ASHE

Sedona Ashe doesn't reserve her sarcasm for her books; her poor husband can tell you that her wit, humor, and snarky attitude are just part of her daily life. While she loves writing paranormal shifter reverse harem novels, she's a sucker for true love, twisted situations, and wacky humor.

Sedona lives in a small town at the base of the Great Smoky Mountains in Tennessee. She and her husband share their home with their three children, adorable pup, five cats, two pet foxes, chickens, three crazy turkeys, two cows, and over a hundred reptiles.

When she isn't working, she enjoys getting away from the computer to hike, free dive, travel, study languages, and capture the essence of places and people in her photography. She has a crazy goal of writing one million words in a year and spending six months exploring Indonesia.

SOCIAL LINKS

Hi my beautiful readers!
If you are looking for something else to read while you wait
for my next weird and sort of funny book to drop, please
check out my other series!

REVERSE HAREM SERIES
But Did You Die?
Dragon Goddess Series
Royal Storm of Atlantis
Three of Me
Dino Magic
Hey There, Hop Stuff

MF SERIES (JUST ONE GUY)
Flawed Fates
Slaymore Academy

Or click HERE to see all my books!

Made in the USA
Monee, IL
13 October 2024

67172646R00204